Kingdom Keepers

DISNEY AT DAWN

BOOK TWO

ALSO BY RIDLEY PEARSON

Kingdom Keepers I—Disney After Dark
Kingdom Keepers III—Disney in Shadow
Kingdom Keepers IV—Power Play
Kingdom Keepers V—Shell Game
Kingdom Keepers VI—Dark Passage
Kingdom Keepers VII—The Insider
Kingdom Keepers—The Return—Disney Lands
Kingdom Keepers—The Return—Legacy of Secrets
Kingdom Keepers—The Return—Disney At Last
The Syndrome—A Kingdom Keepers Adventure

Steel Trapp—The Challenge
Steel Trapp—The Academy

For a complete listing of Ridley's published books
visit www.ridleypearson.com

WITH DAVE BARRY

Peter and the Starcatchers
Peter and the Shadow Thieves
Peter and the Secret of Rundoon
Peter and the Sword of Mercy
The Bridge to Never Land

Escape from the Carnivale
Cave of the Dark Wind
Blood Tide

Science Fair

RIDLEY PEARSON

Kingdom Keepers

DISNEY AT DAWN

BOOK TWO

DISNEY • HYPERION

Los Angeles   New York

The following are some of the trademarks, registered marks, and service marks owned by Disney Enterprises, Inc.: Adventureland® Area, Audio-Animatronics® Figure, Big Thunder Mountain® Railroad Disneyland®, Disney's Hollywood Studios, Disney's Animal Kingdom® Theme Park, Epcot®, Fantasyland® Area, FASTPASS® Service, Fort Wilderness, Frontierland® Area, Imagineering, Imagineers, "it's a small world," Magic Kingdom® Park, Main Street, U.S.A. Area, Mickey's Toontown®, monorail, New Orleans Square, Space Mountain® Attraction, Splash Mountain® Attraction, Tomorrowland® Area, Walt Disney World® Resort

Buzz Lightyear Astro Blasters © Disney Enterprises, Inc./Pixar Animation Studios

Toy Story characters © Disney Enterprises, Inc./Pixar Animation Studios

Winnie the Pooh characters based on the "Winnie the Pooh" works by A. A. Milne and E. H. Shepard

Printed in the United States of America
First Hardcover Edition, August 2008
First Paperback Edition, August 2009

Library of Congress Control Number for Hardcover Edition: 2007042049
ISBN 978-1-368-04626-8
ILS# FAC-025438-20071

SUSTAINABLE
FORESTRY
INITIATIVE
Certified Chain of Custody
Promoting Sustainable Forestry
www.sfiprogram.org
SFI-01054
The SFI label applies to the text stock

This book is dedicated to all those readers who,
by e-mail, demanded it be written.
You see?
Someone's listening. . . .

1

LIGHTNING FLASHED ON THE HORIZON. A breeze swirled around the Cast Members. The air tasted dusty, almost bitter, with electrical charge.

Finn Whitman, one of five kids on top of the final parade float, pointed to the far gate where the Magic Kingdom's DHI-Day parade was to pass through, where five *identical* kids, wearing *identical* clothing to theirs, stood waiting.

DHI stood for Disney Host Interactive or Daylight Hologram Imaging—depending on whom you asked—a recent addition to the Magic Kingdom that offered the holograms of five teenage kids as Park hosts. The five kids who had auditioned for those roles were typically forbidden to enter the Magic Kingdom. But tonight was special: it was a DHI celebration.

Finn sensed trouble coming, wondering if it had to do with the electronic illusions waiting by the gate.

"How weird is that?" he said, seeing himself as a hologram not thirty yards away. The Finn Whitman standing by the gate looked no different from himself, except for a slight sparkle, a glow, when viewed from a certain angle.

"It gives me the weebies," said Charlene, regarding her identical, though electronically projected, twin. She too wore a cheerleader's outfit; she too had her blond hair pulled back severely into a ponytail, not a hair out of place; she too looked slightly embarrassed to have the body of a young woman, instead of a girl. Charlene was an athlete and champion gymnast and had clearly been recruited as a Disney Host for her clean, cheerleader looks and her uncanny physical ability. She was good with people and could make friends with anyone. Most kids at school were jealous of her—but the other DHIs appreciated the skills and abilities she brought to the team.

The hologram of Charlene stood next to the hologram of Finn, but the software had all five holograms in PAUSE, making them look more like glowing mannequins than kids. They awaited the start of the parade with the patience of the robots they were.

"We've been here before *as* them," said Willa, "but never *with* them."

"I was, once," corrected Finn. "Only the one time, and I was being chased by Security. I have to admit, it was plenty strange to see myself guiding some guests while I was also running for my life."

"What's that?" asked Philby, pointing up at the rise behind the tall boundary fence inside the Magic Kingdom.

"Cinderella Castle," answered Charlene.

"No, the gray balloon," Philby said. "It's massive."

"Looks like a weather balloon," said Terry Maybeck, who seemed to stand more than a head taller than all of them. An African American, Maybeck currently wore his hair in dreads, making him look older than the others.

The swarming clouds suddenly swallowed the large balloon.

"It doesn't make sense," said Philby. "You don't release a weather balloon in an electrical storm unless you're Ben Franklin."

"Not our problem," said Maybeck. "All we've got to do is ride the float and wave to the guests. Let's stick with the program."

At that moment, music started and the first float moved toward the open gate. The five holograms came to life, as if a switch had been thrown. They formed a line at the front of the parade, waving to the bushes, as if guests were waving back.

"Sometimes our DHIs look *so stupid*," Willa said.

"Sometimes?" Philby said sarcastically.

"They paid us well," Maybeck reminded them, "and we got gold passes for our families. We've got nothing to complain about."

"And they're having a parade to celebrate our DHIs

returning to the Kingdom," Finn said, "and we get to be part of it. Things could be worse."

"Who here doesn't miss the way it used to be? *Before* they patched the source code?" Maybeck met eyes with each of them.

Finn had been the first to "cross over" during his sleep: to wake up as his own hologram in the Magic Kingdom. Initially it had seemed impossible, but encounters with pirates and dark fairies had made him reconsider what was real and what was make-believe. Soon, all five kids had come to the same realization: when they went to sleep at night they awoke *inside* the Magic Kingdom as their DHI holograms. In reality, it had not been a corruption in the software's source code but the ingenious work of a veteran Disney Imagineer named Wayne, who had needed their help. But no one at Disney knew this other than them, so recently programmers had inserted a software patch to correct "the problem."

None of them knew if Wayne could, or would, undo it, allowing them to return to the Magic Kingdom as nighttime holograms. But all of them secretly hoped he would.

"Here we go!" said Finn. "Hang on!"

Their float jerked and climbed up the sloping asphalt just behind another float carrying Aladdin and

Jasmine. With all the floats strung out in a line, the kids had lost sight of their matching holograms out in front, leading the way.

The music swelled, and a man's voice dramatically announced, "Welcome to DHI-Day at Magic Kingdom!" The sound of applause rose above the lush jungle landscaping.

"Keep your smiles on," said Maybeck, "and hang on tight."

But at that moment, all five kids lost their balance and stumbled into each other. Jasmine and Aladdin also slipped off their pillows as their float accelerated to close a sudden gap that had appeared in the parade line.

It took Finn a moment to spot the problem: one of the floats—the villains float—had been pulled out of the line and off to the side. The Aladdin float, and the one carrying the DHIs, had sped up to close the gap.

"What's with that?" said Maybeck. "Broken down?"

"No," said Philby. "It's empty."

He was right: the float's platform lacked a character or Cast Member. It was just an empty wooden rectangle. Below it, the Cast Members responsible for preparing the floats scurried around frantically, hurrying to get the empty float out of the way and to fill the void created by its absence.

"What happened?" Finn called down to one of the

Cast Members just before reaching the gate and the adoring guests.

The man didn't answer immediately. But his face gave away his concern. "He was right there a minute ago," he mumbled, nearly drowned out by the music. "I swear he was!"

"Who?" called Finn. "Which character?"

He and the others had long since learned to take nothing for granted. Not when there were Overtakers in the Park, who wanted to gain control of the Magic Kingdom. There were no accidents here: everything happened for a reason, even if the other Cast Members didn't recognize it.

"That float should have Chernabog on it!" said Philby, shouting to be heard above the music. "Only he's not there." He turned and looked back at the empty float as they passed fully through the gate and into the Park. Finn had turned around as well. So had Maybeck.

"Who's Chernabog?" grumbled Maybeck.

Philby answered, "Only the most powerful villain Walt Disney ever created."

Finn's voice was overpowered by the joyous music and the crush of applause. "And he's gone missing? That can't be good."

2

FINN FELT THE QUICKENING BREEZE of the lightning storm bearing down on the Park. He hoped the weather would hold off at least until the parade finished. It was an evening parade with fireworks to follow. He didn't want it canceled. It wasn't every day he was asked to ride a float in Disney World.

He kept checking the sky as the line of floats reached a view of Tom Sawyer Island. He noted that the water looked oddly green and mysterious. His four friends waved and smiled at the crowds—big crowds. All but Maybeck, who nodded with his whole body but never actually waved, his head bopping and moving to the parade music.

As their float moved through Frontierland, Finn caught sight of a girl among the crowd. She was like a beam of light or a bright star in the night sky, the way she stood out. Amid the hundreds of guests—thousands?—she had appeared almost magically. Nut-colored skin, thanks to an Asian mother and African American father; a tangle of dark hair bouncing as, running now, she kept up with the steady movement of the parade. She seemed almost to float above the ground. Immediately behind her followed Jess. And though they claimed to be sisters, it had to be by adoption. Amanda's skin was a rich caramel, her hair so dark brown it was mistaken for black. Jess had once had jet black hair as well, though it was no longer so. But her pale, translucent skin set her apart, not just from Amanda, but from every girl Finn had ever met; it had depth, as if you could see into and through the first layer to some part of her that lay beyond.

"Amanda!" Finn shouted, breaking a strict rule that required silence of any Cast Members on a float.

The other kids hurried over and waved enthusiastically at both girls.

Amanda and Jess waved back, glad to have been spotted. Amanda gave Finn an enthusiastic thumbs-up—or at least he thought she'd intended it for him. He hadn't seen or heard from her in weeks. She hadn't been in school. She'd disappeared the same day her sister had somehow been transformed by Finn—an event he still didn't fully understand. Jess had gone from evil twin to a sweet, even angelic, girl, all in less than a minute. Only then had Amanda dropped the bomb that Jess was her sister, an explanation that had never been fully clarified.

"Where did they come from?" Charlene asked.

Even now Finn heard a tinge of jealousy in her voice. Or was that suspicion? There was a lot unanswered about Jess and Amanda. "And check out that hair color. Since when is she a strawberry blonde? Last time we saw her she had hair like my granny's."

"What the heck are they doing here?" Philby called out. He didn't mean the sisters.

Two big monkeys were moving in the bushes, swinging and keeping perfect pace with . . . *was it possible?* . . . the float. *Their* float.

"Since when are there monkeys in the Magic Kingdom?" Maybeck said.

"Are they wild?" Charlene asked, having noticed them as well.

Finn saw something his friends apparently didn't: the monkeys weren't following the float; they were following Jess and Amanda, keeping perfect pace with *their* movements.

"There aren't any primates in the wild in northern Florida," Philby said, ever the expert. Philby was a walking encyclopedia—he knew everything, and what he didn't know he knew how to research. His red hair and rock-climbing, thrill-seeking mind-set played against the geek he really was. A favorite of the girls at school, he wanted nothing to do with them. He spent his weekends with a climbing wall and a laptop.

The parade turned just then, making a graceful arc past the Hall of Presidents. The crowds thickened. Amanda's efforts to keep up with the DHI float failed. She and Jess stopped, caught in a bottleneck of Park guests. Finn waved, and Amanda waved back, but it wasn't a pleasant or friendly wave; it was more like panic.

Growing smaller now and being absorbed by the crowd, Amanda pointed to Cinderella Castle. Then sharply up. Finn nodded, hoping to communicate that he too was aware of the oversize gray balloon. But Amanda shook her head violently, as if he didn't understand. He nodded, again trying to say that he did understand. He felt constrained by not being able to shout down at her. Amanda frantically pointed toward the sky. Then she tore a leaf off a plant and pushed it against her face. Again she pointed toward the castle. Then the float rounded the corner, and Amanda was gone.

Finn looked up at the swirling, dark clouds. *They'll cancel the parade*, he wanted to shout. Maybe she was concerned that he and the others were so high above ground when lightning threatened. But surely the Park authorities had it under control. He wasn't worried about their safety—he just didn't want the parade canceled.

Maybeck edged closer to Finn, pushing past Charlene, who was waving two pom-poms. "What do you suppose they're doing here?" Maybeck asked, while bobbing his head and trying to keep a smile on his face.

"No clue."

"AWOL all this time, and they suddenly reappear for our reopening celebration. Doesn't that strike you as just a little bit odd?"

"Everything about them is odd, if you ask me," said Charlene, overhearing.

"What was with the leaf?" Finn mumbled. No one heard him.

"I like them both," said Willa, joining in. Willa looked constantly on edge. She had chocolate-colored, captivating eyes and a somewhat grating voice.

"You like everybody," Charlene said.

"So what?" Willa complained.

"It just doesn't work. You can't like everybody," Charlene said.

"Why not? Of course you can!" Willa said.

"Oh, forget it," Charlene said, shaking her pom-poms. She looked more eighteen than fourteen.

"Amanda knows where I live," Finn said. "Otherwise I might have said that they came here to catch up with us after reading about the grand opening."

"If she'd wanted to catch up with *you*, she'd have come by your place," Maybeck said.

"So it's you, I suppose," Finn said. Maybeck

believed every girl was in love with him. "She knows where you and Jelly live, too, don't forget."

"I'm just saying the timing's kind of interesting," Maybeck said. "We know there's something strange about those two, and there just happens to be a pair of monkeys following them."

Both Jess and Amanda reappeared, staying with the parade float once again.

With Amanda stabbing the sky and looking worried, Finn pointed back, behind her, trying to show her the monkeys. But before he could tell if she saw them, he lost sight of Amanda.

"She could have been pointing to the balloon," Finn said. "Even though it disappeared, maybe they saw it too. Whatever she saw, she was . . . I don't know . . . agitated. I don't think they came here to celebrate. I think they came to warn us."

"Warn us?" Charlene said.

"About the weather?" Maybeck said skeptically. "I doubt it."

"Could have been about the primates," Philby said.

"Yeah. A couple of monkeys," snapped Maybeck sarcastically. "Now, there's something to set your legs trembling."

"Maybe they were running from the monkeys," Willa said.

"I'm not even sure they *saw* the monkeys," said Finn.

The parade kept moving, and their float along with it. They crossed the lagoon, heading for the Hub, the density of the crowds increasing. Cheers arose. Kids screamed out their names.

"We're rock stars," said Maybeck.

"Our DHIs are the rock stars," clarified Finn. "Let's not confuse the two."

Finn caught a lightning flash out of the corner of his eye. The storm was moving closer. He looked up at the sky to see that it was far darker than even a few minutes ago. Was this what Amanda had wanted him to see? His mind reeled with possibilities. Why had she seemed so agitated? The low clouds and swirling fog obscured any sight of the gray weather balloon. Would anyone believe him now?

Suddenly the music was interrupted. "Ladies and gentlemen!" the booming voice announced. "Welcome to the Magic Kingdom's DHI-Day celebration! Please direct your attention to Cinderella Castle, where the fireworks will begin shortly."

"Look!" Philby said. "They're speeding up the parade!"

Whoever was in charge didn't want the parade caught in the storm.

"Don't you think we should tell someone about that

balloon?" Willa asked. "That's got to be dangerous in an electrical storm."

"They must already know, don't you think?" said Finn.

Philby said, "The string or wire holding it is tied to that window. Maybe it's some kind of experiment."

"Isn't that the window to the apartment?" Finn asked. As DHIs, the kids had previously used the castle's penthouse apartment as a hiding place.

"What if that's what Amanda was pointing to?" Finn continued. "What if she was trying to show us the balloon?"

"But why?" Willa asked.

"What's so important about a balloon?"

"Nothing the Overtakers would like more than to ruin the DHI celebration," said Philby. "What if they're trying to use lightning to set Cinderella Castle on fire or something?"

"I wouldn't put it past them," said Finn.

"We don't know if the Overtakers exist anymore," said Maybeck. "If they do, don't you think Wayne would contact us? Has anyone heard from the old dude, by the way?"

The Overtakers were a group of Magic Kingdom characters, rebels led by Maleficent, the evil sorceress from *Sleeping Beauty*. Their goal was to overthrow the good and take control of the Park for themselves. Wayne and others believed the Overtakers intended to imprison any characters and Cast Members not part of their group. They had been caught preparing vast dungeons beneath Pirates of the Caribbean, which were said to be for this purpose.

The DHIs were now also known as the Kingdom Keepers—one of the most popular attractions in the Park. The last thing the Kingdom Keepers could afford was for Maleficent to gain power again. They had barely stopped her the first time, and she now considered them among her greatest enemies—a distinction they could have done without.

"We should probably tell someone about the balloon," Finn said, moving to the back of the float and the small ladder there. "At the very least, it shouldn't be up in the storm."

The peculiar phenomenon that had been discovered shortly after the Disney Host Interactives had been installed in the Magic Kingdom had carried all five kids into a struggle with the Overtakers and the evil fairy Maleficent.

Wayne had showed them an astonishing three-story maze called Escher's Keep in Cinderella Castle, which led to the little-known penthouse apartment, now a secret hideaway used by Wayne.

Finn wondered aloud if the balloon might be something Wayne was responsible for.

"If Wayne's up there," Philby said, "we should go see him."

"You can't leave now," complained Charlene, waving her pom-poms eagerly for the cheering crowd.

"Cover for me," said Finn. "No one's going to notice if one of us isn't here."

"They'll notice if *you* aren't," Willa said. "They won't notice if I'm not."

"That's not true. Besides, I'm the one going, so I don't think it really matters."

"We never go solo. Remember what happened to Maybeck?"

Finn stopped, one foot over the rail and on the small ladder leading down. Maybeck's DHI had once fallen into a trap that had prevented the real Terry Maybeck from waking up. The so-called "Sleeping Beauty Syndrome" might have killed him.

"It was *your* rule," Willa reminded him. "And it was a good one. We've had no trouble since we started pairing up."

"Okay," Finn said. "So?"

"Someone's going to notice if you leave," Maybeck warned.

"Just keep moving," said Finn. "The more the

three of you move around up here, the less likely I'll be missed."

"You don't actually think we're going to let you do this alone, do you?" Maybeck said.

"We're all coming," Philby said. "Here's the plan. . . ." He pulled them all into a huddle at the center of the float. "The fewest number of guests will be on the bridge to Liberty Square. We get off and start shaking hands and signing autographs like it's all part of the parade. That's also the closest we're going to get to the castle. When we make our break, we all go at once— again, like it's scripted. If we get separated, we meet inside the castle in Escher's Keep."

Lightning flashed again. A few seconds passed before the first rumble of thunder rippled through the air.

"That lightning is still some distance away from here, right?" Charlene asked anxiously.

"Closer than it was. You couldn't hear thunder a few minutes ago," Philby said. "I'll bet they're closing the rides—the mountain attractions and roller coasters. That's going to mean a whole bunch of the guests in and around the Hub for the fireworks."

"If we really saw a balloon, whether they believe us or not, we've got to convince them to check it out before that lightning gets here." Finn couldn't stop thinking about Amanda holding up that leaf to her face. *Green skin?* Was that the message? More than anything, he hoped they might find the two sisters. He sensed they had some of the answers.

"And if they don't care about the balloon?" Willa said.

"We're approaching the bridge, people," Philby announced. "If we're going to do this, now's our chance."

"Okay," Finn said, working his way down the ladder. The others followed.

He happened to look up at Charlene just as she blinked furiously to protest leaving the float. "We can't do this!" she said.

Her blinking revealed a subtle green shadow on her lids, which enhanced the color of her eyes.

Finn spoke what he'd been thinking—what Amanda had been trying to tell him by putting the green leaf to her cheek.

He called out to the others, "Maleficent is inside the castle. That's what Amanda was trying to tell us."

3

THE KINGDOM KEEPERS MET UP AGAIN at the base of Escher's Keep, a confusing maze of interlocking staircases, mirrors, and doors that crawled up the inside of Cinderella Castle. It had been built years ago. One misstep, and you were dumped into chutes or slides, some of which landed you in the castle moat.

"I tried to tell a Cast Member about the balloon," Finn said. "But he thought I was my DHI playing some kind of trick on him. I shook him, and he said, 'Amazing technology! That feels so real!' What a jerk! I tried to point out the balloon, but with the clouds, you can't even see the string or wire or whatever."

"We've got to get up there," Philby said, "Maleficent or not."

"But what if Amanda was trying to *warn* us?" Charlene asked nervously. "Wouldn't that mean we might be walking into a trap?"

"She's got a point," Maybeck said.

Finn quickly reorganized them: he and Philby would ascend Escher's Keep to the apartment; Maybeck and Willa would try to find Amanda and Jess while

Charlene stood sentry on the path to Fantasyland, giving Philby and Finn eyes on the castle from the outside.

They said their good-byes, Maybeck uncharacteristically wishing them luck, his dark, troubled eyes expressing concern. They agreed to meet after the fireworks in front of Prince Charming Regal Carrousel, immediately behind the castle.

"And if you guys don't show up?" Willa asked Finn.

Thankfully, Maybeck dragged her out the door and into the castle gift shop's storage room before Finn had to think of something plucky to say.

"You okay with this?" Philby asked nervously, his foot on the first step of Escher's Keep. It was a route that had to be memorized, and neither boy had attempted to climb it in several months.

"Let's do it," said Finn.

Philby stepped aside, allowing Finn to lead the way. It was no picnic. Sometimes stairs led nowhere. A single misstep would mean falling down a slide to the ground floor or into the moat. The route up to an elevator that accessed the penthouse apartment included invisible bridges, upside-down staircases, and trapdoors. The illusions were the result of mirrors, projections, and trick lighting, their combined effect overpowering.

"Do you remember the way?" Finn asked. He faced four doors, all in different colors. They formed a semicircle on a small platform of polished floor tiles. He and Philby were fifteen feet above the ground floor, having ascended the first staircase correctly—skipping every other tread.

"I want to say second from the right: blue. But it's your call," Philby said.

Turning the wrong door handle caused a trapdoor to open.

Philby stayed off the platform in case Finn chose incorrectly. The plan was to take turns until they got it right.

Finn tried the blue door, and the floor fell out from under him. Down, down, he raced, the slick slide spinning him in tight coils before throwing him out onto the floor. He headed to the slanted stairs and began climbing again.

Philby tried the yellow door. The trapdoor opened beneath him.

Green—for "go"—seemed too simple a choice, so on Finn's next attempt he tried the purple door, and it opened.

"Purple," Finn called down to Philby, who was gingerly skipping steps as he made his way up the slanted staircase.

Once through the purple door, Finn started across an invisible bridge—an effect so convincing he would have sworn there was nothing beneath his feet. He moved across it in tiny steps, just barely sliding each running shoe forward, making sure something solid was beneath it. Philby, behind him, took the novel approach of getting down on hands and knees and breathing low onto what turned out to be glass, and then following the orbs of fog.

"It's a mirror," said Philby, sneaking up behind the slower Finn. The trick was compounded by the fact that a false destination—a second purple door—was projected at the other end of the invisible bridge, making Finn want to head in that direction. In fact, at its midpoint, the bridge veered right, arriving at what looked like a solid wall, which wasn't solid at all. The two boys ended up on a second small platform.

"I remember this part," Philby said. "This is where we go *down* the stairs in order to go back up."

"Are you sure?" Finn tested the "up" staircase: it was real. He thought Philby had it wrong.

But Philby waved his hand across the step four steps above this first step, and then punched his hand right *through* the illusion—the stairs stopped midflight, nothing but a projected image. He led the way down a staircase and then back up a longer staircase, which would make it appear to anyone standing below as though the boys were walking upside down.

"You two!" a low voice called out loudly. "Come down from there!"

Finn caught sight of an upside-down Cast Member. He was dressed as a barbershop singer, in white pants, a red-and-white-striped shirt, and a straw hat: a Dapper Dan Cast Member.

"Security," Finn whispered to Philby. "I faced Dapper Dans just like him that time Amanda and I were here taking pictures of everyone's DHIs. They were trying to catch me."

"You are not permitted in this area!" the man hollered. "Come down at once."

"I don't think we should trust him."

They reached a third platform and ducked behind a false wall with two windows. "You think he'll come after us?" Philby asked.

Thunder cracked high above them.

"I think there's something going on here," Finn answered. "The weather balloon, the monkeys, Amanda and Jess showing up for the first time in forever. And personally, I don't trust *anyone* dressed up like he's selling fried chicken. He could be anybody. That's an easy costume to fake."

"So we ignore him?"

Another crack of thunder. It was getting close.

"*Outrun* him," Finn said, "is probably more like it."

"And if we're caught?" Philby said. "You ever read those contracts we signed? They'll remove our DHIs from the server. They'll replace us with other kids. We'll no longer be Disney Hosts, no longer have the gold passes. We'll lose it all." He hesitated. "All that for some weird balloon? You sure it's worth it?"

"You're the one who saw it, not me. Listen, I'm not sure of anything," Finn said. "You want to head down, I'm not going to stop you or anything." He added, "But I'm going after that balloon, Security or no Security. Amanda was pointing at the castle, and that's good enough for me."

"How could she possibly know anything about it?" Philby asked.

"How can we possibly go to sleep at night and wake up as DHIs inside the Park? When was the last time *any of this* made sense?"

Philby pursed his lips. He nodded. "Yeah, okay. You're right. If they toss us, so what? We go down fighting."

"Exactly." Finn peered around the edge of the wall.

"What do you see?"

The man in the straw hat was gone.

"I think he's coming after us."

4

MAYBECK DUCKED INSTINCTIVELY as the sky flashed, and, only moments later, thunder boomed and rolled in a long series of endless echoes. A few early raindrops splattered in huge globs onto the footpath, and the air smelled dusty and sweet—ozone—foretelling the electrical charge it carried.

Charlene stiffened with the crack of thunder. "I . . . do . . . not . . . do . . . lightning," she said.

The Park guests scattered for cover, quickly emptying the paths.

"Then forget what Finn said and come with me!" Willa said, taking Charlene by the hand. "The parade blocked Jess and Amanda from coming over the bridge. They'll probably head past the Haunted Mansion and through Fantasyland to reach the castle. We're going this way," she said, pointing in the direction of Prince Charming Regal Carrousel, "to cut them off. Maybeck, you go around past the Mansion. Hopefully, one of us finds them before we meet up somewhere near Peter Pan."

"See you in a minute," Maybeck said.

"It's hard to see much, so pay attention," she said. The swirling clouds had brought an early darkness.

"Never fret. Eyes like a hawk," said Maybeck.

"What about the monkeys?" Charlene mumbled. "What if that was some kind of omen?"

"I'll keep that in mind," said Maybeck.

They split up, Willa dragging Charlene by the arm. Maybeck jogged off.

Park guests waved at Willa and Charlene. Some braved the increasingly steady rain to chase after them, calling for autographs. Willa pressed on.

Charlene said, "We're getting wet."

"That's what usually happens with rain," Willa said.

"We can't get wet!" she complained. "DHIs don't get wet. The rain runs right through them. We can't disappoint the kids like that!"

"Are you worried about the kids, or your hair?"

"Both, I guess."

"Okay. So let's run faster."

5

AMANDA AND JESS RAN THROUGH the light rain, dodging clusters of guests who were determined to stick it out and wait for the fireworks.

"It's not far now," Amanda said, spotting the spires of Cinderella Castle.

Jess didn't answer.

Amanda glanced back. It wasn't like her sister to avoid a chance to make a snide comment. "Keep up! You're falling behind," she called out. Jess was a fast runner; it made no sense that she should lag. She seemed to be running at a steady pace, no faster, no slower, no matter what Amanda said or how fast she ran.

The rain made the walkway more slippery. Amanda slowed and shortened her strides to avoid falling. When she looked back, Jess was still running at the same pace, the same stride. She apparently had magical footing— she didn't slip.

Amanda stopped and turned fully around and stared at her sister. *How could she not slip even a little bit?*

Despite the falling rain, Jess's shirt was . . . dry, her hair perfectly in place.

What a princess, Amanda thought.

But then she tensed.

Jess's feet landed on the wet walkway. No splash.

"Jess? Stop! Answer me, Jess!" Amanda cried out.

But Jess just kept on running toward her. The same perfect form and posture. The same perfect Jess.

Jess finally did stop, though she remained several yards off, like a fearful animal.

There was a reason her shirt and hair were both dry: the rain fell *through* her, hitting the walkway below.

Amanda stepped forward, now only inches from her sister. The rain fell harder, soaking her own hair and shoulders. Jess remained dry.

"Say something," Amanda whispered.

She reached out her arm and swung it from right to left, cutting her sister in half, her hand passing right through.

A hologram. A DHI.

"Where's my sister?" Amanda managed to choke out, the drops of water now flowing down her cheeks having nothing to do with the rain. "What have you done to her?"

6

"**H**E CAN'T POSSIBLY KNOW the way up here," Finn whispered. "Only Wayne understands Escher's Keep. He said so." But he could hear the swishing of the man's clothing as he climbed the upside-down staircase. He not only knew the way, he seemed to be quickly closing in on them.

"I don't think that actually matters right now," Philby said. "We are going to be in some serious—" He gasped. "What are you doing, Finn?"

Before him, Finn Whitman, the fourteen-year-old boy, transformed into a glowing version of himself with a slightly shorter haircut. He was now his DHI hologram.

"Willa said she s-saw you do this." Philby stuttered when nervous. "But I d-didn't believe her."

"It's not very stable. I can't hold it for very long," Finn said. "Go. Black tiles. Never two in a row. It's the left staircase when you reach the other side. There's the final invisible bridge and then the black hole. I'll meet you there. Wait for me."

Philby waved his arm through Finn just to confirm what he'd seen him do. "But if you're here as your DHI, then where's the real you? Not back asleep in bed? And why can't any of the rest of us do this when we're awake?"

"Philby, I don't know. Maybeck said he's had the same thing happen. Willa, once or twice. We can discuss this later, okay? For some reason, I'm able to will myself to cross over. I don't understand it, but I don't try to understand it. It just *happens* if I let it. Wrap your mind around *that*. It doesn't last long, and it's exhausting. So I'll meet you in the black hole, and I'm going to need your help from there on."

"And you're going to stay and . . . what? . . . *fight* this guy?"

"Yeah, right," Finn said sarcastically, his voice sounding a little bit different, like the buzzing of something electronic. "I'm going to make him wonder what he's chasing. I'm going to freak him out of his shorts. If I'm lucky . . . well . . . Let's hope I'm lucky." He waited only seconds. "GO!"

Philby took off across the checkerboard floor, making sure the toes of his shoes landed only on the black squares, and never two black squares in the same horizontal row. It required a kind of dancing across and down the floor that made him look like a kid in *Riverdance*.

Finn's ability to cross over while awake had to do with achieving a kind of meditative state. If he focused on having no fear, no worries, he temporarily crossed over. He didn't know the rules or how it worked, only that he could make it happen—though only inside the Magic Kingdom, where hologram projectors existed throughout the Park. He took a moment to test his ability, aware of its unpredictability and his lack of control over it. He grabbed for the nearby doorknob. His hand landed on it, and he was able to *turn* the doorknob. Then he pulled his hand away, closed his eyes briefly, and concentrated on just a single idea: light. He opened his eyes and reached for the doorknob once again. This time the doorknob passed *through* his hand. It sparkled and glowed as he swept his hand on through the doorjamb and back out.

So far, he seemed to be in control of his hologram, but he knew from previous attempts that his hologram quickly deteriorated. A few minutes was all he had, until Finn, the fourteen-year-old boy, came back to replace the DHI.

He stepped out of the way as he heard footsteps approaching. The man arrived at the platform. Finn hid behind him. The man was big, with thick, heavy legs and broad shoulders. He looked a little foolish in his red-and-white-striped jacket and straw hat. He studied the checkerboard floor like a person trying to remember the code, bringing his thick hand to his scrabbly chin in contemplation.

"White or black? Odds or evens?" Finn said, startling the man.

The man spun around, his face a knot of anger. "You're not allowed here," he said in a deep, dry voice. Incredibly quickly for his size, he jumped toward Finn and swiped at him, his hands passing *right through* the DHI, at which point he stood up in astonishment, looking at his own hands as if they'd betrayed him.

"One wrong step, and you fall," Finn said, darting past the man and out onto the checkerboard floor. He concentrated on the idea of light—*pure light*. A DHI weighed nothing, and only weight triggered the tiles in the floor. But he knew he couldn't maintain this pure state for very long. He had to lure the man out onto the floor quickly. There wasn't much time.

He tried another tack. "I'm a Cast Member," Finn said, "like you."

"I don't care. You're not allowed up there," he said. By saying this he confirmed he knew about the penthouse—Walt Disney's former apartment— the secret room Wayne had offered the DHIs as a place to hide.

An Overtaker? Finn wondered. The group loyal to Maleficent, dedicated to changing the balance of power in the Parks.

"I said you're not allowed up there," the man said.

"White or black?" Finn said, his DHI standing on one of each.

The pleasant warmth of the DHI gave way to a slight chill, and Finn knew the internal light was giving way to flesh and blood. He wished he understood how to control this transformation better, but that was for another time. He took advantage of his brief weightlessness and crossed the checkerboard floor to a platform that presented another three ascending staircases. He had one last trick left.

The man stepped out onto the checkerboard, keeping his eyes on the squares. It was a long fall below— thirty feet or more, though the floor had been painted in perspective, which made it appear more like three hundred: a bottomless, rocky cavern. He took that in, and then, as he looked across at Finn, his face turned scarlet with anger.

"You won't talk your way out of this, son." He stepped onto a black tile. Then another. *He knew the pattern!* Making sure he avoided any two black squares in the same horizontal line, he progressed cautiously but quickly across the floor.

Finn felt the DHI fading. He'd managed to maintain it for a minute or more, but he suspected he weighed something now. Would he trip the sensors that opened the floor, or could he make it across?

His plan was to run *right through* the man. He believed if he concentrated, he could summon his pure DHI for the fraction of a second it would take to pass through him. In doing so, he was certain to cause the intruder to misstep, which would send him plummeting. But Finn would have to move quickly to avoid being on the floor when it fell out and gave way.

He stepped out onto two black squares. He could *feel* his weight on his feet. He was about equal parts boy and DHI. *How much longer?*

The Dapper Dan stopped halfway, his face a scowl. Then something occurred to him, and he belched out a laugh. "Going to wrestle me, are you?" He grinned mischievously. "I'll save you the trouble." His right foot reached out for a white square.

Finn had not considered that the fastest way for the man to catch Finn was to make Finn fall *with* him.

Finn ran forward on the black tiles, simultaneously letting go of all fear. He felt the warmth return like a blast from a furnace. But well before he reached the other side—in fact, before he even reached his adversary—the floor went out from under him.

The man fell, letting out a short scream as he was funneled into a red plastic chute.

Finn was floating. The trapdoor had opened beneath him, but his DHI simply hovered. He was suspended ten feet above the evacuation chute, with only air beneath him.

He felt the chill returning. He managed three steps toward the edge of the open pit and then fell. His fingers caught the lip of the hinged flooring, and his body smacked into the hanging trapdoor. Normally not good at pull-ups, he must have been partially DHI, because he managed to lift himself, hook a leg, and pull himself up. Seconds later, the trapdoor snapped back into position. He stayed on the black squares and recrossed.

Middle staircase. Red door. He remembered this section well.

He heard the Dapper Dan hit bottom and, seconds later, the sound of him climbing stairs again. Faster now. Ever more determined to apprehend Finn.

Finn stepped forward into total darkness, a matter of extreme trust. The first time he'd followed Wayne in here, he'd nearly puked from fear. The black hole.

He ran smack into Philby.

"There's no elevator," Philby said.

"What?"

"No elevator. It's not here."

"It has to be here," Finn said.

"No such luck, Sherlock."

"But that means—"

"Somebody's up there," Philby said. "Already in

the apartment. And what do you want to bet it's not Wayne?"

"There's got to be another way up," Finn said. "Fire stairs. Something for an emergency."

"In case you hadn't noticed, it's pitch-black. You don't happen to have a flashlight on you, I suppose?"

"Turn your back to me," Finn said. He mustered his strength. Transforming into his DHI sapped his energy. He felt exhausted from having challenged the man just now, but knew he had to do this. He closed his eyes. He felt the warmth return. He couldn't hold it for more than a few seconds. He came out of it, his legs weak, his head swooning.

"Oh, man! How cool is that?" Philby said excitedly. "Hold on to my shirt, lightning bug. I saw some stairs over here."

Finn reached out and held on, as much to keep his balance as to stay with Philby. They reached a set of metal stairs, the handrail cool to the touch.

"Going up," said Philby.

They started climbing the spiral stairs. Higher and higher.

From below them came the heavy breathing of the man pursuing them.

He'd already caught back up. He sounded incredibly close.

7

MAYBECK PROVED HIMSELF the faster runner, arriving next to Amanda at nearly the same instant as Charlene and Willa despite having come the long way around. The rain was falling in punishing waves, and thunder was cracking menacingly overhead.

Amanda, soaking wet, was on her knees, crying. Jess just stood there, the rain passing through her. It took Maybeck and the girls a few seconds to realize what Amanda already knew.

"Oh, man," said Maybeck. "How long ago did this happen?"

Willa and Charlene helped Amanda to her feet. Everyone but Jess was now drenched. Charlene held her hands over her hair, as if that would do any good.

"She didn't keep up," Amanda said. "I thought she was probably fiddling with her iPod—trying to protect it from the rain. She won't stop messing with that thing. So I looked back, and . . . *she* was there." She pointed to the DHI of her sister.

"But how is that possible?" Willa asked. "Jess isn't a DHI."

"She is now," said Maybeck, contradicting. He ran his hand right through Jess's body and out the other side.

Some kids cheered and called out from the crowded wait line in front of Peter Pan's Flight, where they stood protected from the rain.

"Somebody did this," Amanda said. "They programmed a DHI for her. But it's not much of a program. She's just . . . standing there."

"But why?" Maybeck said.

"Who?" Willa said. "The Imagineers wouldn't do this without Wayne telling us."

More kids called out from the line, this time wanting autographs.

"We can't stay here," said Maybeck.

"I have to find her," Amanda said. "The *real* her."

"We need Finn and Philby," Willa said.

Hunched over and miserable in the rain, Charlene added, "Could we maybe move this meeting somewhere dry?"

Maybeck said, "We saw you two not five minutes ago. If they grabbed her . . . if they made a switch . . . it had to have happened between then and now. Somewhere really close to here."

"Are you saying she was . . . kidnapped?" Charlene said, a little too concerned with her hair to have stayed with the discussion.

"If humans take you, you're kidnapped," Maybeck answered. "I doubt there's a name for it when it's a band of Disney villains. But yeah. She's missing."

"But why?" Charlene asked Maybeck. "Why kidnap Jess?"

The three kids stared at Amanda, waiting for an answer. She pursed her lips as if she'd swallowed something bitter. "If I told you—which I can't—you wouldn't believe me."

"Try us," Maybeck said.

"You'd be surprised at what we can handle," said Willa.

"The Overtakers?" Maybeck asked, winning Amanda's attention.

"You don't know the half of it," Amanda said.

"Try us," Maybeck repeated.

"Please tell us," Willa pleaded. She wiped the rain from her eyes. "We want to help, but we need to know what's going on, what we're involved in."

Charlene proved she'd been paying attention after all. "This has to do with Finn, doesn't it? When Finn got tangled up with Jess, and you said some kind of spell had been removed. Maleficent's spell."

That incident had happened months ago, though the kids remembered it as if it were yesterday. Maleficent had kept Jess under her control to prevent Jess's own powers from interfering with Maleficent's plan. The DHIs had managed to trap Maleficent, and Finn had helped free Jess from the spell—though her powers had yet to be explained to any of them. Maybe this was why the sisters had vanished recently: to keep from having to explain themselves.

"We have to hurry," Willa said. "For one thing, those kids are blowing our cover. For another, every second counts. She can't be far."

"Since when are you a detective? You've been reading too many American Girl books," snapped Charlene.

"No, she's right," Maybeck said. "Time is in our favor, but not for long. Amanda and I will retrace her route, looking for her. Willa, you and Charlene get Finn and Philby out of the castle and meet up with us."

Amanda jerked her head toward Cinderella Castle. "He's *in* there?" she gasped, and then mumbled, "I'd nearly forgotten."

"Forgotten what?" Maybeck asked.

Amanda looked back and forth from the sputtering and sparking DHI of her sister to the colorful lights illuminating the castle.

"Something horrible's going to happen," Amanda whispered. "Jess dreamed about it. We came here to warn all of you." She met eyes with Maybeck and then Willa. "He's actually *in* there?"

"She dreamed about it?" Charlene said, distrustful and sarcastic. "Your sister can dream the future, I suppose? Is that what you're trying to tell us?"

"Fairlies have abilities you wouldn't believe."

"What's a Fairlie?" Willa blurted out.

"I told you you wouldn't believe me."

8

Finn followed Philby up the tightly wound spiral staircase in complete darkness, his lungs and legs burning, his head pounding. Transforming himself into a DHI—twice in a matter of minutes—had taxed him. He climbed, half in, half out of consciousness, sliding his hand along the cool steel handrail, faint of head but not of heart. Someone was trying to attract lightning to Cinderella Castle. He envisioned the penthouse apartment converted into a Frankenstein laboratory, some Disney monster strapped to a stainless-steel table with wires attached to his head and heart. He didn't know what to think—except that the Overtakers had sent the Dapper Dan to stop them. That had to mean something big was going down.

Thunder cracked outside, sending a rumble up his legs. Climbing higher in a lightning storm was not the smartest move. He felt another tremor in his chest.

Speaking in a breathless whisper as they climbed, Finn said, "What if it's all a trap? An elaborate trap? What if this guy is supposed to drive us to the top of the castle? What if the weather balloon and lightning are intended for us? To *kill* us?"

Philby stopped, and Finn bumped into him. He had trouble catching his breath. His heart was about to explode.

The staircase vibrated; the man was climbing toward them.

"But if that's the case, then this guy's suicidal," Philby said, "because he's right behind us."

"But if he's an Overtaker, how do we even know he's real?"

"How do we know if any of this is real?" Philby quipped. "Not one of us has ever told our parents about what happens to us at night. Why do you think that is?" He answered his own question. "Because they wouldn't believe it."

Shadows flickered on the wall. A flashlight. *The guy!*

"Climb!" Finn hissed.

They started climbing higher, running up the stairs as fast as they could. Their pursuer wasn't nearly as light on his feet as they were. The beam from his flashlight and the strange, shifting shadows it cast propelled them hurriedly up, up, up. At last, they faced a door.

It was bolted shut; there was no doorknob or handle.

In the dim light, Finn caught sight of a handwritten sign taped to the wall:

OPEN <u>ONLY</u> IN EMERGENCY

"Do we dare?" Finn asked.

"It has to lead into the apartment," said Philby.

"Agreed."

The light from the flashlight rose more quickly now. "And we're trying to get into the apartment."

Finn moved the bolt, and the door popped open.

Together they entered into another dark space. Finn reached out. It was narrow and tight. The sound of bells . . . no . . . Finn knew that sound. It wasn't bells. It was . . . *hangers*.

"We're in a closet," Finn said softly. "A closet inside the apartment, I'll bet."

"The stairs are the apartment's fire escape," said Philby. "Makes sense." But why lock a fire escape from the *outside*? Finn wondered silently.

He groped in the dark and touched another door in front of them and opened it a crack. The closet led into the apartment's small bedroom, the shiny bedspread a hideous shade of grass green. The air smelled stale and dusty. The boys slipped into the bedroom. It felt unbearably warm.

Heavy footsteps clomped up the stairs.

"Hurry!" Finn hissed. He and Philby shut the closet door and, working together, slid the bed to block it. At the very least they had bought themselves a few seconds.

They hurried to the bedroom door, and Finn put his ear to it.

"Anything?" Philby asked, one eye nervously on the blocked closet behind them.

"It sounds like someone mumbling." Finn opened the door carefully and then quietly stepped through. Philby followed. They were in a small hallway with a view into a larger living room. The décor might have once been called modern. Now it looked slightly cheesy.

Finn angled his head around the corner to get a better view into the living room. Then he jerked back.

Maleficent—the most powerful of the Disney fairies and Finn's greatest enemy—stood by the apartment window. Amanda had somehow known! Maleficent had enormous evil powers, including the ability to conjure spells with nothing more than incantations. Finn had once seen her transfigure a trash bag into a rat. She had demonstrated powers of fire and electricity, conjuring a cage of glowing "wires" around him. Her one weakness was temperature—she could only conjure when cold, which helped explain her being jailed in an apartment kept so warm. He doubted she was at her full powers, given the warmth of the apartment, but that could change in an instant. She had her back to them, and her dark robe hung to the floor. Now Finn understood what he'd heard: Maleficent was chanting while facing the open window. It was blocked on the outside by a heavy iron grate—like a jail cell.

Casting a spell? Finn wondered.

His legs shook with fear. The last he'd known, she'd been locked in a jail cell in the catacombs beneath Pirates of the Caribbean. What was she doing here?

She stepped away from the window but continued chanting. Through the window, the sky darkened. The storm roared as lightning flashed and thunder cracked. Finn tensed with the next lightning strike: a tremendous flash was followed instantly by a crack and boom. Was she summoning the lightning? Another loud crack. A bolt of electricity struck the iron grate. It glowed red hot, and then sparks flew. The iron grate melted and fell open, the window no longer blocked. The evening's cool breeze blew through.

Maleficent climbed up onto the sill. The crowd cheered from below.

Color filled the sky—the fireworks display had begun.

"Stop!" he shouted.

She turned. "YOU!"

It was no trap. Their being here clearly surprised her.

Her red eyes locked on to his. Her green, hideous

skin scrunched tightly around her eyes. *If looks could kill* . . . he thought.

Finn stepped back, afraid. *The cool air* . . . Three loud bangs of thunder mixed with the fireworks, making a war zone out of the sky. A fiery backdrop played out behind the green creature standing in the window.

She glanced back at him one more time and then climbed outside.

Finn and Philby hurried to the smoldering window opening and looked out.

Maleficent was climbing the castle wall, her cape swirling in the wind. She moved like an insect.

He looked down and gasped. They had to be a hundred feet up.

"I'm not going out there!" Finn said.

"The stairs!" Philby said.

With every second she would be cooling off, regaining her powers. The boys hurried back to the bedroom, determined to follow her. The Dapper Dan was pounding on the closet door from the other side.

"Ready?" Finn said, his hands against the bed frame.

Philby, selected as a DHI in large part for his brainpower, did not need to hear what Finn had in mind. He knew intuitively.

"One . . . two . . ."

On *three* the boys shoved the bed out of the way. The door flew open.

The Dapper Dan, who'd been pushing hard on the closet door, fell through and tumbled down onto the carpet. Finn and Philby ducked into the closet, hurried out the emergency door, and threw the bolt before the Dapper Dan had climbed to his feet. They had trapped him inside.

They hesitated on the landing.

"Up or down?" Finn asked Philby, the challenge obvious to both boys.

Philby looked down the stairs, knowing this meant safety. Then he looked at Finn. "If she gets free, we'll never be safe again," he said.

"Up!" the two boys said in unison.

The boys climbed the dark staircase, slowly at first, but then, holding the rail, Finn picked up the pace.

As they neared the top, the sound of the crowd grew louder. The stairs ended in a small stone chamber with an open window.

It took only seconds for Finn's eyes to adjust. There was a young woman tied up in the corner. She had wings, and for a moment he thought she, too, was an Overtaker. Then he recognized her as Tinker Bell. She was a Cast Member, in costume.

Maleficent stood in the open window, her robe

fluttering, the fireworks flashing colors in the sky beyond her. Now Finn saw the metal wire secured to the wall.

"Silly boys!" Maleficent said in a raspy voice. "The end is near."

She jumped.

Finn ran to the window.

But she hadn't fallen. Instead, she flew off, away from them.

She could fly!

But then Finn understood: near the conclusion of the fireworks show, Tinker Bell flew from the castle. Tinker Bell was actually a Cast Member riding a zip line from the castle onto a roof in Tomorrowland. But on this night, it wasn't Tinker Bell riding the zip line.

Maleficent let out a bloodcurdling screech—to the delight of the crowd—as she rode the wire high in the sky. She grew smaller and smaller.

The crowd went crazy with cheers and screams.

Her hideous screech rang in the air until swallowed by the next thumping blast of fireworks—the grand finale—that joined the rippling of thunder echoing off the Florida landscape like the aftereffect of a bomb exploding.

9

THE LIGHTNING STRIKE that hit Cinderella Castle charged the night sky with intense light as fire rained down. The bolt of lightning had grounded out on the thin wire holding the weather balloon. Next, the lights went out in a large area encircling the castle, including the street lamps surrounding the Hub, most of Liberty Square, and as far away as Tomorrowland. Spotlights that normally lit the sky went black, leaving the colorful glow of the fireworks' grand finale.

Then something—or someone—flew out toward Tomorrowland, and it was quite obviously *not* Tinker Bell. The caped figure was chased by a ball of swirling orange flame. A chorus of cheers arose. No one was exactly sure what they'd just witnessed, but whatever it was, it was amazing.

Willa and the others heard the cheer. Only moments later a swirl of rumor reached them: a witch had flown from the castle. Maybeck said a few words that would have gotten him detention in school.

"Which witch?" Charlene wondered aloud.

"Three guesses," said Amanda.

The three others looked at her sharply.

"Finn!" Charlene muttered, her worry hanging in the air.

"What do we do now?" Willa gasped.

"You've got to tell us what you know," Maybeck demanded of Amanda.

"It's Jess that saw this coming, not me," Amanda said.

"Saw *what* coming?" he asked.

"Trouble."

"You already said that. You gotta give us more."

"I told you: Jess is different."

"She's your sister!" he complained.

"Yeah," she said, sounding apologetic. "Kind of. I guess you could say I'm a little different as well."

"Different how?"

"Just . . . different."

"She's not on trial," Willa complained to Maybeck. "She and Jess came to *warn* us!" She addressed Amanda. "What did Jess think was going to happen?"

"She *saw* things. She wrote them down—drew things—in her journal. Kept track of them—dreams mostly. And daydreams. But . . ." She cut herself off and looked at each of the others searchingly. "The really creepy part is she showed me a sketch she made of lightning striking the castle. She knew it was going to happen, and I think she knew that Finn was going to be inside."

"You owe us an explanation," Maybeck said impatiently.

"And you'll have it," Amanda agreed. She glanced around—a number of guests were braving the rain to get a better look at the castle. "But not here. Not now. You have to help Finn. He's in danger. More danger than from just the lightning. It's the Overtakers. They did this. They're responsible. Jess . . . I have to find Jess. They're afraid of her . . . powers. She can stop this by warning you and others, but not if they control her."

"Stop what?" Maybeck asked.

"I wish I knew."

"The lightning?" Willa asked. "We're a little late, if that's the case."

"It was more than that," Amanda said. "Listen, I've got to find Jess. You all need to help Finn and Philby. They're in danger. Jess saw that coming. *That* was what she was trying to prevent."

"Okay," Maybeck said, "enough chit-chat. Let's get going. Amanda and I are going to head back to look for Jess while you two check out the castle and find Finn and Philby."

"With the power out, they'll close the Park," Willa warned. "They're not going to let us run around for long. And if they recognize us, they're not going to want us in the Park at all."

"Well, then, pull up your hood. Mess up your hair. We gotta do this," Maybeck said. "If they close the Park, we'll text and figure this out." He grabbed Amanda's arm and tugged. She hesitated, then moved with him.

They took off at a run.

"Everyone check the group text at midnight," he yelled over his shoulder.

Charlene and Willa headed for the castle, which was shrouded in darkness and a veil of smoke left over from both the fireworks and the lightning strike.

Behind them, they left the sputtering hologram of Jess, who, as another series of street lamps flickered and failed in the spreading blackout, sputtered and went dark.

Gone, just like the real Jess.

Some kids cheered from under awnings. Rain continued to fall.

One of them shouted, "The Kingdom Keepers *rule!*"

Willa winced at hearing the nickname that a local newspaper had adopted for the kids and their DHIs. She felt a chill down her spine and a pain in her stomach. They weren't superheroes; they were teen models mixed up in some confused technology that no one fully understood—not even the people who'd invented it.

She'd gotten a good look at the thing flying.

She knew what she'd seen—*whom* she'd seen—and the chill was replaced with a spasm of terror.

Maleficent had escaped. Jess had been turned into a DHI.

To think that those two events were some kind of freak coincidence and unrelated was just plain wrong.

10

It sounded like dozens of footsteps were hurrying up the spiral staircase as Finn and Philby rushed to untie the woman dressed up as Tinker Bell. Finn got the tape off her mouth.

"Are you all right?"

She looked terrified. "Who . . . *what* . . . was that?"

Philby said, "Finn, we're cooked."

The approaching footsteps were noticeably closer. They belonged to either security guards or Overtakers. Either way spelled disaster for the boys.

"Who's coming?" the Tinker Bell woman asked.

"We don't know."

"I'm not sticking around to find out," she said.

The boys looked paralyzed.

She said, "Harnesses," pointing to the wall. "They're rescue harnesses, in case I get stuck out there." She hesitated only a second before grabbing one. "Put them on!"

She helped both boys into the harnesses and double-checked them for safety. "Have you ever ridden a zip line?"

55

Finn shook his head.

Philby said, "In camp once."

"Same thing," she said. "I'm going to go first." She clipped a pulley to the guy wire. "That way I can catch you two as you arrive on the other end. Ready?"

Whoever was coming up the spiral stairs was moving fast.

"See you down there," she said. With that, she jumped.

Finn watched as she zoomed away, into the dark of the night. She disappeared.

"I am *not* going out that window," Finn declared.

"Listen," Philby said, "we have two choices: we can get busted and blamed for everything that just happened, or we can go out that window."

"You're insane."

The sounds coming up the stairs grew even louder.

Philby grunted and pushed Finn toward the window. "You're first," he said.

"I don't think so."

"Those guys are going to be here in about two seconds."

"What if it doesn't support us?

"This is Disney. The thing will probably support a tank."

"What if Tinker Bell doesn't catch us?"

"My advice? Don't look down."

Philby tested the pulley and pushed Finn.

Finn felt a blistering wind on his face.

He was . . . *flying*. It was, for an instant, the coolest thing he'd ever done. He was zooming down the wire, high above the grass and the water, headed for the lights of Tomorrowland.

The whine of the pulley rose to a high-pitched whir. Philby was behind him now. Down, down, down they raced. Then the wire leveled off, and their speed decreased. They were headed above a set of rooftops. Finn caught sight of the MONSTERS, INC. LAUGH FLOOR sign to his left. With the wire more level, they continued to slow.

Tinker Bell caught them at the far end, in front of a set of pads. She unhooked the pulleys and helped them both out of the harnesses.

Finn looked back to see several men huddled in the tower they'd just left.

"Nice timing," he said. Seeing how far they had traveled, his knees went weak. "That was not a smart thing to do."

"It was *incredibly* stupid!" Philby agreed. He looked at Finn sheepishly. "But man, was that fun!"

Tinker Bell led them down a very steep metal

staircase and into an alley. A moment later, she'd showed them how to reenter the Park. They hurried toward the Hub.

"FINN!" He heard his name shouted from far away. It took him a moment to see in the glow of a few emergency lights what Philby saw first: two figures up near the castle. Girls.

"It's Willa and Charlene," Finn said.

"How can you be sure?" Philby said, squinting.

"Trust me. It's them."

The boys ran toward the girls, circled carefully, and hid on the other side of a stone wall, waiting. They squatted down and caught their breath.

Finn dared to raise an eye above the wall: he saw a pair of Cast Members that he took to be security guards, searching the crowd.

"They're looking for us," he told Philby. "Might be Overtakers. Might just be Disney Security."

"We'll get across the Hub and catch up to the girls. We're just two kids now among all the others."

It was true: the rain had stopped and the crowds had returned. An announcement was repeated several times, apologizing for the fact that the Park would close early due to the weather. Cinderella Castle had been roped off.

The two boys crossed the busy Hub outside of the

castle. As they reached its center a number of lights came back on, and the look and feel of the castle was restored. Some firemen were packing up.

And there, waving from the castle plaza, were Charlene and Willa.

"We've got to get out of here now. All of us," Finn told Philby. "We'll fill in the blanks later."

"No argument from me," Philby said. "I just want everybody safe."

11

AT TWO MINUTES BEFORE MIDNIGHT, as Finn was preparing to text with Philby, Maybeck, and the others, his laptop's messaging window showed an extra user. His parents made a big deal out of how unsafe the Internet could be. And while he thought his parents overdid their warnings, he knew that the appearance of an uninvited guest into a group chat was cause for alarm.

Finn typed: **Anon I, who are you?**

I'm from the firehouse.

Finn's breath caught. Wayne Kresky, the Disney Legend and former Imagineer, lived above the firehouse in the Magic Kingdom. Could this possibly be Wayne? The man had been missing for a long time now.

WAYNE? Finn typed, but nothing appeared in the text window. The program was blocking that name from being written. Finn considered how to work around the problem. Then he typed again.

W . . . A . . . Y . . . N . . . E . . . ?

You always were the clever one. my name was supposed to be blocked, but separating the letters! brilliant!

Finn wasn't convinced it was Wayne on the other end of this written conversation. Whoever it was could be an imposter.

Finn typed: **You have something I found, but you kept. it's magical. what is it?**

He anxiously awaited the answer. This question, he felt, would determine if it was in fact Wayne.

Uncle walt's pen

Finn laughed at the screen. It really was Wayne. No one but he and the other DHIs knew that answer.

An unusual feeling overcame Finn. For months he'd wondered if Wayne had died or been captured by the Overtakers. Thrilled to now reconnect with him, he let his fingers hover over the keyboard.

Where to start?

A Disney old-timer, Wayne knew more about Disney World than any living person. He had once counted Walt Disney himself as a personal friend. A legend in Disney circles, his name often appeared on blogs.

He was responsible for Finn and his friends becoming DHIs in the first place. He had created the concept and had overseen the development of the software. More important, as far as Finn could tell, he controlled a secret group of Cast Members that opposed the Overtakers' attempt to gain control of the Magic Kingdom.

Finn received a video chat invite from Anon1. He accepted.

* * *

"It's really you," Finn gasped, seeing the man's weathered face on his laptop's screen. There was no telling how old Wayne was, but he wasn't young.

The video signal wasn't perfect: static overlaid Wayne's face, and the sound of his voice was crackling and uneven. He looked and sounded older than Finn remembered him.

"You don't have much time," he said, causing gooseflesh to ripple up Finn's arms.

"Excuse me?" Finn replied.

Wayne was continually checking over his shoulder, as if afraid of being found out, which Finn found disturbing.

"You were lucky at the Park tonight," Wayne said.

"You were there?"

"Never mind about me. *You* were there. That's all that matters."

"It was Maleficent."

"Tell me exactly what happened."

Finn kept his summary of the evening's events as

short and succinct as possible. He described spotting Amanda and Jess during the start of the parade; of later seeing a pair of monkeys in the bushes near the crowd. Wayne quizzed him about the monkeys. Then Finn described his being chased up Escher's Keep, and finished with Maleficent's daring escape out the window and down Tinker Bell's zip line.

"We'd moved her there," Wayne said. "Third move in as many weeks. We had intelligence that the Overtakers were planning for her escape. We thought by moving her around frequently . . . But it obviously wasn't enough."

"What about the weather balloon? The lightning strike?"

"The apartment was locked down like a jail cell. Sealed tight. We had to provide a way out in case of fire, but the closest exit was locked from the inside. Our security guard would have had to open that door for her to escape."

"The Dapper Dan chasing us . . . was he one of your guys?"

"You had no way of knowing that."

But I should have, Finn thought. The Dapper Dan had known the way up the Keep. Only Wayne could have taught him the route.

"We put on an ankle bracelet that would send an alarm if she moved more than fifty feet from the transmitter," Wayne explained. "It housed a GPS transmitter, so we could track her down. They used the power of the lightning strike to break open the bars. Nothing short of a small bomb would have accomplished that. The lightning also temporarily knocked out the power, which was crucial for her to escape. They bought her enough time to cut the ankle bracelet off. We found it up there in the Tinker Bell tower."

That didn't sound good. "So she's just . . . gone?"

"I doubt very far. A green face tends to stick out. It's control of the Park that she's after. She'll stay in the Park, we think. But to accomplish her goal of domination, she'll have to rebuild, and reorganize the Overtakers. And she'll need the five of you out of the way. You defeated her last time. She won't risk that happening again."

Finn didn't like the way Wayne said that so calmly. Out of the way? He tried to wrap his mind around the fact that they were talking about a Disney character—villain or not—as if she were human. And after all that he and the other DHIs had been through, it wasn't so hard. Something weird was going on, and somehow they were now a big part of it. Whatever kind of being Maleficent was, however it was that she existed, her presence was very real, as was the threat to the DHIs.

"She needs cold, don't forget, or at least the illusion of cold. She loses her powers in the heat. For this and other reasons, we think she's likely gone to Animal Kingdom."

"Because?"

"There are several attractions there that are kept quite chilly. And of course there's Everest."

"Is that where Jess is?"

Wayne's face tightened. "You want to explain that, please?"

Finn told him the rest of what had happened. He explained what Willa had told him briefly upon their meeting by the castle: that Jess had been replaced by a DHI and the real Jess had vanished.

"That's why I was I was about to text with the others just now," he explained. "To figure out how to get Jess back." He listened to himself say that, and wondered what chance they had against Maleficent. Having ignored it, he switched over to the group text and asked them all to wait for him. Wayne showing up complicated things.

"Amanda," Finn told Wayne, "supposedly said something about Jess being . . . different. Like she's a Cast Member or something."

"She's not a Cast Member," Wayne said knowingly. If he knew something about Jess, he hid it well, for although the reception was poor—sparking and sputtering—his expression didn't change.

"What I'm going to tell you now," Wayne said, "is done so in the strictest confidence. Do you understand me, Finn? You can share what you must with your friends, but only if absolutely necessary, and only if they promise to protect the information. It's critical to the safety of all of us."

"I promise."

Wayne glanced suspiciously over his shoulder for the umpteenth time. "I'm in hiding, as you must be aware by now. The Overtakers are said to have obtained the DHI technology. They are working on projecting me—turning me into a DHI so that they could mislead our efforts to defeat them. And if they managed to contain my DHI when I was sleeping . . . well . . . you saw what happened to your friend Maybeck."

Months earlier, Maybeck's DHI had been prevented from crossing back over—a process that was triggered by a small black remote control device that Wayne possessed. As a result, the human Maybeck had remained asleep in bed in a kind of induced coma while his DHI had been trapped in a maintenance cage in Space Mountain. Finn had freed Maybeck's DHI, and Wayne had then crossed them over, allowing the human Maybeck to awaken from his comatose state.

But the idea of that happening to Wayne or any of the other DHIs ever again was terrifying. Unthinkable.

"What you've just told me about Jess's disappearance," Wayne said, "figures into this theory, I'm afraid. It suggests the Overtakers do, in fact, have the DHI technology at their disposal, and that presents us with some difficult choices."

"Our DHIs went back online tonight," Finn muttered.

"Precisely! You're aware of the DHI expansion plan?"

Finn had heard rumors that Animal Kingdom was planning to use DHIs of various animals to guide guests through the park. A lion or baboon would show a family around in the same way holograms of Finn and his friends guided guests around Magic Kingdom.

"Animal Kingdom this year," Wayne said. "Then they'll put your DHIs at Disneyland and the cruise ships within two years. You and the other DHIs have become so popular that the Imagineers are ramping up expansion into all the Parks around the world: Paris, Hong Kong, Japan. You have developed an enormous fan base."

The video briefly sputtered and went dark, but a moment later Wayne's face grew larger as he leaned toward the camera.

Wayne spoke softly. "Imagineering won't confirm or deny my team's accusations that Animal Kingdom's DHI server was cloned, but now with what you've told me, I'm sure of it. The Overtakers have a second DHI server, Finn. No one around here is ever going to admit it, but that doesn't mean it's not true. They have stolen the software responsible for projecting you five kids as holograms. If they've created DHI data for me, as I believe—and for Jess, as you've just told me—then it's in an effort to trick us or spy on us or manipulate us. What if my DHI is used so that I give my people orders that they, the Overtakers, want given?"

"That would give them control of the Park." Finn paused, deep in thought. "But wait a second. If they have the same server, the same software, does that give them control over our DHIs too?"

"You see? You understand things so quickly. There's a reason you're the leader," Wayne said, his eyes briefly looking brighter.

"I'm not the leader."

"Of course you are."

"We've never voted on a leader."

"Not all leaders are elected, Finn. Some just rise to the occasion."

Finn ignored that. He and his friends worked as a group. Wayne wouldn't understand that.

"So what you're saying," Finn said, "is that the Overtakers may be able to use our DHIs like they used Jess to trick Amanda? They could have us doing stuff we wouldn't want."

"It's not only that, I'm afraid. If they have a second server up and running—and by everything you've told me about Jess's disappearance, they must—then the greater concern is their generating DHIs for each of you inside Animal Kingdom. If they trap those DHIs and prevent them from crossing back over when you're asleep . . ."

"We'd end up like Maybeck was."

"Sleeping Beauty Syndrome," Wayne said.

"Yeah: SBS," Finn whispered so softly to himself that Wayne didn't hear. It was the nickname Wayne had given to the comatose state. "But why would they want to do that to us?"

"Because Maleficent wants you out of the way. For good. They can only accomplish that if you go to sleep," Wayne reminded Finn. "That's the key, you see? If none of you goes to sleep, there's no way you'll cross over in the first place, no way you could be trapped in the Syndrome. They cannot gain that control over you as long as you remain awake."

"I thought the software was rewritten so that we couldn't cross over again? And if we don't cross over we can't be trapped in SBS. SBS couldn't happen again. Wasn't that the real reason the DHI server has been down for the past couple months? The Grand Opening was to celebrate everything working again."

"Yes, yes, yes. And I'd like to think the same rewritten software had been installed at Animal Kingdom, but that installation has been going on while the original software was being debugged. I know a software update was made available to Animal Kingdom, but I can't get anyone over there to confirm it ever took place."

Finn stared at Wayne's flickering face, his thoughts whirring. Wayne was warning him that the Overtakers had a DHI server with the original flawed software that allowed Sleeping Beauty Syndrome. "You're freaking me out," Finn said.

"Yes. I can understand that."

"How do you know any of this is for real?"

"I don't. All I can tell you is, as a precaution, I've been taking twenty-minute naps—never a minute longer, hoping to keep them from crossing me over. So far it has worked. But for how long? The crossing over has to do with the dream state. We designed it that way. It occurs in the first few moments of REM sleep, which is about twenty minutes into a decent night's sleep. The crossing over feels to you like it happens immediately—instantly—but that's not the case. And another thing: I designed the crossing over to synchronize—that is, if you all go to sleep at about the same time, all five of you would then cross over at roughly the same moment. It saves the code from having to reload for each of you."

"But what about the remote control? If we got in trouble, couldn't you use that to cross us back over?"

"If your DHIs were all in the same place at the same time. Yes, that's more than likely possible. But they could prevent that easily enough."

"By keeping our DHIs apart." Finn didn't like what he was hearing. "So, what am I supposed to do?" he asked. Wayne was making it sound as if there was no hope: they were doomed.

"You need to stay awake. You need to find where the real Jess is being kept," Wayne explained. "And you need to find that second server and take it back. At the very least, you need to crash it. But only once Jess is safe and you see that she's fully awake. I wouldn't mind if you contacted me then as well. If you crash that server before saving Jess . . . well . . . I'm not sure you or anyone else will ever see her again."

"And if they catch you sleeping, then the same applies to you," Finn said.

"Never mind about me. It's Jess we must concentrate on."

"Why? Who is she?" Finn asked, hearing something different, something urgent, in Wayne's voice. He knew something he wasn't sharing.

Wayne grimaced. He looked sternly into the camera. "It's not for me to say."

"But you know?"

"I suspect. Knowing and suspecting are two different things."

"Then tell me."

"I can't. That wouldn't be fair to her or you. For one thing, I could be wrong. Listen, Finn, there are powers at work far greater than my own. It's not for me to guess. If you're to learn about Jess, it will have to come from another source."

"Amanda."

"Perhaps."

"They're sisters."

"That's a loosely thrown-around term, now isn't it, Finn? We're all sisters and brothers, depending how far back you go."

"They aren't sisters," Finn said, seeking an answer.

"It isn't for me to say. That's the best I can do."

"Find Jess," Finn said, repeating his instructions. "Find and crash the second server. Recover it if we can."

"It's challenge enough, I know," Wayne said. "But the bigger challenge will be how quickly you can accomplish any of this. You absolutely must have Jess safe and the server crashed before any of you fall asleep. If you sleep, you very well may be crossed over into that second server, the Overtakers' server, and that would leave you—the real Finn—"

"SBS," Finn said, cutting him off. "The Sleeping Beauty Syndrome."

"Yes, I'm afraid so."

"*You're* afraid?" said Finn sarcastically. "How do you think I feel?"

"There's one last thing I need to explain."

Wayne was constantly doing this: holding stuff back, and Finn found it frustrating and annoying. It was as if . . . as if he were testing him.

"I'm going to put a secure Web address into your group text. Have you ever heard of VMK, Virtual Magic Kingdom?"

"No," Finn answered him.

"It was a video game that was closed to the public years ago, but it's still alive and active with the Imagineers. You'll like it. I've created a secure private room for you and the others to use. You can message there safely. And listen, you may need access to it when you're in Animal Kingdom since it won't work on mobile phones. You can use the Disney Vacation Club screens with the access code: yen-sid—underscore—now. Memorize it, don't write it down."

"Got it."

"Once you're inside VMK, if you need my help, type my name. It won't show in the text box, but I'll see it and I'll come find you. Don't trust any of the other avatars you encounter in VMK."

"But you said they're Imagineers!" Finn protested.

"The Overtakers are everywhere, Finn. Take every precaution possible."

"Yeah, okay."

"You must find Maleficent and destroy the second server. So, yes. You and the others will be going into the Animal Kingdom to accomplish that. And remember, your DHIs aren't protected there."

"I remember."

Wayne looked back over his shoulder again. "Oh, no . . ." he said, his voice strained. The screen sparked static, and Wayne was gone.

* * *

Finn explained things in the group text, then found his way to to the DHIs' private room inside VMK. Their avatars had clearly been drawn with an attention to hair color and style. Nothing else about any of them looked even vaguely similar. Maybeck was sitting on a virtual couch. Willa and Charlene were over in a corner, their text boxes filled with dialogue.

What had to be Philby stood near to the room's only door, as if guarding it. Text bubbles appeared above an avatar when anyone typed a message.

Philby: Maybeck, help me out here

Philby's and Maybeck's avatars pushed the couch in front of the room's only door to block it. Philby remained there, just behind the couch, while the others moved to the far side of the room. Charlene brushed her hair in the mirror. Maybeck's avatar shot free throws at a basketball hoop on the wall.

Finn described the meeting with Wayne as simply as possible.

Finn: Animal Kingdom is installing a DHI server — animal hosts as guides. our old friend thinks the new server may have been cloned, possibly when Maleficent was hiding out in the server room. remember that? if that's right, the Overtakers may have their own DHI server, or they may have control of the new one at AK. that means if we go to sleep they may be able to cross us over — to control us and prevent our return. we'd be in perma-sleep the same way

Maybeck was at Space Mountain. Sleeping Beauty Syndrome.

Willa: Jess's DHI

Finn: Exactly. that was them. it confirms some kind of second server is up and working.

Philby: Are you saying we can't go to sleep?

Finn: He's warning us not to.

Philby: Exactly how long does he think we can stay awake?

Finn: Depends on how much Coke we can drink.

Charlene: I'm already tired. Charlene's avatar finally turned away from the mirror.

Maybeck: This is crazy.

Finn: We can do whatever we want. he's just warning us.

Maybeck: Not to sleep.

Finn: Yes.

Maybeck: And I'm saying that's crazy.

Philby: So what's the drill?

Finn: We find Jess and get her to safety. then we find or destroy this cloned DHI server and put it out of commission.

Maybeck: All before we go to sleep.

Finn: That's the safest for all of us

It was a long time before any dialogue lines appeared above any of the avatars. Finally, Willa's avatar stepped away from the others.

Willa: If it was my sister, i'd be freaking out.

Charlene: Same here.

Maybeck: Do we know they've got her in AK?

Finn: Remember the monkeys we saw tonight? they've got to be from the Animal Kingdom! and it fits with what the old guy said about the server— that's AK as well.

Philby: AK's a big park

Charlene: I love Animal Kingdom

Maybeck: We can't get in there at night without being busted. i don't need any trouble. my aunt is using my DHI money for my college.

Finn: The guy who chased philby and me . . . turns

out he's with the old guy . . . he can get us in around 5 AM, when the park is waking up. there's work to do before then. we need to know everything there is to know about the park

Maybeck: Such as?

Finn: Layout and cast members — that'll be willa. electronics and security — philby, of course, including the coldest buildings. maybeck will find out everything about the animals — their feeding, where they're kept, how dangerous they are. charlene, we may need costumes, ways to blend in. i'll talk to amanda. she mentioned Jess's diary. amanda will definitely be part of this. Anyone have any trouble with that?

No one typed a thing.

Finn: Okay. good luck getting out of your houses. i'm going on bike. we should all charge our phones so we can keep in touch

He waited. No one challenged him.

Finn: Meet up with a food truck at 4:45 AM outside the entrance to the Animal Kingdom Lodge. the dapper dan guy will be driving. if anyone can't make it early, we'll all meet after the main gates open on the path leading in to the Rainforest Café. agreed?

Maybeck: I'm in

Philby: Me too.

Willa: Likewise

Charlene: What if we can't find Jess?

Finn had half expected a question like that from Charlene. But he wasn't prepared for the sinking feeling in his gut as he read it. His fingers hesitated briefly above the keyboard. And then he typed.

Finn: That's not an option.

12

Finn DIDN'T GET ANY great joy from sneaking out of his house at 1 a.m. His parents were pretty good about giving him his privacy and space. The two things they asked in return were honesty and trust. He broke their trust by opening his second-story window and shinnying down the fire rope installed for emergencies. The only justification for his actions was that this qualified as an emergency—though he'd never be able to explain it to them. If caught, he'd be grounded for all eternity.

He quietly walked the Hawk Tracer BMX out to the sidewalk. Then he climbed onto the bike and took off down the sidewalk. It was the most beautiful bike he'd ever owned—silver-and-black frame, monkey bars, alloy levers—and it ripped along, teasing him into trying a few tricks, such as jumping curbs and popping wheelies, which he resisted because of the dark.

He kept to the residential streets as much as possible, avoiding the busier avenues, afraid that a policeman would stop and question a kid on a bike. It was a long ride, and he settled into a rhythm of slowing at stop signs, looking in all directions for headlights, and then crossing—but never fully stopping. The residential streets were totally quiet and empty of cars. Soon he had two miles behind him. Then three. He crossed two major avenues, finding his way into Orlando's older neighborhoods, one connecting to another. Finally, the residential gave way to the commercial. He flew past shuttered buildings, businesses of every kind: psychic readings, dry cleaning, a yarn store, a bakery, dozens of restaurants and coffee shops, dog grooming, curtains and drapes, lamps, a half dozen banks, and a copy shop. He spotted the red tile roof and stucco walls of a building he'd been to once before. Amanda's house.

It had a tall, stained-glass window in the front, just below a squared-off steeple that showed a white angel against a blue background. Maybe it had once been a church.

He pulled the bike around back to an apron of cracked blacktop that had once been a parking lot. He locked the BMX to a metal railing and then circled the building, wondering, *What now?* He'd never been inside Amanda's house before, though he assumed, from what she'd said, that she and Jess had separate bedrooms. Each ground-level window had a grid of heavy wrought-iron bars on the outside to protect against burglars; it gave Finn a ladder to climb. He went from the railing to the bars on a window, grabbed hold of an iron pipe running from the gutters, threw a knee up over the edge, and pulled himself onto the Spanish-tile roof. He walked gingerly, for the first tile he stepped on cracked.

A shade was pulled down blocking the first window he reached. Finn edged around the corner to another window with its shade up. There was a small solar panel propped up on the window ledge. It was dark behind the glass. Finn cupped his face to the glass and was able to make out an empty bed. There were no posters on the wall—no artwork at all. The place looked dumpy and unlived-in. He took this to be Jess's room. There were no bars across the second-story windows, so he tried to open one, but it didn't budge. He moved along slowly; the roof was steeply pitched. The Spanish tile felt smooth and slippery beneath his sneakers.

The last window on this side had its shade up, but gauzy curtains were pulled across it. It also had the same kind of solar panel outside—this one taped to the jamb. He tried cupping his eyes with his hands to the glass but could barely see anything in the dark room. What he did see was a pair of sneakers on the floor: Amanda's black high-tops. Convinced he had the right room, he tapped lightly on the pane. Waited. Tapped again.

All at once, black objects fled from the overhead eves. Bats! Finn instinctively jumped back, slipped, and fell face-first to the curved tile roof. He reached out and clawed his fingertips into the windowsill. Just then, the curtains sprang back, and there was Amanda looking out the rain-stained window at him, her face a sleepy, twisted knot of curiosity. She wore a spaghetti-strap top and plaid pajama bottoms.

Finn's fingers slipped an inch, leaving scratch marks on the sill. Another half inch, and he was gone.

Amanda threw open the window and grabbed both his wrists. They locked grips. She put her foot to the wall and heaved and pulled. Finn grabbed the inside of the sill, got his knees under him, and, with her help, climbed inside.

"Sorry," he whispered.

"The front door is easier," Amanda said in a normal voice. "Or you could have called."

"Shhh!" he said, ducking low, as if that would help.

"Why?" she said, again in her normal voice. "I'm the only one here."

"What?"

"I . . . ah . . ." Amanda switched on the light. It was a dim compact fluorescent bulb hanging from a wire that led to a car battery. A second wire led from the battery to the window and the solar panel beyond. As Finn took all this in, Amanda spoke, but unlike the Amanda he knew, she wasn't telling the truth. "Our mother . . . my mother . . . she . . . she . . . her sister down in Boca needed her. She had to leave suddenly. Left me by myself."

"All alone?"

"I'm a big girl."

"You're fourteen. My parents *never* leave me alone overnight." He paused as their situation sank in. "You're alone? We're alone?" He spoke in his normal voice.

He took in the light, the battery, and the solar panel outside the window. He saw no light in the hallway. He'd seen no other lights from the street.

"We are. Stay there." She went to a closet and put on a robe. She sat down on the edge of her bed and pointed to a rickety chair at the desk.

Finn moved the chair closer.

"It's two in the morning," she said. "Just for the record."

The air from the open window was cool. The curtains danced at the sides. Amanda stood and closed the window. "Whoa!" she said. "Check it out!"

It took Finn a moment to spot the bat hanging upside down from the eaves above the window. It was *big*, though Finn didn't want to appear scared by a bat. It had a blue iridescence to its black wings, tucked at its sides. It looked dangerous.

"Creepy," he said.

"There are a lot of bats here," she said. "I think they

live in the attic. Though that's the biggest one I've seen, by far."

She pulled the curtains, shuddered, and sat back down on the bed. "They make the weirdest sounds at night. Sometimes I have trouble sleeping."

"Flying rodents. Never been a big fan. I'm not one of those guys with rats for pets. No thanks."

"I've never had a pet."

"Seriously?"

"We moved around a lot." She blushed and looked away; he wondered what that was about.

"You remember Wayne?" he asked.

Her eyes went wide. "I thought he'd disappeared."

"Yeah, so did I." Finn went on to explain his encounter with Wayne, and then the meeting that had followed. Amanda interrupted several times, clarifying the connection between Jess's disappearance, her DHI being seen at the Magic Kingdom, and the possibility that the DHI server had been cloned.

She sat for several long minutes with her head in her hands, her hair cascading over her forearms and forming a veil she hid behind.

"I'm going to trust you," she said.

Finn felt a shiver. He looked up at the bat, a long, dark silhouette seen through the translucent curtains. "Okay," he said.

"I can trust you, right?"

"Right."

"Because I'm not supposed to tell anyone."

He didn't say anything, but she had every cell in his body focused on her.

"Most people, they would never believe it. And that's a *good thing*. It's better if people don't believe it. It's safer for everyone. There's some saying about hiding behind ignorance, isn't there? There should be, if there isn't. Am I rambling?"

"Sort of."

"Nervous."

"It's just me."

She came up from under the veil of hair and met Finn's eyes. Hers were close to tears, shining like marbles. "You, of all people, might understand. You and the others. I can't think of anyone else. Maybe you won't believe—and that's okay," she said, reaching out and touching his knee. "I won't be mad or anything."

"I can't believe it if I never hear what it is," he said, a little impatiently.

She nodded, her eyes apologetic. "Jess and I are different," she said.

"I know that," he said quickly. "You're very different."

"No . . . I don't mean from each other. I think it might be better if you just listen. No offense or anything, but this is kind of hard to explain."

He nodded, thinking he shouldn't speak.

She saw this and giggled. Covered her mouth. Looked as if she might cry. When she spoke, it was very softly.

"I guess the only way to explain this is just to say it."

Works for me, he thought, but didn't say so.

"We're Fairlies."

"You mean: fairies?"

"No. Fairlies. As in, fairly human. It was supposedly a joke a long, long time ago, but it stuck. Fairlies. Go figure. We're not witches or fairies, or anything like that. We're just kids with . . . unusual abilities."

"Such as?"

"I'm not allowed to say. Sorry. Rules, you know?"

"You and Jess are sisters?"

"Sort of, I guess. Not exactly. We're both orphans. All Fairlies are orphans. My parents drowned. Jess's went on this trip to South America and never came back. They think pirates—*real pirates*—got them. She and I were raised in the same foster home. That's why I call her my sister. Fairlies display certain qualities at a very young age: spoon-benders, mind readers, clairvoyants. There was a boy who could set fire to things by just *looking* at them. Very strange. But real. Jess dreamed the trouble here in the Parks. This was way before you guys were hired to be the models for the DHIs. She and I . . . we kind of ran away. Not recommended, I might add."

Finn understood the solar panels then: there were no parents. Jess and Amanda lived by themselves.

"The day we got here, Maleficent put a spell on Jess or bewitched her or something. Jess didn't even recognize me. Then you and the DHIs came along. Somehow, you released her right before Maleficent was captured. I wanted to go back after that, to the . . . foster home, but Jess had more dreams."

The way she'd paused told Finn something, but he wasn't sure what.

"She keeps them in a diary, a journal," Amanda explained.

"So, she can dream the future?" Finn asked skeptically.

"Believe whatever you want to," Amanda said, "or not. *I believe* the Overtakers have taken Jess prisoner to prevent her from interfering with whatever they have planned."

Finn's skin crawled. He felt slightly sick to his stomach.

Amanda stared at Finn long and hard, her eyes fiery

pinpricks. "I can't expect you to believe any of this. Asking that is probably too much. I hope you do some-day. I hope this makes us better friends, not worse. I'm trusting you in ways I've never trusted anyone." She paused. Her breathing was labored, her skin flushed. Finn felt as if he might explode with anticipation.

"And your powers?" he asked.

"Sorry," she said squinting. "Can't say. Not now. Not yet, anyway."

"You and Jess are squatting. Here, in this house, this church. Whatever it once was. The solar power." He pointed.

Amanda eyed Finn cautiously. "You're not going to tell."

"I've got bigger secrets than this, believe me."

"It was closed up. Abandoned. We always enter by the back. We're very careful. Only once have I used the front door, and that's when you and your mother dropped me off here. I wasn't even sure it could open."

"And the neighbors?" Finn asked.

"What neighbors?" Amanda said. "It's stores and stuff. No one's ever said anything to us. It's only been a couple of months. The water's on. It's cold; no hot water, but it works. We shower at school. The toilets work."

"This is way cool."

"It's not great, but it's what was available. We had to think fast."

"Don't Fairlies have money?" Finn asked.

"If you're going to tease me, we're done here."

"Can't take a joke?"

"Not about that," Amanda said. "And yes, I have an after-school job. But right now, I think we both could use some sleep." She yawned.

"No! We can't sleep," he said. "Wayne says if any of us—the DHIs—go to sleep, we might get trapped the way Maybeck did last time. He said the only way to protect ourselves is to find Jess, get her to safety, and then find and crash the second server." He let this sink in. "We need your help. That is, only if you want to."

"Of course I want to."

He liked the idea of her being involved. She was the most unusual girl he'd ever met. He wondered what powers she might have and why she wouldn't tell him about them. "You were going to join our group text," he reminded her.

"Yeah, well . . . my computer access is through our local library. A little late for that."

"So what about her journal? Can I see it? Maybe she left clues or something. We don't know what we're looking for, and it's a huge park. We're all real tired, and we haven't started. We don't know for sure she's in the Animal Kingdom. Wayne thinks so, but no one knows for sure. I don't know if you can help, but—"

"Absolutely. I absolutely want to help if I can."

Amanda took off, out of the bedroom and down the dark hall. A light popped on in the next room, casting a trapezoid of light against the far wall, where a mural of a woman's stern face had been painted. She seemed to be looking at Finn. He ducked back into Amanda's room.

She returned, clutching a leather journal. Reluctantly, she passed it to Finn. "This is private stuff, remember?"

Finn nodded and flipped through the pages. The diary was filled with writing, drawings, sketches. Clippings and photographs had been pasted, paper-clipped, and stapled to the pages. Fortunes from fortune cookies. Ticket stubs.

In the upper-right-hand corner of a page crowded with sketches was a drawing of a castle being struck by lightning. Finn pointed to it. "Okay," he said. "Now I believe."

13

Finn CLIMBED BACK UP the fire rope to his bedroom window, while below him, barely seen, Amanda waited for him, straddling his mother's mountain bike, which he'd loaned her.

His mission was to get hold of his father's mobile phone so Amanda would have one for the day, and to make sure his parents didn't worry about him or question where he'd gone.

He reached his parents' bedroom on tiptoe and quietly opened the door. His mother was snoring; his father lay on his side facing the window. The clock on his mother's end table read 4:08 a.m.

He found his father's dresser in the dark and patted around, searching for his phone. On Friday nights his father made a point of turning off his phone for the weekend. With any luck, he wouldn't look for it. If he did, he wasn't going to find it.

He returned to his mother's side of the bed and quietly turned the clock so that it faced away from the bed, where it couldn't be read by his mother. Then he gently shook her awake. She was a heavy sleeper, and he was counting on her not coming fully awake.

"Mom . . ."

Her eyes squinted open, saw him, and then shut again.

"Finn," she complained.

"It's just after six," he lied, wishing he didn't have to. "I'm going on my bike over to the skate park. Might go to Blizzard Beach later. I'll call."

"Don't forget sunscreen." She opened her eyes a little more and looked for the clock, but she made no effort to turn it around. This he'd been counting on.

"Okay, no problem."

Finn put away the fire-escape rope and left the house by the back door, joining Amanda and climbing onto his bike.

"How'd it go?" she asked.

Finn handed her his father's phone. "Worked out great. I'm good to go for the rest of the day."

"Your parents let you leave the house in the middle of the night?"

"Not exactly. But sort of."

Had he looked up, he would have seen a large bat with the blue tint on its wings. The bat hung upside down from the gutter of his house. It fell free and flew away, flapping frantically. Circling above the two bikes, the winged creature moved nearly silently down the empty street as it followed a pair of red safety lights flashing in the dark.

14

THE FOOD-SERVICE STEP VAN had double tires in the back and mud flaps that carried silhouettes of silver mouse ears on their black rubber.

The van's driver, wearing a Dapper Dan Cast Member costume, had florid cheeks, blue eyes, and bushy eyebrows. He spoke in a deep voice.

"Everyone in back. Find places to hide in case they check back there." He popped open his door. "It'll be pitch-black in there once I pull that door down, so hurry!"

Finn rushed the others into the back. They climbed up into a refrigerated area of cardboard boxes filled with fresh fruits and vegetables stacked onto wooden pallets and strapped to the walls. Each stack offered a place to hide behind. The kids doubled up. Charlene and Willa hid behind a tower of raspberry and strawberry flats. Maybeck and Philby ducked behind the lettuce, leaving Finn and Amanda to press into a small space behind six stacked boxes of carrots.

"Okay," the Dapper Dan said. "That's good. Stay like that. All set?"

The door came down hard, with a bang of finality. It was dark as a cave inside. The refrigerator unit up near the cab wheezed loudly as it blew an icy wind, freezing them.

"Dang . . ." Maybeck said. "This is how I always imagined prison."

"What if one of us is afraid of the dark?" Charlene asked timidly.

"Then she should hold on to Willa, Charlene," said Maybeck.

"I didn't say it was me!" Charlene said.

"Right," said Maybeck.

The truck grumbled and groaned. It lurched around a series of corners toward the back side of the Animal Kingdom. Pretty soon the brakes squealed and it came to a stop.

This wasn't the first time Finn and the others had arrived at the security gates at the back of the Magic Kingdom. Supplies, VIP visitors, merchandise, and employees came through these entrances. Credentials were checked, manifests and work schedules cross-referenced. From the back of the truck, the kids heard some talking, though the words were indiscernible. Then a single *thump*. The Dapper Dan had elbowed the back wall of the cab, trying to warn his passengers.

"I dropped my purse," Charlene announced in a

harsh whisper. "I can't find it! I can't find my purse."

Finn knew that if Security saw a purse, they would probably climb up into the back of the truck to retrieve it. And if so, then they'd spot the kids.

"I can't see!" she hissed again.

Sounds of the door hardware rattled at the back of the truck. The back door was definitely about to be lifted.

"My purse . . ." Charlene moaned.

Finn stepped out from behind the stack of carrots. Amanda reached out to stop him, but she was too late.

He felt around the floor. *Nothing*. He used his phone as a flashlight.

There was the purse, laying on the truck bed. Charlene's arm shot out from behind a stack of boxes, and she grabbed it.

The door rolled open a crack. Finn shoved the phone into his pocket, snuffing its light. His knees didn't flex. He didn't move. He just stood there. Light flooded into the back of the truck. He turned, but it was too late. The door continued up.

In an instant everything changed: he was suddenly pasted to the ceiling—floating—hidden by the rolling door, which was carried on tracks like a garage door.

"Clear," one of the Security guys announced.

Finn sank toward the truck bed. In the dim light

he saw Amanda facing him with her arms extended. As she lowered her arms, Finn sank.

The back door clattered shut and the *clunk* of hardware confirmed they were locked inside again.

"You did that!" he whispered so only she could hear. "You held me up there, Amanda."

"No idea what you're talking about," she whispered back.

"Thank you! You saved us all," Finn said.

"That was way cool, Finn," said Maybeck. "You mind telling me how you did that?"

Amanda whispered warmly into Finn's ear. "No . . . not yet."

Finn said into the dark: "Ah . . . I could show you, but I'd have to kill you."

Maybeck chuckled.

"I want some, too," added Philby.

"Later, dudes," said Finn.

Again, he felt Amanda's breath warm against his neck as she whispered softly, "Thank you."

He wanted to say something, but his voice had gone dry, and he couldn't get a word out.

15

A MOMENT AFTER the truck finally pulled to a stop, the Dapper Dan climbed up inside and then lowered the folding door behind himself, leaving it open just enough to admit some light from the nearby light poles.

"This is as far as I go with the truck. Finn gave each of you an assignment, as I understand it. Our friend in the firehouse asked me to tell you, Philby, that he's arranged a way for you to monitor what's going on in the Park while you're here."

"That sounds good to me," Philby said.

"There are video cameras in the Park," explained the Dapper Dan. "The cameras can be moved and zoomed to monitor what's going on."

"Makes sense," Philby said. "But we'd need access to the system."

"Yes. Our friend arranged that. The screens at the Disney Vacation Club booths. I have the password for you."

"I could do that," Amanda said. "I mean, if no one else wants it, I'll do it," she added carefully.

Everyone nodded.

"Sounds good," Philby said. "If you see anything weird, you can text us."

"No problem," Amanda said. "Happy to do it."

The Dapper Dan asked if they knew their way around the Animal Kingdom. All of them had been there plenty of times. To prove it, Willa recited the various areas of the Park. "Asia, Africa, Pandora: World of Avatar, and DinoLand USA. And obviously Discovery Island in the middle. Five areas and five of us, so I'm assuming we each search one area and try to find Jess."

"It will be better if you blend in," the Dapper Dan said. "If you look like Cast Members there's less chance you'll be stopped and asked questions."

Charlene said, "The best thing we can do is dress up as rangers."

Willa said, "There's a costume repair shed outside the Park, behind DinoLand."

Finn said, "So, we'll all dress up as conservation rangers or animal care Cast Members. All except you, Charlene."

"Because?"

"Your gymnastics make you the perfect DeVine. She's the camouflage Cast Member on stilts. She blends into the trees and jungle, meaning you can spy without being seen."

They were all staring at Charlene.

"Will you do it?" Finn asked.

"Of course!" Charlene said excitedly. "I'd love to be our spy!"

"Wayne wanted me to remind you," the Dapper Dan said, "that Maleficent can transfigure herself to look like any animal. So be careful. Consider everything and anything a possible enemy."

"If that's supposed to make us feel confident, it totally failed." Willa frowned at the Dapper Dan, who then shrugged.

"Any questions?" the man asked as he passed out laminated badges. "These are your fake IDs. Memorize your new name and clip these onto your costumes once you've changed. They make you legitimate Cast Members. But remember, you look young, so keep away from the others as much as possible."

He opened the truck's rear door. The sun had not yet risen. They found themselves in a vast, empty parking lot, alongside several trailers. The sky was fully aglow with the push of dawn. The kids climbed out of the truck and hurried toward the Cast Member entrance. The Dapper Dan called out, "Good luck!"

16

Even if the lights had been on, the costume repair shop would have felt creepy.

The six teens stood just inside the door, staring at the endless rows of various Animal Kingdom costumes. The emergency lighting made the air look thick with dust.

There was a noise then, like the wind: a swishing, whooshing sound, as if someone had left a window open. But no one felt a breeze, and not a hair moved on anyone's head. However, quite a few hairs raised on the back of Finn's neck.

"You hear that?" Finn asked.

Maybeck closed the door. The boom echoed around the building.

The ceiling arched thirty feet overhead, steel beams with cross supports—all unfinished and basic. Displayed before them were fifty or sixty rows of clothes hanging from steel pipes. The rows stretched from where they stood to the far side of the building.

"Oh . . . my . . . gosh," gushed Charlene. "It's huge."

"But what about that sound?" Finn asked. "You heard that, right?"

"Probably just hangers," Maybeck said.

The racks held every kind of Animal Kingdom costume and Cast Member outfit, in every size. That, and accessories like hats, boots, belts, buckles, and backpacks.

"Wow . . ." Willa said.

"Okay, there are dressing rooms over there. Let's get in costume."

*　*　*

Suspended above the impossibly long rows of clothing and costumes hung large hand-painted signs. They divided the space into sections.

Maybeck cruised ANIMAL CARE costumes while Willa searched the racks for PARK RANGERS. Charlene browsed the area marked PERFORMERS, looking for DeVine costumes.

The same noise happened again. Like wind. Or wings. It was followed by the tinkling of hangers sounding like dull bells.

Charlene called over to Finn. "Okay, I heard it that time."

"Don't forget Small World," Finn called back, his voice echoing off the ceiling.

As DHIs, the kids had once ridden through It's a Small World late at night only to have all the dolls come alive and attack them. It was a memory—more like a nightmare—none of them cherished. Other parts of various attractions in the Magic Kingdom had come alive as well, often threatening them, or outright causing them harm. It had instilled a reluctance in them all, a distrust of what might happen next, that had stayed with them long since, and whether they spoke of it or not, haunted them.

"You're just buggy because it's dark in here," Maybeck said. Maybeck, who claimed to be afraid of nothing.

"Well, I'm not buggy!" Charlene announced. "And I heard hangers banging around over there. Hey, you all, Willa and I are going to check it out," Charlene said.

Together the girls moved in the direction of the unusual sound. They explored the racks cautiously, a few garments at a time. The bell-ringing of the hangers stopped all of a sudden.

"Whoever it is heard us," Charlene whispered to Willa.

"Why did you have to volunteer us for this?" Willa asked.

"Because the boys are always acting like we need them, and that's so not true."

"Agreed," Willa said. "But maybe this one time we could make an exception?"

"No way!" Charlene barked as she laughed quietly.

Just then a large bat dropped from the rack. Both girls shrieked. It was black and hairy and over a foot tall. The thing unfolded its wings, and flapped violently. Willa ducked. Charlene screamed and went over backward, falling to the floor.

The bat spiraled into the upper reaches of the warehouse. It looked like a flying cat, fluttering, weaving, diving. One moment it was up high near the ceiling, the next dive-bombing toward one of the Kingdom Keepers.

Finn and Amanda ran toward Willa and Charlene. Philby hurried to open the door, hoping it might fly outside. Maybeck grabbed a butterfly net from the props section and went after the bat like a lacrosse player.

"Find the lights!" Maybeck shouted, following the bat down a row of grass skirts. "Bats don't like light!"

Where the others might have been satisfied with scaring the bat out of the building, Amanda and Finn understood the tension in Maybeck's voice. Finn had seen a huge bat at Amanda's. The same bat? Not a great believer in coincidence, he, too, wanted to catch it. Clearly Maybeck also believed it was no ordinary bat.

"Philby," Finn shouted, "the lights!" He had no idea how to turn on the lights in a building this size, but

if there was a switch, Philby would find it before anyone else.

True to form, the overhead lights came on only
seconds later, and the warehouse lit up like the school
gymnasium. As the lights flashed on, the bat dove as if
it had been shot. Maybeck left his feet, lunging as he
swung the net. The bat and Maybeck's net met in a tangle of nylon mesh and high-pitched squeals. Maybeck
hit the concrete floor like a base runner sliding into
home plate. He flipped the net, trapping the bat inside.

The others let out an unplanned cheer.

They had captured a prisoner.

17

Maybeck approached the employee entrance to the Animal Kingdom holding a pillowcase that wouldn't stay still. The Cast Member entrance—employees only—was a revolving door of steel tines that moved only clockwise and required the employee card to open. The unattended entrance—he was grateful for that—required him to swipe the ID card the driver had provided. A red light turned green, and Maybeck pushed through the turnstile. Use of the pillowcase prevented the contents from being seen: the bat. Still, it was too close for comfort, and he was only too happy to dangle it away from his side as he cleared the entrance.

The pillowcase danced again.

"Settle down!" he said harshly, aware that he was speaking to a white pillowcase. Or more precisely, its contents: a Livingstone's fruit bat.

It quieted.

Willa, an animal lover, had identified the bat the moment Maybeck had caught it. This led to a group discussion of what to do with the thing. Charlene wanted it released and out of the building as quickly as possible. Philby suggested doing something to it that wouldn't have been approved by the SPCA, and while Willa thought it was "cute" and that it might make an interesting pet, Maybeck and Finn came up with a solution that seemed to please everyone—except Philby, of course, since it meant keeping it alive.

"We can't let it go," Finn had said. "I know it's completely ridiculous to think it might be Maleficent . . ." Willa groaned at the mention of this. "But what if it is? Or what if we've captured Maleficent's spy? Amanda and I saw a bat at her house. What if that was this same one?"

"If it is Maleficent, don't you think she'd turn back into herself and do something bad to us?" Willa suggested sarcastically. "I'd say this would be a good time for that."

"Good point," Charlene said.

"Wayne told me the heat slows the powers she uses to transform herself. It's like her kryptonite. We don't know what she's capable of," Finn said. "I just don't see how it's worth taking any risks."

"It's not," said Maybeck. "We've got to lock it up . . . do something with it, so it can't follow us."

"You all know what I think we should do," said Philby. Everyone ignored him.

"It'll be light out soon. Bats don't fly around in the

daylight. The main thing is: we don't want it to find us or Maleficent."

"Why can't we just hide it among the other bats?" Maybeck said. "Have you even seen the bat enclosure? This thing won't be going anywhere. And it's not like Maleficent can walk in there and take it out."

Finn said, "That's brilliant!"

"Earth to Maybeck. It's just a bat. It is *not* Maleficent, or she'd be in our face right now," said Willa emphatically.

"So you'd just let it go?" Finn asked.

"Not me," Maybeck said, speaking directly to Finn. "At the least it deserves a bat jail. I can bluff my way into the bat enclosure."

Maybeck rarely lacked self-confidence.

"And if you're stopped?" asked Charlene, always the cautious one.

"I'll tell whoever stops me I'm returning a bat that was sick. You think anyone's going to want to get up close and personal with this *thing*?" He jiggled the pillowcase. The bat turned and flapped its enormous wings and tried to nip at Maybeck through the fabric.

"Okay. That's settled," said Charlene. "Let's just get it out of here."

And now Maybeck, inside the Park, was telling the contents of his pillowcase to settle down, and much to his astonishment—it obeyed. He told himself that his tone of voice was responsible, that the bat had responded to his anger. But what if it had actually understood him?

At a few minutes past 6 a.m. there were more Cast Members in the Park than he would have expected. He realized that employees must arrive between six and seven, because they were suddenly everywhere: sweeping, opening up attractions, zipping around in golf carts. It was a frenzy of activity. He followed a road to his left, a road he'd seen a number of Cast Members take, not entirely certain where he was. He'd entered to the left of the main entrance—that much he knew. He sneaked Philby's map out of his back pocket. Philby had done his homework, supplying both a Disney illustrated map with a key and a Google Earth satellite view of the area. On the satellite map he'd drawn and labeled some red circles, including DeVine's entrance gate, the two monkey temples, the Conservation Station, the Park's main entrance, and the group rendezvous spot.

Once on Discovery Island, Maybeck headed for Asia and the Maharajah Jungle Trek.

Some birds called out from the top of a tree. He moved a little faster.

He crossed Discovery Island, to the right of the Tree of Life, aiming for a bridge to Asia. He texted.

Maybeck: I'm inside, Discovery Island.

Finn: Okay.

Maybeck: Heads up! there are already a bunch of cast members around.

If Maybeck had looked over his shoulder, he would have seen many more birds than had been there only moments before. The birds settled in a nearby tree. As more joined them, the group flew to the next tree. And the next. They were following Maybeck and the pillowcase.

Philby: Okay. we all meet at home base after the park opens

Maybeck crossed the bridge and walked until he saw the Maharajah Jungle Trek just ahead. A cacophony of bird calls surrounded him. He could hardly hear himself think. That was the first time he bothered to look up.

What he saw surprised him, even frightened him. Two trees packed with birds. For a moment, it seemed as if they were following him.

Nah . . . he thought. *Couldn't be* . . .

Finn had heightened Maybeck's curiosity. What had they discovered in the short time it had taken him to enter the Park?

More obnoxious bird noises overhead.

He looked up.

Four trees. Hundreds of birds.

What the . . . ?

18

PHILBY SWIPED THE ID through the card reader at the door to the AK Maintenance facility. A small red light turned green, and Philby pulled on the door. It opened, and no alarms sounded.

Finn held out his hand to Amanda, who looked down at her sister's diary and then reluctantly gave the book to him.

"I'm not sure she'd want me doing this," Amanda said, still holding one hand on the diary.

"I promise, only the pages we talked about," Finn said, pulling out his phone.

"We don't know that they have anything to do with this," Amanda warned. "I'd rather you not use your phone to make copies. Phones can be hacked, or the photos can be shared or posted. I don't want that. Jess wouldn't want that."

"You're the one who said she could dream the future. Maybe her drawings will help us find her."

"I get that. But some of it is personal, you know?"

"And maybe, without knowing, she left us clues how to find her. She drew lightning striking a castle.

There are drawings of monkeys in there." He tugged gently on the journal, but Amanda would not let it go.

"Please," Finn said to her.

For a moment the journal connected them.

"Use a copier. There has to be one in here. Or scan it and print it, but no phones. You need to promise."

"I promise," Finn said, meeting eyes with her.

Amanda let go of the diary. "Thank you."

"Stand guard while Philby and I get this copied," Finn said. "Text if you see anyone coming."

"Okay," she said. Her eyes remained filled with concern.

"I promise, all we're going to do is make copies," Finn reminded her.

"And what about bats?" she asked.

"We'll be careful."

Finn followed Philby inside to a reception area, where a well-organized desk held a telephone and computer. Some Disney cartoons were taped to the computer monitor, and there were framed pictures of three kids. The few lights that had been left on cast murky shadows and offered a dimly lit corridor running in both directions off this front room. There were two signs, each with an arrow: one read MAINTENANCE and pointed left; the other read ANIMATION TRAINING LAB and pointed right.

"Cool," Philby said, turning right. "I've got to see this."

The animation training lab was a garagelike work-shop that reminded Finn of the workshop in his grandfather's basement. The L-shaped room had coun-tertops that ran along every wall, behind which were pegboards holding every conceivable kind of tool. Computers and hand tools littered the counters. But what made it much different from Grandpop's base-ment was its purpose. The room was designed for the repair of the Audio-Animatronics—the talking robots—that were used extensively throughout the Park. The result was the disturbing presence of human torsos, heads, hands, and legs in every stage of creation, from pieces that looked like robots to painted faces dressed in costumes that seemed so real Philby kept spinning in circles, afraid one or more of them might suddenly move or attack. Of equal concern were the dozens of animals under construction, including pieces of tigers, lions, Stitch, Donald Duck, and a fantastic hand—possibly from a gorilla—that was nearly three feet across and supported by a metal superstructure that held it four feet off the floor.

"Whoa . . ." Philby said, taking a look around. Both boys spoke in whispers, as if the "body" parts might overhear them.

"Somehow I don't think we'll find a copier in here," Finn said, holding Jess's journal.

"Oh, I bet you're wrong. Give me a minute." Philby walked the lines of workbenches. He muttered words like "impressive" and "interesting" and "incredible." Then he addressed Finn. "Articulated, motor-controlled limb movement—very cutting edge." He stopped in front of a six-foot tyrannosaur head with wires sticking out of a missing eye.

"What about a copier?" Finn reminded him, not so impressed.

"Yeah, okay," Philby said. "But I could stay here for hours."

"Let's save the extra-credit work for another time."

Philby's curiosity carried him to the far end of the room, where the lab opened out into a large space that appeared to be used for assembly. Most of the robotic dummies stood on their own here—cables and wires running from them—and many were at least partially clothed and had faces. Most of the Audio-Animatronics were of animals in various poses, all of which looked incredibly lifelike. But it was the far end of the room that intrigued Philby.

"Check it out," he said, approaching the area somewhat cautiously and with great respect. "Remember this?" he asked.

The three walls at the end of the room were covered in jungle-green paper, as was the floor. There were stage lights and tripods and cameras and a dozen computers on rolling stands.

"I do," said Finn. He and the other DHI kids, upon acceptance by Disney, had been computer-modeled by Disney Imagineers. Their movements were recorded to create the DHIs. The empty cages off to their left suggested the obvious.

"Animals," Philby said, immediately understanding the setup. "They motion-modeled animals here to create DHIs."

"Wayne told me they were doing that," Finn said. "Animal hosts." The cameras were all set low to the ground. Then there were the cages and—he realized as he stepped closer—paw marks seen faintly on the green-paper floor covering.

"Check it out," Philby said again, this time directing Finn's attention to five photographs thumbtacked to the wall nearby. There were several monkeys, a baby elephant, a pair of tigers, and a gorilla.

"Got it!" Finn said, pointing to a flatbed scanner hooked up to a computer. He touched the computer's space bar and the machine woke up.

Philby laid Jess's diary on the scanner bed and began scanning the pages. As he printed them out, his phone buzzed in his pocket.

Amanda: 2 guys out front coming toward here!!!

"Visitors!" Finn whispered to Philby.

Finn: Hide somewhere safe.

The lab's only door was a long way away. There was one EMERGENCY ONLY door to the right of the green-screen area, but it had an alarm, and Finn had no desire to draw the wrath of Security upon him and Philby before they managed to even get into the Park.

"I've got an idea!" Philby said in a harsh whisper. He pointed to an area where dozens of parts and partial bodies of the Audio-Animatronics figures had been heaped into a kind of junk pile. Many of the human robots had faces that looked phenomenally real.

Finn grabbed the printouts, and the boys jumped into the junk pile, worming their way down into the parts so that only their shoulders and faces showed. They blended in with the robotic human parts.

Two men entered the room, both wearing dark blue coveralls. Neither seemed surprised to find the lights turned on—something Philby had done upon entering.

"It's always something," the thinner of the two said. "I could have told you the sound system was going to go out at some point. They should have rewired the Asia system when they installed Expedition Everest. Not my fault."

The men scrounged around on the workbenches, apparently looking for parts.

"Finding the break in the wire, if there is one, is going to be a bear," said the heavier man.

"Don't mention bears," said the other one. He pointed to an Audio-Animatronics figure of a standing bear cub designed for the Country Bear Jamboree. "This one will get jealous."

Both men laughed—harder than the joke deserved.

The thin one suddenly turned and headed directly for the junk pile where the boys were hidden. "Didn't we loan these guys our acoustic coupler?"

"It's the tester we're looking for. Forget the coupler."

The thin man picked up a piece of one of the robots. He was about two feet away from Finn, who held his breath in an attempt not to be noticed.

"You know what?" the thin man said, looking right at Finn, then at Philby, then at the stack of robots. "This place gives me the creeps sometimes. Some of these things look so real . . . I gotta tell you."

"Found it!" the bigger man said. He held up a box with a lot of wires running out of it. "I knew the guys had borrowed it."

He tucked the box under his arm. The two men reached the door. The thin man stopped at the light switch.

"Hey," he said, "did you turn on the lights when we came in? Because I didn't."

"I don't think I did."

Finn felt sweat trickling down his rib cage. He calculated the distance to the emergency door, ready to run for it.

"Well," said the big man. He switched off the lights.

19

FINN'S FIRST DECENT look at the contents of Jess's diary came as he, Amanda, and Philby awaited the Park's opening. The main parking lot was a steady stream of arriving vehicles. Awning-covered trams were used to transport visitors to the Park entrance. The trams were stacked up at the back of the lot awaiting use. The three kids sat on a tram bench together and reviewed their personal photocopies of Jess's journal in detail.

Finn had always pictured a girl's diary to be line after line of neatly written cursive on well-organized pages, the contents of which held secrets about her love interests. What he saw here surprised him. Jess's was a stream-of-consciousness collage, a collection of images, sketches of animals, and musings. There were clothing receipts pasted into the pages; pieces of postcards, stapled; a fortune cookie fortune taped to a page; there were recipes, movie ticket stubs, pieces of torn photographs; ribbons and candy wrappers. There was an arch that looked like the letter *M*, with a blob of ink on the right side. Surrounding and interweaving it all were lines from poems, song lyrics, comments, and what looked like quotes from conversations she'd had. It was all mixed up into a mess of heavily scribbled pen and pencil.

"Are these supposed to mean something?" Finn asked, fingering the three photocopied pages.

"They mean something to her," Amanda said. "Jess took her journaling very seriously."

"And at what point did she cut off her ear?" asked Philby. "Go van Gogh." He won a smile from Finn. Not from Amanda.

"Look," Finn said, pointing to the photocopy. "That's a castle and a lightning bolt."

"That's what I told you about," Amanda said. "And look down here." She pointed to what was obviously a monkey.

"Yeah, but this could be coincidence, right?" Philby said, sounding somewhat apprehensive. "Are we actually going to believe a person can see into the future?"

Finn looked over at him with a dumbfounded expression.

"Okay, okay. But it doesn't mean everything on this page is significant," Philby protested.

"How do we know it isn't?" Finn asked.

"This is several nights' worth of dreams," Amanda said. "You can tell because some are pencil, some pen. The movie tickets and postcards—that stuff is memories, reminders."

"But what about this decal, or whatever it is?" Finn asked.

"No idea. A stamp, maybe," Amanda said.

The letters were reversed, the image backward.

"There's a tiger, a gorilla, and . . . what's this, a bowling pin?" Finn turned the page upside down, but couldn't quite tell what he was looking at.

"I think they're all clues," Amanda said.

Philby exhaled loudly, so as to be noticed. "We *all* want to find her, Amanda. But if we go chasing down sketches from her diary, then that's a lot of valuable time that could have been spent looking for her."

"I think we can trust this," she said.

"We need more proof," Philby complained.

"We have a castle and a lightning bolt!" Finn pointed out.

"There's also an aqueduct, some balloons, and a railroad track."

"These are dreams, not instant replays," Amanda told Philby. "She had visions. Glimpses. How much of your dreams, your nightmares, do you remember? Bits and pieces are what I get. Sometimes more than that, a piece of a story, but not that often. Maybe we all dream pieces of the future but just don't happen to know it. How often do we write them down or make sketches and keep track? She left us clues, Philby." She waved the photocopy in the air. "This is the map of her dreams. Maybe she didn't know she was leaving it for us, but there's no ignoring the castle and the lightning, is there? So maybe not everything on here is helpful. It probably isn't. But we won't know that until we check it out. Right? We've got to check out each thing on here, because if even *one* other thing on this page can help us find her—" She covered her mouth with her fist, on the verge of crying.

"I'm just saying we don't have much time. I'm nodding out like every other minute. We fall asleep and we may stay asleep forever. That's what Wayne said. I just want us to use our time efficiently, that's all." He studied the sheet. "For instance, who's Rob?" In several places on the cluttered page Jess had written, *Change Rob*.

"Rob Bernowski," Amanda said. "From school."

"A friend? Boyfriend? Or what?" Philby asked.

"A little of both, I think."

"And she wants to change him? And this is relevant to us, how?"

"I don't know. Sure, I guess. She put that into the journal in a bunch of places." Amanda opened up the journal and flipped through several pages around the ones they had copied. "The way she writes it, it's like she's really set on it."

"So are we supposed to talk to Rob about this?" Philby asked sarcastically. "You think Rob has her?"

Amanda glared at him.

Finn asked, "What can it hurt to call him? I don't see why we don't follow up on everything we can. Am I missing something? What if this *is* important, and we ignore it?"

"That's why you called the meeting, isn't it?" Philby asked. "I say we put it to a vote. We could spend all day chasing a bunch of meaningless ramblings, and we haven't got all day. How much longer can we stay awake?" He yawned, and then Finn and Amanda yawned right along with him.

"Stop it," Finn said.

"We're out of time here," Philby complained, "and we haven't even started. I'm going to have to call my mom at some point, or she'll have the cops out looking for me."

"We'll put it to a vote," Finn agreed. "But in the meantime, we're going to make a list of everything on this page and what it might mean, no matter how far out." He addressed Philby. "We'll do it scientifically." He said this knowing it would appeal to him.

"I can get behind that," Philby said.

Amanda looked over at Finn, her eyes red and shining behind tears she struggled to hold back. But her eyes also had a twinkle in them. She seemed to be thanking him. Finn reached out and took her clenched fist in his hand.

"We're going to find her," he said.

20

MAYBECK APPROACHED the bat enclosure from the Maharajah Jungle Trek path. The enclosure was quite large, with colorful prayer flags strung between the facade of a fake building, rock walls, and the large boxlike frame that supported a wall and roof of mesh netting. A three-stage viewing room had been built along the path. A ranger would be on duty once the Park opened at 9 a.m., but for now it stood empty. Maybeck avoided the viewing room, just in case, staying outside, moving along the perimeter wall of the netting. He left the path and entered the jungle, keeping close to the enclosure's netted wall.

It was then he saw the birds again. His first reaction was one of astonishment. He thought it beautiful in a way—a thousand or more dark birds so crowded into the treetops that large branches bent under their weight. He thought how fortunate he was to see such a phenomenon—that it probably only happened in the early hours before guests arrived and scared away all but the most brazen of the wild creatures that had adopted the Animal Kingdom as their home.

Then he noticed something strange about the birds: they all seemed to be looking right at him. He knew this was impossible, and yet . . . The thrill of astonishment gave way to the electric jangle of raw nerves. They *were* looking right at him.

Two things happened then: he spotted a door into the enclosure about ten yards farther into the jungle, and the first of the birds left their perches and flew toward him.

He knew he shouldn't panic. It was only birds, after all. But the way they surrounded him . . . the way the jungle went suddenly silent . . . the way the bats in the enclosure awakened with a start—*nocturnal* animals—a restless jittering as they hung from their perches sent a spike of terror through him. Birds flew in flocks, certainly. But they didn't *attack* as a group. Did they?

The birds attacked.

It was as if someone had blotted out the sun. They came at him as a dark cloud of beating wings and unflinching black eyes. Their small bird legs were aimed right at Maybeck. The birds came at him in such numbers that at first it was just plain scary—they landed on his head, his shoulders, his arms, his back. But then it went beyond scary—to dangerous—as the weight of them pushed him down. To an outside eye, it would have appeared as if thousands of birds had landed in the same spot of the jungle at once, but to Maybeck it meant a pitch-black flurry of wings and beaks and scratching claws. He fought them off one-handed—grabbing, poking, sweeping his arm, and knocking the birds away. But back they came.

He knew he could not sustain the weight of the birds. The pecking.

Now, crushed by the heaviness, feeling it might break him in two, Maybeck released the pillowcase to defend himself.

A tiny hand reached out . . .

A monkey hand! It snatched up the pillowcase, and the monkey took off running. As it did, the birds flew off. In a flutter of feathers, the sun reappeared, and Maybeck watched as the monkey, pillowcase in hand, hurried down the path.

Maybeck took off after it.

He looked himself over as he ran—not a scratch on him. If he were to tell anyone what had happened, they wouldn't believe him. He had no proof whatsoever. *A thousand birds attacked me!* It would sound like a lame excuse for his having lost the pillowcase and the captive bat. He had originally thought Finn's claim that the bat might be Maleficent was a bit of a stretch. But now he reconsidered. Birds didn't organize like that, he reminded himself. Monkeys were known thieves, but what was a monkey doing *loose* inside the Animal Kingdom, even if the Park was not yet officially open? He had questions that needed answering.

He ran as fast as he could.

When the monkey stole off into the jungle, Maybeck followed.

21

WILLA CROSSED DISCOVERY ISLAND, feeling as if everyone were staring at her. Could they tell she was underage? She didn't think she looked all that much younger than the other girls. The formality of the uniform helped her look older, adding a good three or four years to her fourteen. But what if they were staring because they recognized her face as that of a DHI? If caught, she could lose her family's Gold Pass, as well as her performance contract. She might no longer be one of the Kingdom Keepers. She kept her head down and wished she'd used more makeup at the costume warehouse. The ID badge Wayne had given her was clipped to her waist, helping to make her look official. With her eyes to the ground, she walked with her back straight and took determined strides, knowing the importance of body language.

She had volunteered for what was probably the most dangerous assignment that Finn and Philby had come up with: to infiltrate and search the Kilimanjaro Safari grounds. The idea was a simple one: if someone was hiding Jess in the Animal Kingdom, why not stash her someplace where people were prohibited from going? When the Park was open, the safari teemed with hundreds of wild animals. People riding on the safari were restricted to the backs of the safari trucks with a driver/guide who pointed out animals and took guests on a "mission" to save a baby elephant from make-believe poachers. But, according to Philby's research, throughout the safari grounds there were feeding stations, way points, and even some hidden gates offering backstage access. The Overtakers had once hidden Maybeck in a maintenance cage inside Space Mountain; it seemed possible, logical even, that they might hide Jess in a similarly impossible-to-access place. But if one of them got there before the animals were released . . .

"It's done in stages," Philby had explained. "Thomson's gazelles are pretty tame and harmless. Some aren't even rounded up at night, but most of the other animals are. They're fed and washed and doctored, if need be, after the Park closes to the public."

"But what about early morning?" Willa had asked.

"Before the Park opens, they return the animals in a specific order that offers the fewest problems. The trick for you is to get inside before eight a.m."

Willa had about an hour. She quickened her steps, off Discovery Island now, and headed toward the entrance to the Kilimanjaro Safari. A tremendous flock of black birds passed overhead—there must have been thousands of them. They streaked across the morning sky and were gone.

"If you hurry, you can catch the last one." She looked up. It was a cute guy wearing a uniform identical to her own. He stood below the sign for the Kilimanjaro Safari.

"Ah . . . yeah," Willa said. But she tensed as she felt his eyes following her. Did she look old enough to carry an ID badge?

She walked quickly through the empty waiting area, turning and winding her way down to the loading dock, where one of the trucks was waiting. There was an older woman—she had to be nearly thirty—leaning forward from the front bench, coaching the driver. Willa was the only passenger beside the instructor. It was obviously some kind of training run. The truck rumbled off down a path that wound through the jungle.

Willa called out, "I'll be hopping off at Ituri Forest."

The instructor, without so much as looking back, lifted her arm and waved.

Willa heaved a sigh of relief and held on as the driver avoided puddles and recited some memorized lines. Willa had taken the safari ride many times. She enjoyed the story behind it as well as the animal-watching. But the emptiness of the place at this hour gave her the shivers. The truck rounded a bend and slowed.

"Is here all right?" the instructor called back inquisitively. Suspiciously?

The Ituri Forest, Willa realized.

"Fine!" She hopped the three feet down to the muddy ground, hoping the instructor wouldn't see that she was wearing running shoes and not the required ranger boots. She slapped the side of the truck, and it lumbered off. The minute it was gone, she regretted getting off.

Alone on the truck route, in the midst of a thick forest of bamboo and sea cane, Willa spotted a pure white ibis as still as a statue. The bird stood on one leg, perfectly balanced.

She unfolded the map Philby had given her, tried to establish her position, and punched through the forest to her left, expecting to come across a feed station within the next thirty yards. It was tough going, the forest thick with vegetation.

Had she looked behind her, she would have seen a lizard following. It was five or six feet long, with a thin tail and little claws on its feet. Not so much a lizard— more like a Chinese dragon.

22

MAYBECK LOST GROUND to the small, agile simian that moved through the jungle's tight growth in a seamless, fluid motion. He wondered if the monkey was under Maleficent's control. But if so, then why had it not been ordered to release the bat? His answer came as a slice of first light caught his eyes. Bats were nocturnal; it was sunrise. Releasing the bat was not an option.

Maybeck had to get it back. He smashed into bamboo and rubber trees, baby banyans and mangrove. He sloshed through the flooded jungle floor, quickly gaining on the monkey.

Maybeck's progress registered on the monkey's face as wide-eyed terror. It shrieked and exploded into a frenzy, briefly increasing its lead on Maybeck. But only briefly.

Maybeck broke out of the jungle and felt something hard beneath his feet. He looked down: train tracks! The Wildlife Express Train was going through its morning test run. Maybeck jumped out of the way when he heard a blast from the train's whistle. "You crazy?" the conductor shouted through the open window.

He'd been spotted. As the train passed, he saw the conductor reaching for his radio.

Not good.

The train whistle pierced the morning air, sending a flock of sandhill cranes into the blue sky. Maybeck spotted the monkey. It had been crouched in the center of the birds. He closed the distance to ten yards, then five.

The train had followed a long, sweeping curve of track but was now coming around and catching up to them. It reappeared to Maybeck's right. The monkey changed directions, going straight for the train. Maybeck skidded to a stop, caught a toe, and went down hard.

He looked up to see the monkey slip *beneath* a train car, the pillowcase in hand. Maybeck hurried to his feet and ran toward the train. The train conductor hung out of the locomotive, shouting at him. Maybeck squatted in time to see the monkey racing across a short distance of grass toward more jungle. There was no way Maybeck was about to crawl under a moving train. He waited it out impatiently. It seemed to move very slowly. Finally, Maybeck took off toward the end of the train and came around it, once again crossing the tracks.

He found himself next to the Yak and Yeti restaurant. He came to a halting stop, looked left . . .

right . . . *there!* A flash of the white pillowcase was all he caught—just rounding a bend in the path. He took off, heading away from Flights of Wonder. Again, his size and speed overcame the monkey's efforts.

The monkey sensed its pursuer and skittered back and forth in a zigzag, chattering loudly. It crossed the path and shot straight up a dangling rope toward a concrete tower. It reached the turret, nearly thirty feet off the ground, and briefly disappeared. The next time Maybeck saw it, the monkey—still carrying the pillowcase—hurried across a set of ropes toward a crumbling Asian temple encased in bamboo scaffolding. This was on an island surrounded by a narrow moat.

Maybeck stopped at the concrete tower. The end of the rope the monkey had climbed was frayed as if it had been chewed through. He studied the layout, noticing that the rope bridges connected back to the temple, which meant that the monkeys weren't supposed to be able to get down off the towers. The moat was meant to prevent their escape from the island. But the monkeys had managed to drop a rope that had yet to be spotted. By doing so, they'd given themselves an escape route.

The monkey disappeared into the red brick temple, dragging the pillowcase behind it, and was gone.

Maybeck, understanding the importance of acting quickly, rolled up his pant legs, pulled off his shoes, and waded into the murky water. A pair of ducks startled and splashed away to the other side of the temple, squawking and quacking.

Maybeck felt the cold mud ooze between his toes. Bubbles rose to the surface all around him, giving off an unpleasant odor.

He faced a wooden door with iron bars over its small, square window. It was the only way into the temple that he could see.

He arrived there in five giant steps and, sloshing out of the water, reached for the door's handle.

23

WILLA CHECKED PHILBY'S MAP once more: he had marked the location of a feeding station—disguised as a large stump—at the edge of the savannah. Its proximity to a nighttime animal holding pen qualified it as a possible hiding place where Jess could be kept and never discovered. A clock ran off the seconds and minutes in her head—she had several such places to check before the animals were released.

She pushed though the forest, following the map, and reached the edge of the sprawling savannah: a flat plain of low grasses interspersed with trees and rocks and a few small ponds, all of it surrounded by low rolling hills. It glistened in the first golden rays of dawn.

There, quite some distance away, she saw a stump, thinking immediately that it couldn't possibly be Philby's stump because it looked so real. But the location was right, so she decided to have a look.

The problem was, there was no way to sneak up toward a stump in the middle of a field without being seen. She had to cross a hundred yards in the open. Not

that there was anyone to see her, but another training truck could come by at any minute. She decided
rather than run out and look suspicious, she would walk
casually—just another day on the job. Hopefully, the
ranger uniform would do the rest.

Then, taking in her surroundings, she happened to
look back.

At first, she thought it was an alligator. Terror
gripped her: alligators ate people. It happened all the
time in Florida. She'd heard they could run faster than
humans, and when you saw one you didn't want to run
because it teased them into chasing you—and if they
chased you, they considered you food. So she continued walking, though slightly faster than before. The
stump—or fake stump—rose at least three feet off the
ground. If she could only reach it in time . . .

But then she looked again. It wasn't an alligator
after all, but a giant lizard, maybe six feet long. She'd
studied Komodo dragons in school, and this looked
pretty much exactly like one. Komodos didn't eat
people, but they were known to bite and do serious
harm. She didn't know the rule about Komodos—did
you run or walk? The lizard turned sideways for a second, as if to size her up, and once again she changed
her mind: it wasn't a Komodo; it looked more . . . prehistoric, with thick scales and . . . was that possible? . . .

wings, tucked in along its back. It looked more like . . .

A dragon. She'd read stories about dragons. Had seen movies. She'd always considered them mythological creatures. But now she was looking at one.

It had a disgusting, pink tongue that flicked like a snake's—but about two feet long. The tongue curled as it drew back between the rows of gray, stubby teeth.

She wanted to think of this as coincidence—the two of them had just happened to cross paths, and it was now following her. *Tracking her* was more to the point, she thought. But then something even more strange entered her thoughts: what if Jess was indeed locked up in the stump—the food locker—and the dragon was some kind of patrol for the Overtakers? After all, the safari was filled with all sorts of animals, from giraffes to zebras, but a scaly Asian dragon with wings?

The Overtakers.

It was the first thing to come to her: if Jess was being kept out here on the savannah, it seemed obvious who would guard her. And if there was a dragon mixed in with all the rest of the animals, could that possibly be a coincidence, since dragons hadn't existed for the past few million years—if ever?

So what exactly was the dragon waiting for? It just lingered back there, a dozen yards away, trolling back and forth across the grassy landscape as if sniffing around for food. If he was going to attack her, why not get to it?

Could a dragon possibly think? Could it be waiting to see if she headed for the stump? She subtly increased both the quickness and the length of her strides. She glanced back to see that the dragon had stayed right with her. It didn't seem to be moving any faster, either, and yet . . . there it was.

Now more convinced than ever that she was its intended target, she looked around and realized that she was all alone out on the savannah. She saw an ostrich in the distance—perhaps they had begun releasing animals already. A herd of Thomson's gazelles shot across the field, but some nights they were left on the grounds; it didn't mean much to see them. If, on the other hand, the animals were already being released and introduced to the savannah, then Willa hoped they might distract the dragon from its current obsession with her.

She moved increasingly closer to the stump, and now, looking back, she saw the dragon following her. If she climbed on top of the stump, she would be out of reach of the dragon. But what about the wings? Could something like that possibly fly?

She heard the sudden beating of hooves, seconds later mixing with the rumble of a truck engine. A herd of zebras had been released—again to her left—and from somewhere behind her a truck was approaching. If she was going to inspect the stump it had to be now—right now.

She ran the last few yards, and if she'd harbored any doubts as to the dragon's intentions, they were answered by its light-footed sprint to keep up with her. There was no turning back now. No changing her mind. The dragon raced toward her, its mouth open, snapping at the air.

She reached the side of the stump—though shaped like a stump, it was made of metal, with a small door in the side. She worked the snap lock off the hasp and opened the door.

The dragon charged, seemingly not touching the ground at all. It flicked its long tail back and forth, moving in a snakelike fashion, quickly closing the distance between them.

Willa dove inside and pulled the door shut behind her. It was incredibly warm. Enough light filtered in to allow her to see that Jess was not there. There were sacks of food and salt licks. It smelled like a pet store. A coiled hose hung from a hook.

The dragon smashed into the door, then slammed its powerful tail against the stump. Her ears rang. A rumbling in the ground grew louder. Willa looked out a crack in the access door to see the herd of zebras bearing down on her as it crossed the savannah.

The dragon took off for a distant tree and climbed it in a creepy, effortless way.

Willa sagged down to sit, trying to catch her breath.

And then she saw it: freshly scraped into the fake stump's rusty metal was a simple message that made absolutely no sense—and yet somehow she knew it had been written by Jess.

It read: *Change Rob.*

She curled up and held her breath, waiting to flee the stump once the storm of zebras had passed.

24

MAYBECK STOOD INSIDE a dark enclosure the size of a large closet. It had a concrete floor from which a low brick wall rose to waist level. From there, framed lumber intersected by long bamboo poles rose geometrically overhead, wrapped on the outside with heavy brown vinyl: fake brick. Together, it added up on the outside to what looked like an Asian temple. But inside it smelled bad—really bad—like one of those Porta-Potties at the state fair. It was surprisingly cool inside—a place for the monkeys to escape the heat. There was a white plastic tub with a metal handle sitting by the door. Alongside it was a neatly coiled green hose connected to a spigot.

The door clapped shut behind him. He turned in time to see the monkey overhead, carrying the pillowcase, climbing effortlessly, up, up, up, pulling himself between the bamboo poles and jeering down at Maybeck.

Sunlight seeped in through several square openings at the top of the temple. The temple provided shelter for the monkeys, a place to hide from storms and a cool place to sleep. The smell was the problem: the monkeys used the concrete floor as their bathroom. He understood the purpose of the hose then, and felt tempted to give the concrete a spraying off.

If the monkey made it to the top window, the pillowcase and its contents would be gone. Maybeck considered climbing, but that was a race he was sure to lose.

The monkey crossed along the bamboo rafters, and then, to Maybeck's surprise, began to work its way back down. Maybeck's eyes slowly adjusted to the dark. And then something moved from the shadows.

Maleficent.

She stepped out to where Maybeck could see her, regal in her purple-fringed black cape, her startling green skin glowing with maliciousness.

"Hello, Terrance." A voice like grinding stones.

The monkey handed her the bag. She accepted it with an outstretched arm, never taking her eyes off Maybeck.

"Do you know what happens to *children* who play where they don't belong?"

He couldn't get a word out.

"They get . . . burned," she said. A flaming orb appeared in one hand. She cocked her arm back, ready to throw.

Maybeck dove for the hose, swiveled its nozzle, and shot a ferocious stream of water at the witch.

The monkey cried out and leaped up into the rafters.

The water stream knocked the burning ball out of Maleficent's hand but produced a cloud of steam that immediately filled the small space so thickly he couldn't see.

A dark shadow shifted inside the gray cloud of steam: Maleficent moving to cut off his path to the door. He abandoned the hose and sprang for the door. But she was much faster than he'd anticipated. He came face-to-face with the green skin and bloodshot eyes. Her breath was like a dead mouse caught in a trap as she said, "No. I don't think so."

Maybeck didn't hesitate. He kicked out, punching the door open and admitting a flood of light. Maleficent, still holding the pillowcase, moved to block his exit, just as he'd hoped.

He sprang up overhead, through the bamboo, and squeezed out the hole at the top. Hand-over-hand, he swung up the taut connecting rope—five yards . . . ten—as he pulled himself toward the tower.

Maleficent stepped out into the sunlight but jumped back—the heat of the sun's rays already too much for her.

Maybeck reached the tower and found the dangling rope and slid down, burning his hands, reached the ground, and took off running without looking back.

He understood with absolute clarity what was going on: the bat was a spy—*Maleficent's spy*—and she'd dispatched the birds and the monkey to make sure she received the bat's report.

The bat had followed Finn since Amanda's. It knew all about them. And now Maleficent knew, too.

He shuddered with the thought of that as he broke into the jungle and ran for his life.

25

THE MOMENT THE PARK gates opened to the public, Finn, Amanda, and Philby entered through the Cast Member entrance, using the IDs that Wayne had provided. Finn and Philby were determined to mix in with the crowds and reach the rendezvous in time to meet up with the others. Famous as DHIs, their faces were known throughout the Disney kingdoms, a fame that threatened— for they were forbidden from attending except on specially approved days. Getting around without being recognized was not going to be easy. They wore baseball caps to hide their faces, and they kept to themselves as much as possible.

By the time they reached the benches just inside the large gates north of the Rainforest Café, a wet Maybeck and a dirty-faced Willa were waiting. Finn handed out copies of the page from Jess's diary.

Quiet at this hour, it was a good place to meet. They gathered around a bench, awaiting Charlene's grand entrance as DeVine, the ivy-covered chameleon.

Maybeck told them about being attacked by birds, about losing the bat to a monkey, and about his encounter with Maleficent.

Willa spoke of her pursuit by a miniature dragon and her discovery in the metal stump of the cryptic message left by Jess.

"There's something to be learned from what we both went through," Willa said, continuing. "We can't trust any of the animals we see. Maleficent can control them. Whether a flock of birds, or a dragon with wings. We're no longer in the Animal Kingdom, we're in Maleficent's kingdom."

"If she went to all this trouble to be here, there's got to be a good reason." Finn heard something behind him and glanced over his shoulder into the jungle. He saw nothing. Willa and Maybeck were freaking him out.

"Maleficent's weak in the heat. She needs cold to survive. If she's hanging out here, it's someplace cold."

"But why here?" Finn asked.

"We need to keep watch on the bat enclosure," Maybeck proposed.

"I can go places none of you can," said a girl's voice from behind them. Once again Finn looked back into the jungle. Again he saw nothing.

"Up here," said the voice.

He and the others looked up to see a vine-covered leotard, with no face and no arms. It was Charlene, in costume as DeVine, her face painted green and black.

The overall effect was disarming: she'd been standing there all along, immediately behind Finn.

Philby applauded. "Outrageous!" he said.

"Whoa," said Maybeck. "You totally blend in."

"I can't believe it!" said an exhilarated Willa. "I'm looking right at you and I almost can't see you."

"I'll need to leave the area before the real DeVine comes out. But I can go almost anywhere undetected. Even Maleficent isn't going to see me in this."

"Okay, Charlene will watch the bat enclosure," Finn stated with a feigned authority. He remembered Wayne telling him that he was the group's chosen leader, though he still wasn't buying it. But to his surprise, no one argued with him.

Charlene, blending into her surroundings, waited for some Park guests to pass and then said, "Will someone please hand me the page from the diary?"

Amanda produced it, stood on the bench, and passed it up to her.

Charlene studied it. "Monkeys . . . tigers . . . a bat . . . This is enough for now," she said.

"It's possible that everything on that page is significant," Finn cautioned.

Catching Philby dozing off, he punched him in the arm. "And NO falling asleep," he reminded them.

"I'm exhausted," Willa said.

"We cannot sleep!" Finn repeated. "Wayne warned us about that. We've got to believe him."

Maybeck suggested they find some soft drinks.

A few minutes later they were all loading up on sodas. "Maybe Maleficent can't get Jess out of the park until after it closes," Amanda said, "or maybe the plan is to run all of you around until you tire out. If she can trap you all in the Sleeping Beauty Syndrome, she eliminates the enemy and is free to rule without challenge."

"You think she took Jess to bait us?" Willa asked.

"None of this means anything," Maybeck said, "until we find Jess. The challenge is to stay awake long enough to find Jess and crash this cloned server—if it even exists. Then maybe we hunt down Maleficent, if we're still standing. But until we find Jess, none of it matters."

"Listen!" Charlene said from high on the stilts.

The kids turned their attention toward the jungle.

"Not to me!" Charlene clarified. "To the music."

The kids perked up their ears. It was Ashley Tisdale's "Kiss the Girl," coming over the Park's speaker system.

"Yeah? So?" asked Willa. "Radio Disney plays that all the time."

"I know that," Charlene said. "But me and my family come as often as possible, and I've never heard that song in this Park before."

The kids listened some more. "You're right. It's always *Lion King* and stuff like that."

"It's Jess," Amanda stated.

"What's Jess?" Finn asked.

"'Kiss the Girl' is Jess's favorite song," Amanda said. "She abuses that song on her iPod. If it doesn't belong in this Park, then it's her. It's some kind of message."

"I think you're more tired than the rest of us," Maybeck said.

"Which is completely understandable," Willa chimed in, "given the stress . . ."

"Listen . . . listen!" Amanda demanded, raising a finger to try to shut them up. "Raven-Symoné is going to sing 'Under the Sea' next."

"Yeah, right," said Maybeck. "I suppose if your sister can dream the future, you can *hear* it."

"Philby," Amanda said, "Jess had her iPod with her. Is there some way she could use it over the sound system?"

"Hijack the sound system?" Philby said, considering the question. "Depends, I suppose. If she stripped a wire from the earbuds and tapped into—"

But he was cut off by the music changing.

Raven-Symoné was singing "Under the Sea."

All the kids went quiet.

Some visitors walked past talking about going on

Expedition Everest. The parents sounded reluctant to try the ride.

But it wasn't the guests that had silenced the kids.

"Coincidence," Maybeck said in a whisper. He didn't sound at all convinced.

"It's Jess," Amanda countered, her voice noticeably brighter.

"I know for a fact that they never play that song here," Charlene said from up high. "I believe Amanda. And besides, it's softer than the regular music—not as loud. It doesn't sound right."

"Which would also explain why Finn and I overheard two maintenance guys talking about sound-system problems," Philby said.

Finn's face brightened. "That's right!"

"Then why doesn't she just send us Morse code, or something?" Maybeck complained.

"Because she can't give away what she's done," Amanda said, trying to think as Jess would think. "She doesn't want them figuring it out. So she's trying to communicate with us, without it being really obvious."

"Wait right here," Philby said, taking off at a run. The kids watched him go.

They used the downtime to review the page taken from Jess's diary.

"The animals could symbolize different things," Willa suggested.

"Like what?" a skeptical Maybeck questioned. "Listen, I see the drawing of the lightning striking a castle, and even I've got to admit it's pretty coincidental. But the rest of these? They're animals. So what? She likes animals. It doesn't mean they *mean* something."

"It doesn't mean they don't," Amanda countered. "You don't know Jess. They're clues. Clues we're supposed to follow."

Philby came running toward them.

As he did, there was suddenly no music at all: a rarity in any of the Disney Parks.

Then "Under the Sea" began playing again.

One thing all the kids knew: music never repeated in any of the Parks. Not ever.

Out of breath, Philby said, "It's playing on this side of the Park and in Asia. Discovery Island and Africa have different music going."

"That doesn't necessarily mean anything," Maybeck said. "How do we know that isn't always the case?"

Philby explained, "From what I know, the system is designed to be able to move sound around the Park. The parades used to require that the music follow the floats. It's a sophisticated, computer-controlled sound system. I've never read anything about one half of the Park being sent one kind of music, and the other half another."

"That confirms it's Jess," Amanda said excitedly. "She just repeated 'Under the Sea.' We know that song doesn't belong here, and on her iPod it follows 'Kiss the Girl.' Pretty obvious she *wants* someone to hear it. Maybe us. Maybe someone to try to fix it, someone to go looking for the problem."

"Or maybe," said Willa, "the song itself is significant. Ariel. Or Ursula—"

"I hate Ursula," Charlene tossed out.

"Or it has to do with where they're keeping her," Amanda continued. "Or it fits into her dreams in some way."

"We've got to take it seriously," Willa pleaded, looking at Finn, knowing the decision would somehow be his to make.

Finn felt all eyes fall on him. He stifled a yawn. Every minute was precious. His head was clouded and heavy.

"Let's run down everything to do with *The Little Mermaid*," Finn said.

Maybeck groaned. "Isn't that wasting time? The bat is *real*. That monkey is *real*. The dragon was real. Let's follow things we can actually see."

"How do we know that?" Charlene asked from atop her stilts.

"Ariel's Grotto," Willa said. "Magic Kingdom."

"We split up," Finn said, pulling out a pencil and writing on the back of the photocopy of the diary page. "Maybeck will try to locate the animals and images sketched in the diary. The rest of us will look for anything to do with 'Under the Sea' and *The Little Mermaid*."

"I don't know if this counts," Philby said, "but when you stand in line for Nemo, over at Epcot, the ocean is painted above you. You're literally under the sea."

"I like it," Finn said. He wrote it down.

"The same thing's true at Hollywood Studios," Willa said. "On the Voyage of the Little Mermaid, you stand under the sea while waiting."

"Okay . . . Okay . . ." Maybeck said, finally going along. "I don't know if this counts, but there's this poster my little sister loves. Always points it out. It's by the Mickey's PhilharMagic line. I'm pretty sure it's says something like 'A Must Sea,' spelled *S-E-A*."

"That definitely counts," Finn said, writing this down as well. "Anything else anyone can think of?"

One by one, the others either shook their heads or shrugged.

"It's a lot. And they're spread all over the place."

"It's a waste of time," Maybeck cautioned. "It's just a song."

"You have your assignment," Finn said. "Philby will stay and try to figure out the Park's sound system. Get on to VMK if you can and find Wayne. Maybe he can help." He explained how to use the Disney Vacation Club screens to view the Park security cameras as well to access VMK. "Amanda, you will keep watch for Jess using the Vacation Club screen by the Dawa Bar kiosk. Willa will take Ariel's Grotto and Mickey's PhilharMagic—both in Magic Kingdom. I'll take Nemo and the Voyage of the Little Mermaid. Maybeck, you stay and keep after the monkey and bat. Follow the clues in the diary, working with Charlene. Any problems?"

To his surprise, no one complained or tried to change the assignments. Maybe he actually was the leader.

"All of us have to study this page from the diary. We each have a copy. We need to write down where we've seen any of these animals, or images of these animals. This building she drew . . . this dude wearing a turban. And I'll call Rob, since his name keeps coming up."

He met eyes—tired eyes—with Maybeck, and saw Maybeck's frustration and impatience.

"I'm open to suggestions," Finn offered.

A silence hung heavily in the air.

It was broken by the music beginning again. "Under the Sea." Playing now for the third time in a row.

"Two hours," Maybeck said. "We meet back here."

"Agreed," Finn said.

The kids scattered.

26

LIKE THE OTHERS, Willa had put her Animal Kingdom Cast Member costume on over her regular clothes. She'd slipped out of the AK costume and had tucked it into a bush outside the gates of the Magic Kingdom. Using the ID Wayne had given her, she was admitted without a problem.

She called her mother while on the bus. This was critical, because she'd sneaked out in the early hours of the morning before, saying she'd gone to Mass. She did this on her own periodically—something her mother found "dear"—so she knew it wouldn't raise a suspicion. Her mother was no longer a churchgoer, not since her father's accident, so the only excuse she had to make now concerned what she was doing with her morning.

"I'm at Disney World," she told her mother, settling for the truth. For all she knew, the Find My Friends app had already given her away.

"But you're not allowed. They'll pull our pass if they catch you."

"It's important."

"What could be that important?"

"I'm doing it for a friend."

"Doing what?"

"Research."

"You're not tangled up with those other kids again, are you?"

"They're my friends, Mom."

"They got you into a lot of trouble last time."

"I'll be home . . . later. I'll call if it's going to be after dark."

"It is *not* going to be after dark, young lady. I want you home by five."

"I can't promise that."

"You can, and you will. I'm still your mother, and if I say five, then it's five. And remember: stay away from the Magic Kingdom. If they make us give that money back . . ."

"They won't, Mom. I'll call. I love you, Mom." She hung up. Her mother hadn't been herself since the accident. In some ways the two of them were closer; in other ways they'd kind of traded roles: Willa felt more like the parent. She wondered why certain things happened in life—happened to some people but not others. Why had she become a DHI? How very different her life would be had she never auditioned for the part. Now she was caught up in something few would believe; she didn't even believe it herself some of the time. Rescuing a girl who could dream the future? It sounded so *stupid*. And yet . . .

She kept her head down on the way to Ariel's Grotto. If she was spotted, she'd be mobbed by autograph seekers. If busted by Security, they would throw her out and take action. She hoped the little bit of makeup she had on would help disguise her. She promised herself to keep a low profile and get this over with as quickly as possible.

She charged a princess wig and Disney hat onto her credit card. A khaki-colored baseball cap, it was a little large for her head, but it held down the red wig and hid her face well. She walked briskly and turned off Main Street as soon as possible, cutting in along the Monsters, Inc. Laugh Floor and looping around toward the grotto. Not a single glance in her direction. The disguise was working.

She stopped at the rock wall bearing the name ARIEL'S GROTTO and studied the marquee. It had an image of Ariel and a seahorse and looked like a cave.

If she remembered correctly from the night before, the Ariel parade float was adorned with colorful sculptures of Sebastian, Scuttle, Triton, and Ursula. Did Jess's musical clue have anything to do with the parade?

After a long wait in line, she stood inside the

grotto, where girls lined up to meet Ariel and have their pictures taken with her. She was posed on a bench.

"Under the Sea," Willa was thinking, searching for a possible connection to Jess's disappearance. The song played repeatedly inside the grotto. With it, she felt a tangible connection to the missing Jess.

Something in here is important to Jess. . . .

She made herself believe this, having no idea whether or not it was true.

She was now third in line, behind mothers with their daughters lined up to get their photos taken. Behind Ariel, large colorful starfish clung to the aquamarine wall. Nearby sat a small wooden chest.

Nothing here seemed of interest save for the chest, the possible contents of which intrigued her. What was *in* there? she wondered.

She stepped forward, now second in line.

A girl and her mother got their picture taken. The Cast Member playing Ariel was beautiful. She spoke politely to both the mother and daughter, then glanced ahead to Willa.

She motioned Willa forward.

Ariel extended her hand and Willa shook it.

"I have a favor to ask," Willa said.

"How can I help you?"

"Can I ask what's inside the treasure chest?"

Willa said, pointing to the wooden trunk. "What's inside?"

Ariel kept her composure, but her eyes wandered to her attendant, who immediately came over.

"May I help?" a young woman asked.

"This young lady would like me to open the treasure chest," Ariel explained.

"It's important," Willa said in a whisper.

Though the company had never publicly acknowledged the work the Kingdom Keepers had done to save the Magic Kingdom, word had spread through the community. There were few that didn't know the story by now, both inside and outside the network of Park employees. A book had been written and published as fiction, but many knew the truth.

"How important?" Ariel asked.

Willa raised the baseball cap, revealing herself. A shock of recognition overcame the attendant. Willa hoped this was the right thing to do. She lowered her voice. "Did you hear about Tinker Bell last night, during the fireworks?"

Ariel's eyes widened.

"What is going on here?" the attendant whispered hotly into Willa's ear.

"What? I don't know what you mean."

"Don't give me that! First Captain Hook comes

through our line nosing around where he doesn't belong, and now you? And not fifteen minutes apart? What is it with you people?" She leaned in even closer. "Are you *inspecting* us or something?"

"Captain Hook?"

"Don't give me that."

"What did he want?"

"Captain Hook doesn't speak, as you know."

"He was just standing here?"

"They—the others," the attendant emphasized, "never used to pull surprise inspections. And I don't like it."

Willa tried to process all that she was being told. Did she mean the Overtakers? Here before her? Also interested in Ariel? Why?

"You want your picture taken with me?" Ariel asked. "It would be an honor." She'd opened the treasure chest for Willa: *empty.*

Willa felt her head spin. She had to beat Captain Hook—or whoever he was—to Mickey's Philhar-Magic.

"I'm fine!" she shouted over her shoulder, already hurrying away.

27

Finn arrived at Hollywood Studios bone-tired, well aware that if he or any of the other Kingdom Keepers fell asleep, they might not be seen again. Ever. Worse, Jess's disappearance pressured all involved to find her quickly. He was going to be in trouble if this went on much longer. He didn't put it past his parents to go looking for him at Blizzard Beach. When they failed to find him there . . .

He hurried down Hollywood Boulevard toward Mickey's giant sorcerer hat, which towered one hundred and twenty feet over the central plaza. He had his own cap brim pulled down low over his sunglasses as he kept an eye out for any kids recognizing him—he didn't need that. He would take evasive action if necessary. He identified possible escape routes in each direction.

While checking out the PhotoPass store to his left, he spotted a large black crow on the building's roof. The bird was certainly big enough to draw attention to itself, but Finn's curiosity ran deeper: it seemed to be staring at him. The bird had its head cocked so that its large black eye was trained down, not just on the street but on Finn. As Finn moved, so did the bird's head. As Finn hurried up the street, the bird flew and followed, building by building.

Finn might not have taken any notice or interest in a stupid crow, but he couldn't ignore Maybeck's tale about being attacked outside the bat enclosure by a flock of birds. He'd been bitten badly by a parrot once and could remember it as if it were yesterday.

Now, hurrying to the Voyage of the Little Mermaid, it seemed pretty obvious that the crow was following him. This, in turn, made him search the area to see if there were any other animals nearby. He spotted a group of chickadees in a tree outside the Brown Derby—but they didn't seem particularly threatening. A solo jay stood watch from a roof overlooking an ice-cream vendor. Finn's distraction with the animals caused his attention to falter.

He heard the voice too late. "Aren't you . . . *him*?" A boy of ten or eleven. His parents stood a few feet back, his mother's face bright with expectancy. Finn glanced around. How had the boy possibly recognized him? He didn't want this to get out of hand; sometimes signing a single autograph could start a big line.

"Do you like the Magic Kingdom?" Finn asked the boy, who then nodded vigorously.

"The Kingdom Keepers," the boy said. "You're Finn. You beat up Maleficent."

Finn bit back a smirk. "Not hardly. Those are just stories," he said, accepting an autograph book from the boy. "I'll sign this, but only if you promise not to tell anyone." He lowered his voice and said conspiratorially, "I'm here on a mission."

The boy's eye went wide. He shook his head, too awed to speak.

"Good." Finn led the boy over to the sidewalk, where he could sign the autograph book with his back turned to the street. In the Disney Parks, anyone signing anything attracted attention.

The boy followed. As Finn put pencil to paper, he briefly glanced up and into the reflection in the store window. Three brooms, one holding a bucket of water. He spun quickly around, dropping the autograph book. The boy bent to retrieve it.

The brooms stood facing him.

"Thank you!" the boy said, cherishing his autograph.

Finn had nearly forgotten about him. "No problem."

Then something occurred to him. "You see those brooms over there? They look real familiar, but I can't remember why. . . ."

"*Fantasia*," the boy said.

"*Fantasia*," Finn said. "I'm not as familiar with that one as the other classics."

"It's a pretty weird movie," the boy said. "The brooms show up in 'The Sorcerer's Apprentice,' I think. Mickey, the apprentice, can't control the magic—you know? It gets all out of hand. The brooms are part of that."

Uncontrollable magic, Finn thought. Yes, he knew exactly what that was about, just like uncontrollable holograms. The brooms were there *for him*. He felt certain of it all of a sudden.

Finn thanked the boy, who ran back to his mother's side.

Were the brooms part of Park Security? Were they going to bust him for being in the Park? Or were they something more sinister: *uncontrollable magic*?

The brooms swept their way across the street and drew closer.

He walked quickly away. He looked back: the brooms were definitely following.

Finn worked his way into the crowd, glad to see the brooms slow behind him. But then the three brooms split up. The one with the bucket went around the crowd in one direction. One stayed put. The third swept off in the opposite direction. Finn was surrounded. If they weren't Security, then they were something much worse.

Finn dodged his way through the crowds toward Mickey and Minnie's Runaway Railway.

The brooms regrouped and moved through the crowd—but they didn't seem to be in any hurry.

Finn entered the ride. He was directed into one of the cars, joining a family of three on a long bench. He lowered his head to keep from being seen. But he looked up to steal a peek toward the entrance.

For some reason, the brooms hadn't followed him inside.

28

TWENTY MINUTES LATER, with no sign of the brooms, Finn joined the line for Voyage of the Little Mermaid. The ceiling was painted to look like water. His heart beat excitedly: he was "under the sea."

There was no telling what he might find. Big or small, ordinary or out of the ordinary, it could be anything.

He heard a commotion behind him—the people waiting for the doors to open were oohing and ahhing. Finn turned carefully around and spotted the three brooms. They danced and bowed and entertained as they progressively moved closer.

Finn nudged past several people. "Excuse me . . . I got cut off from my family . . . Pardon me . . . I've lost my family and I think . . ." He never quite completed a sentence, thinking this made each excuse less of a lie.

People complained, but no one physically stopped him. He pushed to the very front of the line, putting a good distance between himself and the brooms. What did they want? he wondered. Would they possibly try to hurt him with all these people as witnesses?

The doors swung open. Finn hurried across a row in the middle of the large auditorium. If he kept going he'd have reached the seats closest to the exit doors, but he was afraid he might be more easily spotted there. So he took a seat near the middle.

The theater filled quickly. The brooms appeared at the end of the line. They spread out and moved along the wall to the back of the auditorium.

Before he had time to think, the lights dimmed and the theater went dark. Very dark. As an artificial rain began to fall, Finn took a chance and peeked over his shoulder. The brooms seemed to be watching the show along with the crowd. A wet mist blew from the stage, surprising the audience. A child cried out. Then there were laughs as the audience settled in for the show. The theme music rang out: "Under the Sea."

The song was the connection to Jess, and Finn searched the stage for possible clues as dozens of brightly colored sea creatures, glowing in the pitch-black, began swimming across the stage to the music. Ariel arrived onstage, and the audience applauded.

Flashes of color drenched the auditorium. He stole a look to the back: only one broom.

He fought off a sense of panic. *There!* Midway down the auditorium, a broom on each side. To his relief, they still appeared focused on the show, not the audience. To play it safe, he lowered his head and pulled the brim of his cap down farther. How long until they spotted him? And then what?

The crowd laughed, but not Finn.

The two brooms on either side were looking right at him.

The music grew louder. The auditorium darkened once again.

Finn dropped to all fours and began crawling to his left toward the exit doors. Guests moved their legs to allow him past, creating a commotion. A storm erupted onstage. Finn reached the end of the aisle and hesitated. Light flooded the theater. People applauded.

Finn jumped up and made for the exit.

He ran straight for the broom and pushed it over.

Hitting the blinding sunlight, he took off at a full run, unwilling to look back to see if a crow was following, or a broom chasing him. It seemed to him he'd picked up nothing of value. A waste of time.

Or maybe not, he thought. Had the Overtakers been following him? Why had the brooms seemed more interested in the stage show than in finding him? Maleficent's powers clearly extended throughout all of the Disney Parks—the existence of the brooms confirmed that much.

On his way back to Animal Kingdom, he sent a text warning to the others.

Four members checked in on the group text: Philby, Maybeck, Charlene, and Amanada. All but Willa.

Finn tried several times to reach her, finally giving up and hoping her phone was out of cell range.

But it didn't make sense.

Why wasn't she answering?

29

WILLA TRIED TO USE HER ID to jump the line for Mickey's PhilharMagic, but to no use. So she joined a long line that moved in waves, as a group of three hundred guests was admitted into the auditorium.

With each surge in the line, she passed more posters—all with a funny play on words. The line moved ahead, and it wasn't long before she faced the one Maybeck had mentioned. It showed Ariel and Triton, as Maybeck had remembered. It was titled, "A Must Sea!"

A plaque on the bottom of the frame read: ARIEL BROUGHT PART OF HER WORLD INTO OUR WORLD. . . .

Willa knew this was somehow significant. She sat down to make a note of it, to copy it out exactly as it was written.

Some of the smaller kids were also waiting out the line by sitting on the floor.

Jess had brought a part of her world into *our* world, as well, Willa thought. She'd brought her dreams about the future. She had foreseen things happening in the world that had now taken place: the lightning striking the castle, for one. Finn was right. If they were to find Jess, her drawings were the answer! The poster seemed to confirm it.

Willa wrote the note and put it in her pocket. Then she leaned her head back—*just for a minute*, she told herself—and tried to think of what else the message might mean. The more she concentrated, the heavier her head became. Her eyes began to blink away the stinging fatigue.

She fell asleep.

The rest was a dream. She saw herself being helped to her feet by—of all things—two bears from the Country Bear Jamboree. The kids around her, bored with waiting, were thrilled to see the bears. As she was taken out of the line and through a Cast Member door, she felt her entire body tingle. Not a nice tingle, but like when a foot falls asleep—the same kind of tingle she'd experienced on the nights when, falling asleep, she'd crossed over as a DHI.

Where the bears were taking her she couldn't tell, but there were voices and the sound of an engine. A few minutes later came the sounds of car doors and more voices. A friendly voice welcoming people. She heard the Animal Kingdom mentioned. It wasn't long until she felt incredibly comfortable, and it was quiet again. Beautifully quiet. Wonderfully quiet.

Far, far in the distance she heard the calls of exotic animals—as if someone had Animal Planet playing on their television.

Wherever she was, it felt like she could sleep there forever.

30

PHILBY APPROACHED THE Disney Vacation Club kiosk in Africa. He clicked on Dream Vacations and typed in **yensid_now.** A moment later, the screen refreshed and he was inside VMK's Central Plaza, in control of an avatar. He navigated the avatar toward a bench at the center of the screen.

Wayne? he typed. But as Finn had warned, nothing appeared, only the question mark. He typed the name again. His speech bubble showed only his ID— **Philby**—and a question mark. Growing impatient, Philby walked his avatar around the plaza. A minute passed, feeling more like five. For a third time, he tried typing the name. *Nothing.*

As he circled back around to the benches, a speech bubble appeared above an avatar with unusually white hair.

[ ]: Were you looking for someone? appeared above the white head.

Philby: Uncle walt's pen. finn sent me.

[ ]: Follow me

Philby followed Wayne on a long trip through the Web site to a private room Philby had never seen before. Wayne's avatar shut a door behind them.

[ ]: We can talk here. anything typed is encrypted.

Philby: Okay.

[ ]: Do you have a message from finn?

Philby: We need engineering blueprints for the AK. it looks like Jess may have messed with the sound system. if i can study the way it all works, maybe we can find her.

[ ]: Messed with?

Philby: A song—Under the Sea—was played over the PA. not only does that song not belong in AK, but it played three times in a row, and amanda says it's the same singer Jess has on her iPod, not the singer disney uses.

[ ]: I see.

Philby: Finn thought you could help me get the

plans. i thought about that maintenance place you showed us, but how can i get past the workers?

[ ]: You won't need to. besides, this time of day it's too risky. there's a better way. once we leave this room, we're no longer encrypted. i won't answer any questions out there, so i'll explain everything now. once we leave here, you're on your own, although i'll show you the way. i'll get you inside.

Philby: Inside where?

[ ]: Patience, my boy.

Wayne's avatar moved back to the door. He typed in a code that showed only as asterisks in his speech bubble. The door opened. The avatar stepped out into the hall, looked in both directions, and returned to the room, again shutting and code-locking the door.

[ ]: Can never be too careful. it would appear we're all alone, which is good. VMK was not always a game. originally, the imagineers wanted to create a virtual control room for the various parks. essentially, they were lazy. they wanted a way to fix small mechanical problems, or study the schematics from remote locations—their homes, or while they were traveling. the more employees,

the more sets of plans were needed, and the paper plans were constantly changing and needing updating as systems were improved or modified. a guy named alex wright came up with the idea of putting it all online. they would encrypt access for security reasons, and each Imagineer or employee would have his or her own avatar—a mock human being with hands and feet that could not only study the schematics online but could carry out some minimal maintenance or switching procedures: open boxes, pull switches. the area they created was termed the virtual magic kingdom—vmk—and in their spare time they began to create games with each other. they built rooms and attractions in their virtual world. it was only much later it occurred to someone to allow the public inside. at that time, they sealed off what they call the mechanicals, hiding them behind encrypted firewalls. last year it became apparent the Overtakers were trying to compromise VMK. the site was closed to the public. i can get you access to the mechanicals if that's what you want?

Philby: Does that include the music system?

[ ]: I would imagine. follow me. and don't write anything until I tell you to do so. it is not beyond

consideration that the overtakers are monitoring vmk. they should never be underestimated. they are devious and powerful, and it's apparent they will stop at nothing to control the kingdoms. we must be vigilant.

Philby didn't type anything. He guided his avatar toward the door and waited as instructed.

Wayne approached. Asterisks appeared in his speech bubble. The door swung open.

Philby's avatar followed the white-headed figure out into the hallway. Wayne knew his way around VMK, taking Philby to places he'd never visited. They entered a private room that didn't look particularly interesting. Philby realized this was a trick: the less interesting it looked, the less interested anyone would be in spending time in there. Wayne coded the door shut and then approached the far wall. Again, asterisks filled his speech bubble. A door swung open, and the landscape changed considerably. The walls and floors were silver and black. Dark blue signs with white lettering acted as trail guides: MK $\longrightarrow$ AK $\longleftarrow$ Epcot $\uparrow$ Hollywood $\uparrow$

They turned left, following the signs to the Animal Kingdom.

Access through the door marked AK CONTROL required yet another code from Wayne. The door opened, revealing a room with a flow chart projected on a large wall. It reminded Philby of a war room, like he'd seen in movies. The flow chart showed: MECHANICALS, SECURITY, STRUCTURES, ATTRACTIONS, GATES/ACCESS, BACKSTAGE. Under some of these were smaller titles like ASIA, AFRICA, PANDORA, DINO L. It looked like a giant outline or family tree, with branches connecting a main title to its smaller subtitles.

Wayne's avatar climbed into a cage on the end of a long mechanical arm. As Philby stepped in, it reminded him of the cherry pickers road crews used to trim trees or repair phone poles. Wayne pulled the door to the cage shut, and Philby watched as he pushed levers and the cage rose to pass in front of the titles on the flow chart.

He maneuvered them to stop at MECHANICALS. Wayne reached out and pushed against the screen. Immediately, the projection on the wall changed. Now MECHANICALS was listed at the top, and there were dozens of subcategories, including—Philby noticed— PUBLIC ADDRESS SYSTEM.

Wayne reached out and tapped the title.

The lettering folded back, opening an entrance like a window in the wall. Wayne opened the cage door and led them *through* this new opening in the wall and into a massively complex room. Philby gasped. He heard his own voice and only then remembered he was standing in a small hut. For the past few minutes he had almost become his avatar. He'd been transported. He hadn't remembered where he was. Now, glancing behind him, he looked out through the open doorway. The Overtakers were not to be under-estimated.

He then looked to the screen; Wayne was waiting for him.

[ ]: We're safe now.

Philby moved his avatar forward. He faced a large sound-mixer projected on the floor in front of him. He studied it, realizing this was a photographic image, probably of the actual soundboard somewhere in the Animal Kingdom's control room. And, like the real thing, the virtual soundboard would not only allow him to change volume or inputs throughout the Park, it also displayed cables to switching stations and the hundreds of speakers placed throughout the Animal Kingdom. With a click of a button, he could then overlay either a satellite image or a map of the Park, making it easy to identify the exact location of the various sound-system elements. Wayne was right: it offered an easy method for troubleshooting problems or identifying problem spots without being in the Park.

Slowly, he got the hang of the technology.

Philby: Whoa . . .

[ ]: No one ever accused the imagineers of being stupid.

Philby: This is incredible. i can follow any wire anywhere.

[ ]: And perform tests on it. i should think that was the purpose after all: long-distance testing and repair.

Philby: How much time do i have?

[ ]: No one will bother us here. take as long as you like. since i've gone into hiding, i have nothing but time.

Philby's main interest was the separation of the Park's background music, divided into the five sound areas. Each area had its own output, volume, and tone controls. He located the output wires on the back of the mixer—virtual speaker wires leading out into the Park.

Philby: What are the chances the Overtakers have Jess locked up in the sound control room? she could input her iPod into this mixer pretty easily.

[ ]: I would doubt that. but who knows?

Philby had an idea. He wondered if the sound system could narrow down Jess's location.

Philby spent several minutes following the speaker cables, quickly determining that from where he and the others had heard "Under the Sea" playing over the system, they'd actually been part of the Asia speaker system. He rechecked the soundboard, looking to see if he could explain Jess's iPod having played over the system. There were so many knobs and dials he didn't know exactly what he was looking at. He'd used GarageBand on his own computer, but this was far more complex.

Philby: She's somewhere in asia.

[ ]: Asia is big.

Philby: So we'd better get over there now.

Philby texted to Amanda to focus her attention on Asia's security cameras.

Amanda texted back but never got a reply or emoji.

That was because as Philby turned around, he found himself face-to-face with a very angry tiger.

31

OF COURSE, AT FIRST PHILBY didn't believe it.

A tiger.

He'd never realized how big they were: the tiger stood as high as Philby's shoulder. Orange, black, and white stripes, like war paint. Its eyes were hypnotic; he couldn't pry his own away from them. They stared at him like he was . . . *lunch.*

The tiger blocked Philby from running away. There was no getting past it, even if Philby's legs had worked, and at that moment he had no sensation in his legs whatsoever. He felt nothing but tremendous fear charging his system. It took him over completely. Owned him.

A tiger loose in the Animal Kingdom! Where were the sirens? Where were the animal police?

He opened his mouth to scream, but his throat proved too dry, and he croaked out a pathetic noise that didn't even sound close to the "Help!" he'd intended.

The tiger cocked his head, looking at him from an angle. Sizing him up. Preparing to attack, it crouched slowly and silently. As gracefully as a dancer, it squatted onto its haunches, its leg muscles flexing as if there were steel cables beneath the colorful hide.

Philby couldn't take it anymore. He squinted his eyes shut and braced himself for the attack.

When nothing happened, he slowly edged his left eye open slightly, stealing a look.

At that exact moment, the tiger jumped.

Philby's world went dark.

He felt nothing.

32

Finn arrived at the rendezvous at the specified time. There was a tall guy in a Disney cap and green coveralls hanging out by the gate to backstage, and it took Finn a moment to realize it was Maybeck. With his face in the shadow of the cap, he looked about twenty years old. The two boys met up and stood to the side, near the jungle, amazed at the numbers of visitors that now jammed the Park.

Speaking under his breath, Finn explained his encounter with the brooms.

"Maybe the brooms mean the Overtakers are trying to clean things up," Maybeck said, amused by his own joke. Finn didn't dignify that with a response. "The DeVine Charlene is over by the bat enclosure," Maybeck continued. "I walked around trying to find stuff from the diary. Ended up back at the Gibbons Temple, and I gotta tell you, Whitman"—Maybeck liked to call Finn by his last name—"there was some serious action over there. Bunch of the rangers all making a stink. From what I overhead, some orangutans pulled a fast one. One of the apes supposedly stole a key, hid it in his upper lip, and then pulled off a jail break. Some kind of smarts, these apes. Six of them are missing. There's some serious stuff going down, no doubt about it. And far as I can tell, we're the only ones who have a clue, and not much of a clue at that."

Finn checked his watch. "Where's Philby? And Willa? Philby's never late to anything."

"Haven't seen either of them. Amanda's at Dawa keeping watch on Asia. The attractions, the paths, and all the buildings, inside and out."

"The thing about the brooms—" Finn said, starting to explain the way he'd felt. But then he cut himself off.

"Yeah?"

"Doesn't make any sense."

"As if *any* of this makes sense! Hello? Try me, Whitman."

"Okay. So pretty soon after I arrived at Hollywood Studios, I thought this crow had spotted me. Then the brooms show up. You know? But they didn't exactly come after me. They just kind of *followed* me there. At Voyage of the Little Mermaid it was almost like they were there to watch the show. The way I was."

"I don't get it," Maybeck said.

"You see?" Finn said. "I was pretty sure the brooms spotted me at the show, but I think they were *surprised* to see me there. Or maybe they didn't care."

"I still don't get it," Maybeck admitted, though somewhat reluctantly. Maybeck prided himself on knowing things before others.

Finn blurted out what he'd been thinking ever since the encounter. "Maybe the brooms were at Voyage for the same reason I was: to look for answers. My being there both confirmed they were in the right place and threatened them."

"Threatened them how?"

"What if the crow was some kind of spy?"

"Like the bat," Maybeck said.

"Yeah! Exactly! And what if the brooms were sent to follow me? So they did. Until Mickey and Minnie's Runaway Railway. They didn't follow me into there. Why?"

"I hope you're going to answer that."

"Because by my going in there, they were no longer worried about me. And then when I got to Voyage, they weren't even looking for me. It was the show that they were interested in."

"The show," Maybeck said. "Listen, I'm not getting this. What's up?"

Finn gathered his courage. "I think the Overtakers heard 'Under the Sea,' same as we did."

"Meaning?"

"Think about it," Finn said.

He watched as the mental tumblers clicked into

place and unlocked Maybeck's thought. Maybeck spoke slowly. "They're following the music clue the same way we are . . . because . . . they're . . . looking for Jess."

"She escaped," Finn declared. "They had her in the stump on the savannah. We know that much. Maybe in transferring her, maybe sometime before they ever moved her, she managed to escape. She hid someplace here in AK. And for some reason yet to be determined, she used the music as a clue."

"She's stuck in the Park," Maybeck said, "probably in Asia. And wherever she is she can't get out without our help. So she played the music to send us a clue."

"And we heard it," Finn said, "but so did the Overtakers. We both started looking at anything and everything that had to do with 'Under the Sea.'"

"It makes sense," Maybeck agreed.

Finn tried the group text again, sending a shout-out to Willa and Philby. But they weren't answering.

"So what do we do now?" he asked.

"We can't wait for them any longer. Maybe the dreams in Jess's journal are supposed to help us find her."

"We need Willa and Philby," Maybeck said. "There are a lot of drawings to make sense of."

Finn said what they both were thinking. "What if something's happened to them?"

The two boys met eyes with horrified expressions.

33

AMANDA STUDIED THE thumbnail images, each from a different camera in Asia. Giraffes, elephants, tigers, Park guests, and more Park guests.

In each of the small moving images, she looked for any sign of Jess. Her lips moved sliently. "Come on. I'm right here! Just give me a signal!"

Suddenly something in one of the frames looked familiar. It was Maybeck's confident stride, his way of walking that got him teased by the others. She followed him and Finn camera by camera.

* * *

Finn and Maybeck walked quickly along Asia's Jungle Trek. They kept about ten yards apart; if one of them was spotted, maybe the other wouldn't be. The Trek had an occasional Park ranger at an education station— there to give hands-on demonstrations to the curious— any one of whom might be an Overtaker. Finn paid particular attention to each of these rangers as Maybeck passed, glad to see that none seemed to take any particular interest in him.

Soon, they reached the tiger-viewing yards, where they stood among the ruins of an Indian temple—the jungle and buildings so authentic that, although he'd never been to the real Asia, Finn could imagine himself halfway around the world. The footpath rose here to where it was fifteen or twenty feet off the ground, the walls of the crumbling temple holding in the Park guests, offering views to either side, down into grassy knolls and fields. In the heat of the day, the tigers had taken to the shade at the edge of the wall that contained them. People crowded the temple's viewing windows to get a decent look at the wild cats. The arching windows held no glass but were divided into small squares as if they did, or once had. And while there was no pushing or shoving to win the best view, there was some seriously competitive leaning going on.

But before Finn ever reached the clot of guests at the windows, Maybeck stopped and pulled him aside.

"Check it out!"

Just Maybeck's tone of voice told Finn it was something important. Typically, Maybeck was much too cool to get excited about anything. "Sands of a beach!" Maybeck said.

Finn moved closer to where Maybeck was pointing as Maybeck unfolded the printout of the page from Jess's diary.

The temple's stone wall held a series of stone carvings, four feet by four feet pictographs showing different scenes. The primitive carvings were beautiful. One showed a person with his or her arms in the air, and an eagle flying overhead. Another had a fruit tree at its center, with birds in the branches and deer surrounding it. But it was the monkey at the base of the tree that held Finn's attention.

Maybeck double-checked the printout. "That monkey is so close to the one she drew," he said. "We're here!"

"The windows," Finn told Maybeck, pointing to the knot of visitors straining for a look through open-air windows on the bridge. "They're on her drawing, too!"

He and Maybeck moved toward the crowded area.

"You know," Maybeck said, "until now, I didn't believe that Jess could dream the future."

"And now?" Finn asked.

"Yeah, well, a person's got a right to be wrong."

34

FINN AND MAYBECK steadily pushed to the front of the throng gathered at the windows overlooking the tiger yards, where a blanket of green grass was interrupted by some trees and rocks. A huge tigress slumbered in the thick shade of a bamboo stand, her back against the tall rock wall that contained her. Jess had sketched both this window and the sculpture reliefs they'd just been studying, meaning this location had played a significant role in her dreams.

But what role? Finn wondered.

"It could be she's hiding in the tiger yards," Finn said quietly to Maybeck.

"You see her out there, do you?" Maybeck asked.

"No. But—"

"That's because she isn't there."

"But it makes sense. She wouldn't exactly be able to move if she was stuck in there. Not with tigers roaming the place."

"Whitman, look around."

Finn moved to the opposite side of the walled bridge dividing the two tiger yards. He didn't have to challenge any crowds, because there weren't any. There weren't any tigers seen from this side.

"Convinced?" Maybeck said from behind him. He, too, had switched sides.

"But why would she have drawn both the window and the monkey? Can you explain that?" Finn asked anxiously. "They have to mean something."

"She drew a lot of stuff: a dinosaur, the monkey, the window, a bat, some old dude. How are we supposed to know what it all means?"

"That's just the point," Finn said. "We *are* supposed to know what it means. We're supposed to figure it out. We're supposed to help her."

"Maybe it's about the animals, not the locations," Maybeck suggested. "Something to do with monkeys, tigers, and dinosaurs. What do they have in common?"

"Nothing," Finn said, "except that they're all part of the AK."

"The server!" Maybeck said excitedly. "The second server. Didn't Wayne tell you the plan was to—"

"Make animals into DHIs!" Finn shouted a little too loudly. "You're right." He pulled out the page of Jess's diary and studied it again. "What if these animals are the ones they're turning into DHIs? Jess saw them in her dreams. They meant something to her, something important."

Maybeck texted Amanda.

Maybeck: Amanda. how many tigers do you see

Amanda: Three

Maybeck: Finn and I think some animals may be holograms — DHIs.

Finn joined the group text.

Finn: Overtakers might use DHIs to try to fake us out.

Maybeck: Maleficent cannot be trusted. she could have made herself into a DHI to use as a decoy. there's no way to know.

Amanda: It makes more sense. She's desperate to control the parks! She could use the DHIs to scare the guests, or maybe to put you guys into Sleeping Beauty Syndrome.

Finn: With Jess being able to see the future, she's a real threat to Malef. What if Jess found out what Maleficent has planned?

Amanda: That would explain why Maleficent would want to kidnap her.

Finn: Maybe Jess did the drawings to warn us that some were fakes. Or to watch out for them or something.

Amanda: It's more than that for her. Her dreams involve her. She's part of them. Her diary is about stuff in her life, not ours.

A message bubble filled with asterisks. Someone was typing.

Amanda: Hold on! There's a truck being unloaded behind the bat enclosure. Two cages. Both are covered with tarps, so I can't see inside. You think that's something?

Maybeck: Hard to say.

Amanda: Ok, so the truck driver has a MONKEY on his arm. A live monkey.

Finn: The animal care people would never allow a monkey to be loose. Free. The driver isn't a Cast Member. He's a fake.

Maybeck: How big are the cages?

Amanda: Big! Very big. Big enough for a large dog or a lion.

Maybeck typed quickly.

Maybeck: Or philby and willa?

Finn: Amanda, Keep watch on the videos. We're on our way!

35

FINN AND MAYBECK made their way toward the bat enclosure, just down from the tiger yard along the winding, dark trail of the Maharajah Jungle Trek. Bugs buzzed past their heads as the heat enveloped them, making their chests tight and their breath short. Birds cried out and fluttered past, winning Maybeck's unflinching attention as he recalled his earlier horrifying experience. His phone buzzed. He checked for the message.

Amanda: The camera at the bat enclosure just stopped working. Sabotage?

"She's right, that cannot be a coincidence," Maybeck whispered to Finn. "That camera was sabotaged. Something's going on back there, and we need to know what it is."

Charlene: Hey, guys. Right behind you.

Finn saw a pale green shape amid the dark green of the trees and undergrowth. Charlene was a tangle of ivy, high up on stilts. She was nearly invisible where she stood, ten feet into the jungle. She moved slightly and became more obvious. The two boys moved closer to her.

"I've been keeping an eye on the bat enclosure as Maybeck asked," Charlene said. "There's been a lot of activity, a lot of coming and going through those doors at the rear. The workers definitely kept an eye on that big bat near the red flag over to the left. Twice they've carried the bat out and back. I don't know if that's the one that Maybeck had in the pillowcase. But it might be."

Maybeck moved toward the bat enclosure's viewing station to get a better look. Once there, he turned toward Finn, and shrugged.

Finn whispered to Charlene, "We need to find out what's in those cages that Amanda is talking about."

"I think can help with that," Charlene said. "A way to find out what's going on back there."

"I'm listening," Finn said.

"I'll need a diversion," Charlene whispered. "Something big. Something everyone will watch. And by everyone, I mean the people and the *bats*. Can you do that?"

36

*I*NGENIOUS, FINN THOUGHT as he moved through the swinging doors and into the forward viewing booth. There were three levels of viewing offered at the bat enclosure, three open-air rooms constructed of dark wood that led the Park guest closer to the risk of contact with the flying rodents. The first viewing room offered glass windows; the middle room, screens; and the final room—more of a long booth—nothing but well-spaced vertical wooden bars to keep the large bats at bay. The bars were clearly wide enough for Finn to poke his head through, yet too narrow for the extended wings of the large African bats.

Finn kept his cap pulled down snugly, hoping to avoid being recognized; that was the kind of distraction he could do without. The viewing room was staffed by a college-age girl in a ranger's uniform. Presently, she was busy answering questions. Two young boys were ignoring her. They had too much energy for the small space, and their mother wasn't doing anything to control them. The situation served Finn's purpose well. He slipped the case off his phone as he stepped close to the open-air viewing windows, hoisting his phone to take a picture.

He pressed close to the window's wooden bars. A warm breeze hit his face. The ranger sounded like her patience with the two boys was wearing thin.

Finn purposely fumbled with the phone and case, allowing the case to slip out of his hands and fall through the bars, down into the bat enclosure. He pocketed the phone.

"My case!" he shouted. He jumped up onto the sill and began to squeeze himself through the bars.

Finn was relatively slight of build. He managed to squeeze partway through the bars before the ranger grabbed hold of him.

"GET OUT OF THERE!!" the girl screamed at the top of her lungs, pulling on him. "YOU CAN'T GO IN THERE!!! ARE YOU OUT OF YOUR MIND?"

The effect was exactly what Charlene had asked for: everyone was looking at Finn. Some of the bats spooked and took flight. For a few precious seconds, the ranger pulled. Finn resisted.

"My phone case!" he hollered.

"GET DOWN FROM THERE!"

Finn stole one quick glance. Maybeck helped Charlene, on stilts, through the jungle door and into the enclosure. Charlene's ivy-clad costume pushed up against the rocks at the far end of the enclosure, and within seconds a miracle occurred: she disappeared. DeVine's costume fit into the environment so well that her form appeared as ivy growing up the rocks. There was no mistaking this whatsoever for a girl on stilts. The change was extraordinary.

Finn, apologizing and complaining at the same time, allowed himself to be drawn back into the viewing room, actually grateful for the ranger's efforts, since the swirling bats swooped and dove too close for comfort. The ranger scolded him briefly, then promised to have his lost case retrieved. She tried to contact someone over her headset, but clearly there was no answer. She double-checked both the headset and the radio it was plugged into, obviously annoyed by the lack of response.

She blushed, apologized, and asked Finn to stick around. "I don't know why I'm not getting anyone back there," she said.

I do, Finn thought to himself. *The people behind that door are not the people you normally work with. If they're even people at all . . .*

Once again, his eyes strayed to the far side of the enclosure, where he saw that the ivy patch on the rocks had migrated a few feet farther along, a yard or two closer to the enclosure's center doors. Charlene was moving so incredibly slowly, so expertly, that it was impossible to detect her movements. The ivy seemed to be growing and extending all on its own, blending in perfectly with the ivy already there.

37

W<small>ITH HER BACK TO</small> a false rock wall, Charlene watched Finn being grabbed by the ranger in the viewing booth. The girl stopped him from jumping into the enclosure, and then the two had words. Charlene thought that Finn seemed to be looking right at her a couple of times, and she wondered how good a job she was doing at blending in.

With her face painted camouflage green, white, and brown, only the whites of her eyes threatened to give her away; so Charlene tried to keep her eyes averted. But it wasn't easy. Jangled by raw nerves, she inched her way along the wall, trying not to look at the bats. She hated bats, and the ones in the enclosure were the size of bowling pins: big, gray, winged rats, hanging upside down from clotheslines. As long as they kept their distance, she thought she could make it.

The only people who might spot her were those in the viewing station: the Park visitors and the ranger. When she did look up, it was toward the booth. She didn't know if Amanda had a camera aimed at her, and she'd lost sight of Maybeck, who was somewhere off to her right near the jungle door. She was on her own: fenced in with several dozen giant bats, in a place that smelled . . . well, funky . . . trying to slow-dance her way clear around the curve of the smooth, irregular rock wall to the center doors.

She inched a stilt to her left, stepped the other along, and then froze, allowing her vines to blend in with those growing on the rocks. Then, a minute or two later, she moved again. She and the vines crept ahead, no one the wiser.

Finn left the booth, and Maybeck appeared out on the path with him. They both glanced once in her direction. She saw Finn lift his phone, signaling for her that a text was coming.

Finn: I can't see you at all, Charlie. Great job. We're here if you need us.

The two boys moved away from the viewing station but stayed close.

It was the first time Finn, or anyone else for that matter, had ever called her Charlie, and she actually liked the nickname. There was something pleasing about it, something incredibly personal that made her feel especially good about it. She hoped it might stick, providing she got out of here alive.

The left stilt caught on a rock as she moved, and the rock shot out from under it like a wet bar of soap, raising a puff of dust. This, in turn, startled the bats, already edgy from Finn's distraction. Three of the ugly things flew straight for her, coming toward her face at incredible speed, flying close enough that she could see not only the black-glass, buttonlike, beady eyes, but the tiny gray hairs that surrounded their ratty faces, and the eerie translucence of their wings. Her stomach knotted, her head swooned, and a scream bubbled up from her lungs. She kept silent only by snapping her lips shut and clenching her teeth. The last of the three brushed against her hair, dislodging a carefully placed plastic vine and causing a strand to fall into her eyes— undoing her disguise. If anyone looked directly at her now, they were sure to see a length of blond hair inexplicably sticking out from the ivy—and that couldn't be good. She blew the hair out of her eyes with upturned lips and moved more quickly now, slipping her way around the curving rock wall and nearing the green doors at its center.

She was partially hidden by several trees as she neared the two doors, suddenly realizing that on stilts she was much too tall to fit through without Maybeck's help. Being near the middle of the enclosure, she was also now the center of attention. Without her knowing it, the Park guests were looking directly at her.

She wasn't going to get through those doors, and

she'd come too far to turn back. She looked up: the rock wall rose high above her head, but though it was uneven and craggy, there were plenty of handholds visible. Charlene climbed the rock wall at her gym—she considered herself something of an expert.

The trick was getting her feet out of the stilts without being seen and then leaving the stilts propped against the rock so that she could return to them and effect her escape. She eased down into a squat—not an easy balancing act on stilts—and managed to release her left foot. She freed her right foot, too, and then carefully stepped out of both stilts to leave them resting against the fake rock wall. Some of the ivy strands that wrapped around the stilts continued higher and merged into those that surrounded her leotard. She managed to disconnect the tendrils one by one; far more were sewn to the leotard and remained part of her costume. These also helped disguise her as, by handhold and foothold, Charlene climbed higher up the rock face. With each small ascent she paused for what felt like a very long time, allowing her vines to combine with rock and make it more difficult to spot her. She was helped out by the trees and vegetation between her and the viewing booth. But soon she rose above the crown of the nearest tree, clinging to the odd texture of the fake rock and staying close to the line of real ivy to help camouflage her.

Then, any possible route disappeared above her. She was used to having to plot her way up a rock wall, so she paused and looked for a possible route. The only small handholds she saw moved away from the patch of real ivy. But she had no choice. As she started off in that direction, she realized she was heading directly above the double doors at the center of the enclosure. She was also exposing herself to being seen by Park guests, as she was now directly in front of the viewing booths. Because of this, she tried to move incredibly slowly. But the slow climbing taxed her strength and weakened her.

She couldn't "creep" between handholds and footholds, so she watched the viewing booths, waited for the attention of the guests to stray to one side or the other, and then made her move.

The doors swung open beneath her, and a worker stepped through.

Only then did she realize that some of the sandy texture was shredding off the wall where her running shoes touched. Painted sand rained down toward the ground, falling right on the head of the man who'd come through the doors. If he looked up, he would see her.

Counting on his entrance to have distracted both the guests and the ranger, Charlene no longer took her time. She gathered her strength, reached out, and moved with accuracy—three handholds, two footholds. She climbed quickly and deliberately, clawing her way up to the very top of the rocks, where, enclosed by the bat enclosure's netting, she spread herself flat.

The dust sprinkled into the hair of the man below. He turned to look up. But he saw only a wall—an empty wall. He brushed the sand out of his hair and cursed the people who'd built the enclosure. The darned thing was clearly falling apart.

38

CHARLENE SCOOTED TO the far edge of the top of
the wall and peered over the lip. She had a good view
through the netting of the backstage area. The enclosure's wooden doors opened onto a small, courtyard-
like area between the fake rock wall and a large garage
with a flat roof. The steel wall facing her had been
painted as a backdrop to look like rocks and vines.

She could hear a good deal of activity to her left but
couldn't see what was going on. She spotted a camera
mounted a few feet directly below her and aimed backstage; she assumed this was the camera that Amanda
had mentioned, the one out of commission, an easy
assumption, given that the wire running from it was
currently unplugged.

She reached under the edge of the netting, almost
touching the camera, her fingers grasping for the
dangling wire. If she could only reconnect it, Amanda
could take over the surveillance. It was no use—she
was too far above it, and to move any lower would risk
her being discovered. But Charlene was not one to

be discouraged. She squirmed her upper body slightly farther off the ledge and stretched out, her fingers now only an inch or two from the wire.

She lunged and grabbed hold of it, the wire firmly in her hand.

The worker who had entered the enclosure only a minute earlier, the man whose hair she had dusted with sand, now came back through the twin doors and shut them. There was no time for Charlene to retreat. Instead, she hung over the wall ledge directly above him, her left hand holding the wire, her right keeping herself from falling.

The man stopped and put down a white bucket.

"Well done."

Charlene heard the voice—a woman's sterile voice, uncaring and even rude, if uttering two small words could be made to sound rude.

"Tie him up," the same voice said.

Immediately three big monkeys appeared from around a corner. Fast as lightning, they swarmed the worker. One tied and knotted a length of rope around the man's wrists, holding them behind his back. Another secured his ankles. Within seconds, the man was bound. The third monkey leaped at the man and knocked him over. The man fell, and the two monkeys immediately dragged him across the blacktop and propped him up against a metal box, while the third tied a gag around his open mouth.

Only then did Charlene detect movement to her left, from where the voice had been heard: a flash of purple fabric and green skin.

Maleficent.

Charlene didn't actually see her, but she didn't have to. Purple and green were like Maleficent's team colors. Who else could it be?

With the monkeys' attention on the hostage, Charlene reconnected the camera and wire. The camera immediately sprang to life, tracking left. Charlene quickly retreated back to the top of the wall, flattening herself. She had a choice now: she could leave this to Amanda and the camera or . . .

She spun around and crawled in the direction of the noises. She had to see for herself. Something prompted her to glance back toward the viewing booth. From this height she could see out to several sections of the Jungle Trek path. It surprised her how much she could see—including Maybeck and Finn, who, standing to the side of the path, were shaking their heads furiously at her.

And then she understood: if she could see so much, then Park guests on the trail—like Maybeck and Finn—could see her as well. But rather than go back, she continued crawling, her curiosity ignited by the flash of green and purple, by the eerie sound of the woman's voice, and by a trio of large monkeys who had acted on orders. She crawled past a narrow wall that acted like a buttress, supporting the fake rock wall. It also screened the source of the noises, and by leaving it behind, she now saw through the netting what all the commotion was about.

Four hairy orangutans were directing smaller monkeys while Maleficent stood in the shade watching. The monkeys were unloading bags of ice from a large rectangular truck. They were stacking the bags into a heap, and the ice was melting in the sunshine and leaking out into a large puddle that disappeared beneath the truck. The whole operation looked so human—bosses and workers. And yet these weren't humans at all.

Then she saw the two cages. *Big*, as Amanda had described. They sat on the pavement, pushed up next to the steel barn. Both were wrapped in canvas tarps, but the canvas was not secured well along the bottom, allowing Charlene to see a slice of forest green fabric inside the cage: a ranger's uniform.

Willa!

She couldn't see anything inside the second cage, but she didn't need to: *Philby*. She had no doubts.

"Faster," Maleficent ordered. "We need more room. Bigger! If he's to fit, it must be bigger!"

Had Philby fallen asleep as Wayne had said not to do? Were they taking him somewhere? Smuggling him out of the Park in an ice truck? Or was she talking about some other hostage?

She tried to make sense of it all: the monkeys clearly obeying Maleficent's orders as if they understood her, the cages containing her friends, the melting pile of ice bags, the urgency in Maleficent's voice.

She knew what had to be done: she had to untie the worker and set him free. But did she dare climb down and attempt that? Wasn't it wrong not to? And if she messed up, if she got caught, would she end up like Willa and Philby? Where would that leave Maybeck and Finn, except further isolated?

Backing up slowly now, she decided this needed a team effort. She was no match for the power of Maleficent, who had once, with nothing but a wave of her hands and a mumbled incantation, created an electronic fence to surround Charlene's friends.

The climb back down the wall proved more difficult than her ascent. She had just strapped her feet back into the stilts when she heard: "Look, Mommy! What's *that?*"

The "that" was her, of course—the boy was pointing at her.

She stood absolutely still.

It felt like five minutes passed; it was more like thirty seconds.

"What? Where? The big one hanging from the rope?" the mother asked.

"Not the bats! The thingy. The creature. The vine thingy."

But no one saw her. Charlene had blended into the foliage around her. A few minutes later the unwilling boy was led away, still protesting that he could see the vine lady, and why couldn't anyone else see her?

It took Charlene fifteen minutes to work her way around the rock wall, and a second distraction—this time executed by Maybeck—to leave the enclosure.

A moment later, Finn and Maybeck joined her.

"So?" Finn asked. "Did you see anything?"

"We've got problems," Charlene answered. "Big . . . big problems."

39

FINN IMMEDIATELY UNDERSTOOD what Charlene and Maybeck did not: it wasn't Philby and Willa in the cages. Not exactly.

He took off down the jungle path, forcing Maybeck to hurry to keep up with him. Charlene had been asked to blend into the jungle and keep a strict eye on the bat enclosure. He texted Amanda the same thing. Now that Charlene had repaired the sabotaged camera, Amanda had more opportunity to monitor events backstage.

Though winded, Maybeck kept up. "What's going on, Whitman?"

"You, of all people, should know," Finn said.

"Me? Why?"

"Space Mountain."

Maybeck said, "What about it?"

Finn stopped and pulled Maybeck to the side of the path, out of earshot of the other guests who passed in a steady stream. He spoke in a hush. "When they trapped you in perma-sleep, they put your DHI in—?"

"A maintenance *cage*!" Maybeck answered. "It

wasn't Willa and Philby Charlene saw. It was their DHIs."

"Exactly," Finn agreed. "Even someone as warped as Maleficent wouldn't put a kid in a cage that small. But a DHI is another story."

"But if the DHIs are in those cages," Maybeck said, "then why don't they just walk out?"

"Why didn't you just walk out of the maintenance cage in Space Mountain?"

"I don't know," he said. "It was like I was half asleep or something. Until you showed up, it hadn't occurred to me."

"Because we had crossed over, and you had not. With your body in perma-sleep I have a feeling your DHI is kind of in this suspended state. It doesn't know what's up. Remember, Wayne programmed the server that controlled our DHIs. Maleficent is running the second server. Who knows how their DHIs are programmed?"

"So we need to cross them back over," Maybeck said. "That's the only way to get them out of the control of the second server."

"Exactly!"

"But why would the Overtakers do this?" Maybeck wondered aloud. "Why trap them in perma-sleep in the first place?"

"There's only one guy I know who can answer that. And he's also the guy who holds the button. The remote control that can cross them back over."

"Wayne!"

"If I can get that remote from him, and we can get close to those cages, we can release the sleeping Willa and Philby—wherever they are. And I happen to think I know where they are."

Maybeck didn't dignify that with a question, but he also couldn't wipe the curiosity off his face.

"Animal Kingdom Lodge," Finn answered. "Those are the closest beds to the Park. You can reach the lodge from the savannah, and we know the Overtakers are on the savannah."

"I've got to admit: it does make sense," Maybeck said. "When exactly did you figure all this out?"

"Back there," Finn said. "When Charlene described the cages, it all fit."

"And now we're headed to find Wayne."

"Yeah. There's the terminal in Africa. I can access VMK there," Finn said.

"I thought Philby never came back from that terminal."

"Which is why we're doing this together," Finn said. "Charlene will stay and keep an eye on the enclosure. I'll use VMK to try to reach Wayne, and you'll stand guard. Keep an eye on the group text. You see something, say something."

"And what if we're wrong about the cages?" Maybeck asked.

"We're not," answered Finn.

* * *

Finn's avatar stood by the bench in the VMK's central plaza. The real Finn stood in front of the screen in the Disney Vacation Club kiosk in Africa. The air was burning hot, and he picked up the smell of popcorn, which made him realize how hungry he was. He knew that soon his parents would start to worry. They would expect him home from the water park. But he had things to do.

Knowing it would not print, he typed **WAYNE** into his dialogue box. Sure enough, it didn't show up.

Players' avatars entered the plaza, pausing below the billboards or circulating while waiting to meet each other. Finn's patience was wearing thin when a white-haired avatar finally appeared from his right. Wayne's avatar never stopped moving as **Follow me** appeared in the dialogue box.

He led Finn to the same room where he had taken Philby. Wayne locked the door with a special code.

[ ]: **We're safe here.**

Finn: Philby and willa have gone missing. we think their DHIs are being kept in cages behind the bat enclosure. i need the button.

[ ]: I spoke to philby not long ago. right here.

Finn: He never showed up. i think Maleficent is holding them to protect the second server. we can't crash the server with willa and philby stuck in Sleeping Beauty Syndrome.

[ ]: This is most disturbing.

Finn: Can you get me the button—the remote control?

[ ]: Yes. of course. there's a tree in Pandora that looks like an ear of corn lying down. It has two pink mouths on one side. The fob will be inside the lower mouth.

Finn: That works.

[ ]: If she's trying to protect the second server, then I fear the worst: she will either turn herself into a DHI to fool us or do harm, or she will compromise the animal DHIs created for Animal Kingdom and use them to her advantage. this is a grave situation. in the magic kingdom she recruited Overtakers from within the attractions,

most notably the pirates and the small-world dolls. in animal kingdom there are few, if any, such characters she can recruit for her army. it is our fear she has corrupted the animals themselves. five more orangutans have escaped, along with a half dozen gibbons. several snakes cannot be found. a wildebeest rammed one of the electrical fences attempting to break out. she is clearly gaining strength.

Finn: We want our friends back. Jess drew some things in her diary that have already come true. we think the diary may be—

He stopped typing as a text appeared on his phone. It was from Maybeck.

Maybeck: Mayday!

40

MAYBECK KEPT WATCH from the side of a popcorn cart, where a multicolored umbrella was angled to throw shade onto the Cast Member behind the cart. The tilted umbrella offered Maybeck a way to spy on Finn. Nearby, a gardener was watering some plants.

Maybeck watched this guy and also the sky, for any sign of birds. But it was a lizard, not a bird, that troubled him.

Small lizards inhabited most of Florida. He'd grown so accustomed to seeing them zip up trees, across sidewalks, and down the walls of buildings that he almost didn't notice them at all. His aunt Jelly, who was as close to a mother as Maybeck would ever get, called them "little dragons" and considered them close relatives to the cockroach and mouse. She wasn't beyond trying to beat them with a broom as she shooed them from the house. He'd been catching them since he was five. If you grabbed one by the tail, the tail came off. For a while he'd kept the tails—he'd had about twenty—but Jelly had found them and thrown them out, never saying a thing about it, then lying to him when he asked.

But the lizard he was looking at was bigger—five or six inches, not three. It was also some kind of chameleon, quickly changing from the brown of the wood chips in the jungle to the grayish black of the paved path as the reptile emerged into sunlight. But more than anything, it was the way the lizard headed straight into trouble that won Maybeck's interest. Despite dozens of running shoes and sandals slapping down around it like mallets, the creature never wavered from its mission, dodging this way and that as it risked getting crushed. The lizards that Maybeck lived with spooked easily and skittered away as fast as lightning when approached. He'd never seen a lizard as bold as this one. It headed straight for . . .

. . . the Disney Vacation Club shack.

Finn!

Maybeck looked back into the jungle. Two sets of green eyes glowed in the shade.

Monkeys . . . he thought at first. But the eyes were too wide apart. *Orangutans!* More ape than monkey.

The chameleon stitched its way back into the jungle. It headed straight for the green eyes.

Maybeck worked to figure it out. The orangutans were on some kind of mission. Without a doubt, Finn was their target.

Think! he told himself, knowing he didn't have it

quite right. That's when a lion slinked out of the jungle and Maybeck sent his Mayday message.

"Mayday, dude! Mayday!" he shouted.

The Park visitors saw the lion as well. A man screamed. A woman grabbed her children by the hands and started to run. The crowd scattered.

41

FINN SPUN AROUND to see a lion strolling toward him. A big lion. A lion with a thick collar of fur, a huge head, beady eyes, and glistening white teeth. He instantly knew this was not a case of bad luck: the lion was coming for him just as the birds had come for Maybeck.

The lion lumbered toward him, now only a few yards away. The guests had scattered but now encircled an area about twenty yards across, with the beast at its center.

Heat flashed through him, and all the hairs on his arms and the back of his neck rose with his fright.

He knew what he had to do: he had to cross over. The lion couldn't hurt a DHI. But as the enormous cat began to flex, as if preparing to strike, Finn's fear was not to be conquered. The lion opened its mouth and let out a tremendous roar that seemed to come from all around. It surrounded Finn and shook the ground. It didn't sound natural. Finn threw his hands out, fending off the attack. He swooned, feeling dizzy.

And then, at once, several hands grabbed him and began to drag him away.

He heard applause and laughter.

He blinked his eyes open but was immediately blinded by the sun in the sky.

He averted his eyes and happened to catch a glimpse of one of the hands wrapped around his arm: black and calloused, with long, thin fingers. The hand was connected to a hairy arm.

Finn wrenched his head around.

He was being dragged off by a pair of orangutans. He tried to break the grip of the one on his left, and the thing bared its teeth and lunged toward his face as if to bite him. Finn jerked away, narrowly missing those teeth.

They were dragging him toward the jungle. They were kidnapping him.

And the audience thought it was all part of the show.

42

MAYBECK HEARD THAT ROAR and ran for the gardener who was watering the trees. He stole the hose out of the man's hands. Not really a man—more like a college kid. The guy didn't appreciate someone stealing his hose.

Maybeck's aunt Jelly had a mutt named Porky who considered their small backyard his domain. About once a month some stupid neighborhood dog would decide to visit their backyard without an invitation from Porky, typically resulting in a dogfight of epic proportions.

The first time Maybeck had tried to break up one of the fights, he'd nearly gotten his hand bitten off. He'd been saved by Jelly, who had broken up the fight with the garden hose. Ever since, Maybeck had used a strong burst of hose water to separate Porky and his prey.

He took the hose and sprinted toward the large apes who were dragging his friend across the pavement. He fought his way through the thick crowd, which was actually laughing and cheering.

Maybeck gave the hose one last tug, but he'd reached its limit. It would extend no farther.

He squeezed the handle and shot a burst of water at the lion. The water pressed right *through* the animal. *A DHI!*

Next, Maybeck aimed the hose at the nearest orangutan, hitting him squarely in the head. The ape was real. It let go of Finn to block the water streaming toward its face.

Again, the audience let out a cry of approval, clapping and hollering.

The ape shot a glance at Maybeck as if to challenge him, then quickly seemed to reconsider, and turned back toward Finn.

Maybeck blasted the other ape.

Finn broke loose just as the gardener jumped onto Maybeck from behind, wresting the hose from his grip.

Finn scrambled to his feet, slipped on the wet blacktop, and went down hard. Both orangutans rushed him, and Finn rolled out of the way, causing the two apes to collide. He got to his feet and took off toward Maybeck, who knocked the gardener aside, opening a small hole in the crowd, which Finn charged through.

The two took off at a full sprint, the orangutans following, their backs hunched, their teeth bared.

Finn glanced over his shoulder, but it slowed him.

His phone rang and he answered it. "Don't look

back!" Amanda said. "I can see you on my screen. If you can get to the Lion King show, maybe you can lose them in there!"

"That's way far away," Finn answered her.

"Well, if you have a better idea." She hung up. Finn looked at the phone angrily.

"What's up?" Maybeck asked.

"Follow me, and turn on the jets."

They ran hard, a line of orangutans trying to keep up. Maybeck, a faster runner than him, encouraged Finn. "You've got this!"

"I'm dying over here."

"You're dying if they catch up to us," Maybeck said. Finn ran harder.

Loud music confirmed the Lion King show was under way.

But the orangutans hadn't quit. They were close behind, running on all fours and crying out in loud voices.

Together the boys jumped the line. Cast Members called out for them to stop as the two opened the doors and burst into the show already in progress. Four sets of wooden bleachers rose from a theater-in-the-round, at the center of which were colorfully dressed acrobats performing on a giant trampoline, with trapeze artists spinning overhead.

As Finn slowed, Maybeck didn't hesitate for a second. Perhaps it was the result of forward momentum, perhaps because the Lion King stage set blocked their way; but Maybeck ran right up a ramp, hit the trampoline, and vaulted his way through the air and across to the other side. He tucked into a somersault, rolled to standing, and went running down the opposing ramp—right out of the pavilion.

Trying to avoid a collision with the ramp, Finn skidded and tucked his legs under him as if sliding into home plate. He braced himself to be crushed into the side of the stage, only to fly through the fabric skirt that surrounded it and find himself *under* the movable stage platform and the giant trampoline at its center. He crawled toward the other side, looking back to see two orangutans right behind him.

He glanced overhead. The trampoline's fabric stretched toward the concrete floor as the acrobatic show continued above him. Whenever anyone hit the trampoline, the fabric stretched so low that Finn had to lie flat; he couldn't squat without the risk of being crushed. Watching the orangutans approach, he suddenly saw his situation not as a threat but an opportunity: he could use the trampoline to his advantage.

Doubting that he and Maybeck could outrun the two apes, Finn turned and took a stand. The apes were faster and stronger than he, but Finn had the edge in intelligence. He remained directly under the pulsating trampoline, now turning to face the two apes, who immediately slowed with this challenge.

Finn egged on the apes, drawing them toward him, while keeping an eye on the pattern of the stretched trampoline fabric. There were currently four performers on the trampoline. The pattern of jumps was: the four corners; the center; the four corners.

Finn belly-crawled to the right. The nearest ape took the bait, turning to intercept him. The trampoline suddenly caved in over the ape's head, stretching toward the ground. The ape, caught between the trampoline and the concrete, was crushed by the weight of the acrobat. The ape was flattened. It cried out sharply, rolled away, and took off at a run in the opposite direction.

The trampoline came down immediately in front of the other ape, and that proved enough motivation. This one took off as well, following his buddy. Finn rolled and crawled out the other side and then sprinted for the sunlight outside the pavilion.

Maybeck had waited for him. Maybeck, who never thought of anyone but himself.

They took off running before either said a word, but as they reached full stride, Finn, the slower of the two, managed to pull even with Maybeck, though only briefly.

"Thanks," Finn called out to Maybeck. "I think we now know what happened to Philby!"

"The water shot right through the lion," Maybeck said. "It was a DHI."

"Maleficent's building an army," Finn told him. "An army of animals," he added. Maybeck flashed him a suspicious and disbelieving look. "Wayne told me," Finn said.

Finn turned and led Maybeck toward the Park entrance, still at a full run.

"Where are you going?" Maybeck huffed.

"The button," Finn said. "The remote control. We can't free Willa and Philby without the button."

43

HAVING WITNESSED THE ENCOUNTER with the lion, Amanda kept a close eye on Finn and Maybeck as they headed toward the Park entrance. She had a better understanding of how to navigate the screen. She could both follow the boys and guide them, while she kept an eye out for any Overtakers.

"Hello! What-cha-doing?"

Amanda spun around sharply. A small boy stood looking up at her.

"What are those pictures?" he asked, pointing to the screen. Amanda spun the screen around.

"Nothing. Just doing some research."

"See my tattoo?" The boy held up his arm for Amanda.

A woman approached calling, "Preston?" The boy's mother, probably.

Seeing the press-on tattoo, Amanda stuttered. "Where'd you get that?

"The ranger gave it to me," the boy said.

"Hello," the mother said, just arriving. "Preston, you're not bothering this woman, are you?"

"No, no, not at all," Amanda said, reaching into her back pocket. She pulled out the photocopy of the page from Jess's diary.

The mother was saying something apologetically as Amanda looked at the photo.

Jess had sketched the tattoo of a gorilla on crutches. The boy's tattoo included the caption: "Help Care for Wildlife." Jess's did not, but that was the only difference between the two.

Amanda had thought it was a man on crutches, not a gorilla. Her discovery changed everything.

"A ranger? What ranger? Where'd you get this again?" Amanda asked.

The mother answered.

"We were fortunate to take the walking tour. The Wild Africa Trek. So amazing."

"It was awesome," said Preston.

"That's a backstage tour?" Amanda asked.

"Not exactly, I don't think, but you definitely see things you don't see when on the Safari. It's well worth it!"

Jess had been on the private tour in her dreams. Amanda felt certain of it.

The boy and his mother said good-bye, while Amanda stood there in a kind of trance, her head filled with ideas.

She was wearing a Cast Member ID card that Wayne had arranged for all the Keepers.

Who was going to stop her from walking the Africa Trek and trying to understand why Jess had sketched that gorilla?

She had the answer well before her feet started to move.

No one!

44

FINN AND MAYBECK slowed as they entered Pandora: The World of Avatar. No matter how many times they visited, the raw beauty of the place overcame them both.

The sudden change in vegetation, with oversize trees not found on Earth and plants of fantastic colors, transported them both.

"There!" Finn said to Maybeck. "The ear of corn."

"And the two purple mouths. That's it."

"Right near the front. Leave it to Wayne to make it easy on us," Maybeck said.

"Too many people over there right now," Finn said.

"Yeah."

The odd-looking plant resembled a giant ear of corn tipped over. But the corn silk coming out of the end was purple instead of yellow. The husk was green and brown and purple, and hard like tree bark. The two "mouths" in the side of the thing were dark holes enclosed in purple globs with white flecks. They reminded Finn of cold sores on his lips. A family was taking pictures. Finn and Maybeck would have to wait their turn.

"Eleven o'clock," Maybeck whispered at Finn. Finn carefully looked slightly to his left and identified a casually dressed man wearing sunglasses and a pair of headphones. He carried what looked like a radio in his hands.

"Could be a spy for the Overtakers," Maybeck said.

"Proceed with caution," Finn said.

Once the family moved on, Finn told Maybeck he would need a distraction. They both knew how to play this.

While Finn approached the odd-looking tree with the two "mouths," Maybeck moved closer to the guy with the radio.

With each step, Finn drew closer to the open holes in the side of the leaning tree. His focus remained on the smaller, and lower of the two.

Through their challenges, the Kingdom Keepers had become good teammates. In a soccer game Finn knew when to pass, and when to expect a pass, and working with Maybeck was no different. Finn didn't need to give any kind of signal, and Maybeck didn't need to receive one.

When a single step away from the lower, smaller hole in the tree, Finn looked out of the corner of his eye. At that instant, Maybeck spoke to the man with the radio, probably asking the man for directions. By speaking to him, Maybeck turned the man away from Finn. The move worked perfectly.

Finn reached blindly into the dark hole, not exactly loving the sensation. It felt like bark, though damp with moisture.

Nothing!

He stole another look in Maybeck's direction. The man with the radio was turning toward Finn.

His hand bumping into something, Finn stopped to feel it more carefully. Thick tape with a bump in the middle.

Maybeck leaned in to the radio man and raised his voice, clearly trying to hold the man's attention. But the man's shoulder continued turning away from Maybeck.

Finn took hold and pulled hard. The tape stuck like glue. It wouldn't come loose. He used his fingernail to pick at the corner of the thick tape. It peeled off.

"But which fork?" Maybeck said loudly. "Is it left, or right?" He was acting stupid, which could not have been easy for him.

Finn pinched the tape and yanked. It came free. He stuffed the blob of tape into his pocket before he confirmed it held the remote. "Okay! Okay!" Maybeck said. "Thank you! Sorry I didn't understand."

Finn walked at a normal pace back out of Pandora, wondering if the man with the radio was watching him. Maybeck would have to spend a few more minutes inside Pandora in order to not draw attention to their mission. At some point, he would get away and Finn would be waiting for him.

They had the remote in hand. If they could only find the captured Willa and Philby, maybe they could free them.

45

Having handed off the remote control device to Charlene, who stood watch outside the bat enclosure, Finn and Maybeck rode a Disney bus to the Animal Kingdom Lodge.

Charlene would, once again, use her stilts and camouflage to approach the backstage area behind the enclosure. This time, she would circle around, rather than enter the enclosure, avoiding the scrutiny of the Park visitors. Once she established herself atop the wall near the two cages and the ice truck, she would notify Finn by text.

The boys had to discover where the real Willa and Philby were being kept and be on hand to get them out of the hotel once they awakened. Charlene was to trigger the remote, canceling their DHI state.

They entered the Animal Kingdom Lodge lobby, and both boys gasped. Finn had never seen such a place. It felt as if he'd stepped into Africa itself: the vast floor and the columns were crafted from a dark, unusual wood; the lobby furniture was covered in brown-and-white animal skins; giant chandeliers made of spears and shields hung from the ceiling. African music played, the rhythm enchanting. The bellhops wore brown safari outfits. The lobby stretched two hundred feet or more, leading to stairs and giant windows that looked out onto an African savannah, where Finn could see two giraffes and several wildebeests.

Upon seeing all of this, Maybeck hissed a bad word.

There were people everywhere. Some occupied the sumptuous furniture; others milled about, heading this way or that. The clatter and hum of people eating and talking wafted up from a lower level to the right. A few people waited in line at the registration desk to the left. But all around, there was a feeling of excitement and mystery as families and staff came and went. Into this walked two boys, one in a Park worker's coveralls, the other in shorts and a T-shirt.

No one paid them the slightest bit of attention.

"We're invisible," Finn said softly.

"I hear you," Maybeck agreed.

Finn rarely found a place inside Disney World where he was not self-conscious about being a DHI actor, where he didn't feel the weight of eyes trained on him wondering if he was *him*, the Disney host from the Magic Kingdom. Yet here, in the wondrous lobby of this magnificent lodge, he felt transported across the oceans to another continent, one far away from Mickey and Minnie and the person he had become.

"Any ideas?" Maybeck asked.

"We can't exactly ask someone if they've seen a boy and a girl," Finn said, having already walked past a few dozen boys and girls, most in the company of their parents, but not all.

"No."

"If I could get on to VMK, Wayne might be able to look up what rooms have been checked into in the past few hours, but there would be too many to count."

"Yup."

"Not much help."

"Nope."

"So, do you have any bright ideas?" Finn asked. The two boys passed a small study, like a private library, on their left, and they continued down a long corridor of hotel rooms.

"We can't exactly go knocking on every door," Maybeck said.

"You think?" Finn stepped aside and allowed a family coming toward them to pass. "I was hoping for something more constructive."

"I've got nothing," Maybeck said.

"I noticed."

"We could divide and conquer," Maybeck suggested. "I could take the upstairs or the other side of the hotel."

The lodge was fashioned in a giant Y, with the lobby in the stem, and the rooms stretching out into both wings of the V at the top of the stem. The V stuck out into a savannah, and the long corridors periodically offered viewing stations on either side, where all kinds of wildlife could be seen, from birds that stood four feet high to zebras and Thomson's gazelles.

"We could stay in touch by text," Maybeck continued.

Finn stopped and grabbed Maybeck by the arm. "That's it!" he whispered harshly.

"It is?"

"When I get a new text message my phone beeps. I mean, I turn it off if I'm in a movie, but the rest of the time?"

"Yeah, same. So?" Maybeck asked.

"So," Finn said, "once we're in the hotel, we keep texting Willa and Philby. We listen by every door. If we hear a text tone, then—"

"Sweet," Maybeck grinned devilishly. "Slick! I like the way you think." He lost the smile. "But what if they're being guarded? I mean the guards will just turn off their phones."

"The Overtakers weren't guarding you that time at Space Mountain." Maybeck had once been taken prisoner by the Overtakers and Finn didn't want him to forget it.

"True."

"Why bother guarding some kid who's asleep and can't wake up?"

"Good point."

Finn thought about how it might work. "If I'm the Overtakers, I would put Willa and Philby on a bed, pull the drapes, put a DO NOT DISTURB sign on the door, and leave them be."

"Agreed. Okay! Totally makes sense," Maybeck said. "So we'll start by listening near the doors of any rooms that have DO NOT DISTURB signs out. It's late afternoon. How many rooms can that be?"

"Not many," Finn agreed.

"I feel good about this, Finn. If they're here," Maybeck said, "we're going to find them."

* * *

Finn and Maybeck were taking turns sending texts from the hallways of Disney's Animal Kingdom Lodge. Finn pressed his ear to the door outside another room with a DO NOT DISTURB tag on the handle. He'd found three doors so far. With his ear to the fourth, he heard a text chime, and he told Maybeck.

"This is their room," Finn declared. As Maybeck leaned his ear against the door, Finn sent a text.

Maybeck smiled and pulled away from the door. "Bull's-eye!"

"You're a better liar than I am," Finn said.

"Is that supposed to be a compliment?"

"Charming. I meant to say you're more charming than I am. You're better with the ladies."

"That goes without saying," Maybeck said.

"There's a room being cleaned, back toward the elevator."

"I passed it," Maybeck confirmed.

"I think you left your family's Park Hoppers in this room, and your father's in here asleep with a headache, which explains the DO NOT DISTURB sign."

"I think you're brilliant," Maybeck said.

"Goes without saying. Can you pull it off?"

"This is me we're talking about!" Maybeck boasted.

"Same question."

"You'll need to get yourself gone," Maybeck said.

"I'll hang at the next set of windows."

"I'll text you once I'm inside," Maybeck said.

* * *

Less than five minutes later, Finn received the text message. He returned to the room and knocked softly. Maybeck opened the door.

The room held a big bed and a pair of bunks. Philby was drooling onto the pillow of the big bed. Willa slept peacefully on the lower bunk. They shook both kids, but to no avail: perma-sleep—Sleeping Beauty Syndrome.

"The one thing I remember," said Maybeck, who yawned all of a sudden, "is how much I dreamed when they had me in this state. I dreamed of being locked up. I think I was dreaming what my DHI was seeing."

Finn yawned reflexively. "Don't get me tired, or we'll end up like them."

"A nap wouldn't hurt," Maybeck said, eyeing the bunk. "We could take turns. Ten minutes."

"Do *not* go there."

"I'm tired."

"That's the point. Hang on." Finn sent Charlene a text message.

Finn: Ready when you are.

Charlene: All set.

Both Maybeck and Finn heard the loud scratching sound at the same time. At first Finn thought it was a radio or TV in another room.

Maybeck hurried over and cracked the curtains. "Apes!" he hissed. He held up two fingers.

Two apes, Finn realized. Out on the balcony. The sliding door squeaked as one of the apes pulled on the handle from the outside.

Maybeck pointed to his own chest and then the closet. Seeing this signal, Finn hurried into the bathroom, stepped into the tub, and pulled the shower curtain closed. He heard the door slide open and the sounds of the two apes moving around the room. Were they looking for them? Had the maid told someone about letting Maybeck into the room?

A message from Charlene appeared on Finn's screen.

Charlene: I'm going to push the remote now.

The bathroom door flung open. Finn could hear one of the two orangutans breathing hard, and the room suddenly smelled different. He reached up and turned the showerhead to face the curtains, his hand on the faucet.

Four hairy fingers appeared at the edge of the shower curtain. Finn felt as if he might pass out.

The shower curtain was jerked open.

Finn yanked the lever. Water roared into the face of an ugly orange ape. The ape slapped his own face, screamed, and jumped back.

Finn leaped from the tub, pulled a terrycloth robe from the back of the bathroom door, and tossed it over the ape. He then used the bathrobe's belt to take a strong turn around the confused ape, pulled it tight, and knotted it around the ape's legs. The orangutan fell over, kicking and thrashing and screaming, doing nothing but spinning in circles on the bathroom floor.

The second ape appeared at the doorway. Finn lunged for the other bathrobe, but it drew him closer to the ape, whose big mouth came open, teeth bared. Just as Finn feared the ape would strike, Maybeck leaped out of the bedroom closet and poked it with a hanger that he wielded as a sword.

This provoked the ape. It spun around to challenge Maybeck, giving Finn the extra seconds he needed to take hold of the robe and throw it over the orangutan. He and Maybeck made quick work of tying up this one as well. They dragged it into the bathroom and, as they shut the door, both apes were seen whirling angrily on the tile floor.

Finn shook Willa. Maybeck pulled on Philby's arm. Both groaned and squirmed uncomfortably: they were awakening! Charlene had used the remote on the DHIs in the cages, and it had worked. The cages were now empty—the DHIs gone, zeroed out by the server. Maleficent and the Overtakers with her had to be terribly confused.

And angry.

The orangutans screamed loudly from the bathroom.

Maybeck said to Philby, "I know you feel like a zombie. I've been there. But we have to hurry. We've got to get you out of here."

46

FINN AND MAYBECK helped Philby and Willa to reach the lodge's bus stop. Less than twenty minutes later the four were passing Creature Comforts on their way to the Disney Vacation Club kiosk next to the Dawa Bar.

Amanda had group texted that she'd made a discovery. She'd been secretive. They were eager to talk with her.

Charlene, who was keeping an eye on the bat enclosure, wrote that the ice truck had not been moved.

Arriving at the kiosk, they didn't see Amanda.

FINN: Where are you?

AMANDA: Conservation Station. Waiting for you here. Hurry.

Willa, Philby, Finn, and Maybeck headed toward the Wildlife Express Train. It would take them to the Conservation Station. On their way, Finn called Rob Bernowski, Jess's boyfriend. He put his phone on speakerphone so everyone could hear.

"Rob?"

"Yeah? Who's this?"

"My name is Finn Whitman. I'm a friend of—"

"Jess's. Yeah, I know." The guy didn't sound too thrilled. "She talks about you and the others all the time." *Too much of the time*, his tone of voice implied.

"Have you seen Jess today?"

"No. Why?"

"Heard from her?"

"What's going on?" Rob asked, sounding concerned.

"Just curious," Finn said.

"Because?"

"Yeah, well . . . listen . . . I know this is going to sound stupid, but if there was one thing Jess could change about you, what would it be?"

"Is this some kind of contest or something?"

Finn hesitated. Willa was nodding violently.

"Yeah, that's it exactly," Finn said. "A contest. A school thing. How well do boyfriends and girlfriends know each other?"

"The one thing she would change?" Rob asked.

"Yes. That's the question."

There was a long silence. "Let me see. . . . My clothes. She doesn't like my jeans, man. I wear 'em kinda low."

"Your jeans?"

"Yeah. Did I answer right?"

"I'll have to get back to you on that," Finn said. "That's all you can think of?"

"I can tell you the one thing I'd change about her," Rob volunteered, not giving Finn a chance to stop him. "I'd take her pen and paper away. She's constantly messing with word games. Letters. She's into scrambling the letters of every word she can think of—making other words out of the same letters, you know?"

"Anagrams," Finn said.

"What's that?" Rob asked.

"It's what you call what you're talking about. An anagram is a word that can be made from the letters of another word."

"Never heard of it. But that's exactly what she does." The boy continued. "So what about my prize? Do I win a prize?"

"Ah . . . we'll let you know. Thanks for your answers." Finn ended the call.

"Anagrams," Philby said. "You think it's worth a try?"

"Do we think *what* is worth a try?" Maybeck asked.

"Jess wrote 'Change Rob' in her diary—"

"*And* inside the tree stump," Willa added.

"Some kind of code?" Finn asked. "An anagram?"

Philby was already typing on his phone.

"We can figure this out."

Finn and the others leaned over Philby's shoulder.

He already had searched for a Web site that turned words into anagrams. He typed "change Rob," into the search box and tapped the button marked Generate Anagram.

The phone's screen refreshed. It displayed a long list of scrambled words made from the letters in "change rob."

"'Branch ego,'" Philby read from the screen. "'Corn bag he.'" They all laughed. "'Herb can go.'"

"Let me see." Willa leaned in as they walked. Her shoulder touched Philby's. No one missed the contact, least of all Maybeck. He walked anxiously, staying close behind them both. Willa studied the phone's screen and spoke in a quiet voice.

"We've done this before," she reminded them all. "The clues from the Stonecutter's Quill. Remember? We solved that anagram without a Web site."

"That's because we didn't have a phone. There's nothing here," Philby said.

"Correction: There are no proper names," Willa said.

"So?" Philby challenged.

Willa gently took the phone out of Philby's hand, She studied it closely. Then she handed the phone back.

"Found one," she said, capturing everyone's attention. They turned onto the path for the train and kept walking. "It's not in the right order, but it's there. A one-word name. A *Disney* name."

"Which is?" Finn said.

"Wait! Wait!" Philby barked, not wanting to lose to Willa. "Give me a second."

"Give it up, Philby. If it's a Disney name, then that's it. Enough with you two competing!" Maybeck said. "What is it, Willa? Tell us what it is!"

"Do you give up?" she teased Philby.

"No, wait!" Philby held the phone so close he was practically kissing it.

"He gives up," Maybeck said. "We all give up."

Willa squinted. Philby's lips moved as he read words from the list.

"Chernabog!" Philby shouted out.

Willa smiled, obviously impressed.

"From *Fantasia*?" Finn said. "Looks like a bull standing on two feet."

"I saw that movie." Maybeck said. "That is one mean dude."

Willa spoke. "Not just mean. Chernabog is the most evil of all the villains Walt Disney created. And he just happens to be a demon with *bat* wings!"

The group went silent, their feet shuffling on the path. The air cracked with the train's sharp whistle as it pulled into the station.

Determined not to miss it, the Kingdom Keepers took off running.

47

"He's the worst of the worst." Philby was in fine form, back to himself, alert from the sleep he'd gotten and able to think more clearly than either Maybeck or Finn. They waited in line for the train to the Conservation Station.

* * *

Charlene, in DeVine's ivy costume, was still keeping watch in the jungle near the bat enclosure. She blended in well. Wearing the stilts, she could see over the top of the wall and into the back area.

As far as Charlene knew, Maleficent was still inside the back of the ice truck. It didn't look as if either Maleficent or the monkeys knew the cages were empty. The tarps covering the cages remained in place. All Charlene could do is wait.

* * *

Maybeck, Finn, Willa, and Philby separated for the train ride. Each took a bench away from the others.

As the train arrived at Rafiki's Planet Watch, and

Park visitors trudged up the long path toward the Conservation Station, the Keepers remained apart. They acted as a team.

Finn was last to enter the Conservation Station. He joined the others by the restrooms.

"I'm starving," said Willa.

"Later," said Philby.

"I see her," Maybeck whispered. He pointed out Amanda. They moved to her as a group.

"What's up? You left your post at the videos, so it must be important." Finn spoke to Amanda in a low voice just to be safe. The crowd thinned as a veterinary demonstration began. Two dozen people approached the central display window. On the other side, doctors were operating on a snake that had eaten a golf ball.

"I happened to see this kid. He had this stick-on tattoo," Amanda said.

"I hope this is going somewhere," Maybeck said.

"It matched one of Jess's sketches in her diary." Amanda unfolded the copy and showed them the person on crutches. "It's not a person, it's a gorilla. The vet clinic hands them out. The kid got the tattoo here at the vet clinic. Jess saw something that happened *here!*"

Finn took a moment. "It's definitely worth exploring."

Amanda fingered her pass. "I think these will allow us to go back there. I thought it was better not to try this alone but to get your help. Do this together."

"Agreed," said Finn.

"I don't know about any tattoo," Maybeck complained, "but we just discovered that 'change rob'—also in the diary—translates as Chernabog."

Amanda looked confused.

Willa told her Chernabog was a Disney creature.

"Seems to me that's way more important than a press-on tattoo," Maybeck said.

"The gorilla on crutches is in her diary," Philby reminded. "It's part of the puzzle Jess left us. That makes it mean something. Amanda's right."

"Says the one who just got a couple hours' sleep," Maybeck complained.

"I know this sounds stupid," Amanda said, apologizing to Maybeck, "but I *feel* it's important. I really do. I wouldn't have called you out here if I didn't."

"Everything in the diary has proved out," Finn reminded them all. "The tiger and lion were DHIs. Jess drew the lightning hitting the castle way before it happened."

"Don't forget the apes," Philby added.

"And now the tattoo," Maybeck mumbled. "Okay. I get it. So what now?"

"I'll go back there," Finn said. "Into the vet clinic, since that's where they give out the tattoos."

"I'll go, too," Amanda stated. She wasn't asking.

"Willa, Maybeck, and I can think through what to do about Chernabog."

"And we'll watch for any spies," Willa said.

"Let's have a code for the group text if we see a problem," Finn said. "We'll meet up at the Vacation Club booth by Dawa Bar if we get separated."

"How about we use the code word 'problem'?" Maybeck could sass.

No one laughed.

"Chernabog," said Philby. All eyes fell on him.

"That's the code. At least that way we'll all know it's serious," Philby said.

48

Finn swiped his ID in the card reader. A small light changed to green. An even smaller light went off in his brain: what if the Overtakers had figured out the kids were using fake IDs and were now tracking them through the use of their cards? He shook it off.

He tried the doorknob, and the door opened. He and Amanda stepped through, leaving the sounds of activities behind them.

The hallway he found himself in reminded Finn of the veterinarian's office where his mother volunteered part-time. It also served to remind him of his mother and the fact that he hadn't yet called home. He'd messed up: soon his parents would be at Blizzard Beach looking for him. They were going to be furious. He wondered if any of the other kids were in the same predicament. One thing was certain—time was running out. The Park would remain open only a few more hours. Jess's chance for freedom was fading.

He knew that no matter how they tried, he and Amanda still looked like kids. Tired, even exhausted, kids—but kids nonetheless. There was no getting around it. And he had no idea if unaccompanied kids his age were allowed backstage. With this in mind, he signaled to Amanda to hurry, and they moved down the hallway with an eye out for someplace to hide. Thankfully, most of the doors had glass panels, allowing them to see inside. They passed an examination room, and another, filled with medical equipment. There was one door marked PRIVATE, and another with stickers and cartoon clippings taped to it. It was this door Finn tried first. Inside was a single table and some vending machines—an employee lounge. It was empty. They ducked inside, both wide-eyed and slightly out of breath due to the excitement.

"I'm terrified," Amanda said.

"Me too," Finn admitted.

"We have no idea what we're looking for."

"No. But she must have dreamed about that tattoo. That has to mean something."

"But what?"

"The tattoos are given out to kids who take the private tours. Maybe there's something on the tour we're supposed to see?"

Amanda's blue eyes brightened. "That's got to be it! You're a genius."

Finn felt his face warm. "Hardly," he mumbled

under his breath, wondering how a guy like Maybeck could carry himself so confidently.

There was noise in the hallway, and both of them instinctively looked for a place to hide. But the employee lounge offered them nothing: a few lockers, all padlocked.

A group text pinged Finn.

CHARLENE: Maleficent just left the ice truck.

Finn told Amanda. "What's it mean?" she asked.

"It can't be good."

Amanda looked scared.

"Forget about that for now. We need to look like we belong here."

"Agreed," Amanda said.

A woman wearing green scrubs was giving a tour to two grown-ups and four kids.

"Stay with me," Finn told Amanda. "We're going to join the tour."

He and Amanda trailed a few feet behind the kids, looking like part of the group. The nurse kept talking as she walked, not bothering to look back.

She talking about the rooms and how much they cared for all the animals. It sounded memorized. She said Conservation Station was so high-tech that it accepted sick and wounded animals from all over Florida. Amanda tugged on Finn's shirt to get his attention. They stopped. The tour went on ahead.

Amanda faced a corkboard. Pinned to it were photographs of some of the recovered animals—including *a gorilla with a broken leg.* There were maps and brochures tacked to the board as well.

"The tattoo!" Finn said.

The similarity was unmistakable.

"But what does it mean?" Amanda asked.

"I don't know," Finn said, "but we're obviously in the right place."

Finn studied the rest of the stuff thumbtacked to the corkboard. One of the items was a very large satellite photo of Animal Kingdom. Finn loved looking at and studying satellite photos. It took him only seconds to figure out where the Conversation Station was on the image.

For a moment his breath caught. He felt as if a bone were stuck in his throat. His hands were moving before he understood that he was "borrowing" the satellite photo.

"How stupid could we be?" he muttered.

"Finn? What's happening?" Amanda asked. Concern filled her voice and tightened her eyes.

"Hey!" came a man's voice. "Get away from there! Put that back!"

Finn looked to see a man at the far end of the hallway. He pulled Amanda down the hallway with one hand, the satellite poster in the other.

"Finn," Amanda said heatedly, "we can't steal that."

"They're *both on* here," Finn said harshly. "An *M*, just like she wrote in her diary. And remember 'Under the Sea'?" He wiggled the satellite photo.

The man behind them started running. "Hey there! Stop!" he called.

"Not S-e-a,'" Finn said, spelling out the word. "But *the letter C*! Under the letter *C*." Rotating the satellite photo as they started to hurry, Finn indicated a geographic shape—a wooded area indented by the asphalt footpath, and the footpath itself. Both big C's.

"I see them both! I see what you mean!" Amanda said excitedly.

"She's there, Amanda. Somewhere right there, under the curve, under the C."

"It makes so much sense. Her playing the song! Everything!" Amanda squealed with excitement.

"Those woods. That area. It's the tiger yards," Finn said. He recognized that tight curve and bridge in the Jungle Trek. "Maybeck and I walked right past there."

The man was gaining on them.

"Run!" Finn said, already rolling the satellite photo into a baton. "Run and don't stop running!"

49

AMANDA AND FINN turned the corner. At the far end of the hallway glowed a red EXIT sign. Finn was already in the process of texting a message.

Finn: Chernabog!

Maleficent, the six-foot-tall dark fairy with green skin and a pointed chin, stood between Finn and Amanda and the EXIT door. She held a black kitty cat in her thin arms.

She set the cat down patiently. She waved her open hand over it. The cat stretched and grew, its whiskers lengthening, its eyes enlarging.

It was a full-grown panther.

Amanda and Finn skidded to a stop. The man chasing them turned around and ran away.

"Silly, silly boy," Maleficent said, aiming her finger at him. "Won't you ever learn to mind your own business?"

"Sound the alarm!" the man shouted from well behind Finn.

"Pest!" Maleficent called out. She waved her finger at the man. The panther took off running, past Amanda and Finn. It chased the man around the corner. A scream echoed throughout the building.

Finn pushed the fear from his thoughts. He drove away his anger, knowing his and Amanda's survival depended on it.

He whispered to Amanda, "Examination room on the left. Get the others. We'll meet up at the Jungle Trek."

"What are you talking about?" she whispered back. "I'm not going anywhere."

He couldn't become All Clear if he felt ruffled. The odd state of part human, part DHI was tricky to achieve, and it didn't last long. He worked to clear his mind. The tingling sensation began in his toes and rose up through his legs. He knew from it happening before that he was crossing over.

In the past, he had only been able to sustain his All Clear, waking-DHI state for a minute or two. If he was going to battle Maleficent he was going to have to do better than that.

His voice sounded different as he spoke to Amanda. It was slightly electric or digitized. It was as calm as a glass lake.

"Please go!" he said, ever so gently.

"No, thank you," she said. "I'm staying with you."

Maleficent drew her bony hands toward her face.

Her fingers twitched. Her lips moved as she recited an incantation.

She was conjuring a spell aimed at him and Amanda.

"You have a powerful master," Finn called down the hall. He wanted to upset her and he did. He watched as Maleficent's face became rubbery with surprise.

"I have no master. You know nothing of my ways," she said.

"Is that right? So you and Chernabog are what, partners? Does he see it that way?"

Maleficent cringed. She shaped her hands as if holding a hollow ball.

Finn turned to warn Amanda. "Look out."

She was gone. Vanished. No longer by his side.

Maleficent hurled a blinding ball of fire. The size of a softball, it spun through the air, throwing off sparks and flames.

"Duck!" Amanda's voice, directly over him.

Finn glanced up to see her *floating* horizontally near the ceiling.

Finn had no plan to duck. The spinning ball of fire passed through his All Clear hologram . . . It exploded into a wall.

Black smoke curled toward the ceiling.

Maleficent twisted her sticklike fingers, summoning

a cage of blue-white lines that surrounded both Finn and Amanda.

Finn had been burned by such a cage before beneath Pirates of the Caribbean. This time, he wasn't afraid. His All Clear allowed him to step right through the lines. He walked slowly toward an angry Maleficent.

Amanda, still using her push to float off the floor, slipped through a gap between the electric bars. She lowered to the floor just behind Finn.

"Maybe I've got it wrong," Finn called out to Maleficent. "Maybe Chernabog needs you, or you need him. Are you planning on saving him somehow? Empowering Chernabog? Giving him his true powers?"

"Who are you, child?"

Maleficent took a step back, away from Finn. It was the first time he'd ever sensed retreat in her. He liked the feeling.

But by gloating and allowing himself to enjoy feeling powerful, Finn briefly lost his state of All Clear.

"My partner's powers are not limited," she said. "Not in the least."

She threw an arrow of flame at Finn. Amanda leaped in front of him, having seen the faint blue line surrounding his DHI grow weaker.

The arrow struck her in the chest and was totally

absorbed. Her arms and legs glowed as she sank to the floor.

Maleficent grinned an evil grin.

"Looks like your girlfriend shouldn't play with fire," Maleficent said.

Amanda lay unconscious on the floor at Finn's feet, a burn mark on her shirt. His fear eliminated his state of All Clear, exposing him to Maleficent's powers. Nonetheless, a wild, pent-up anger filled him. It had everything to do with Amanda lying there on the floor. He charged the dark fairy.

Maleficent went wide-eyed, having not expected this. Her lips moved silently as once again she muttered another incantation. But she was too late.

Finn hit her with a body block. He slammed her into the wall and brought his hands to her throat.

Her skin was ice cold.

He said, "Release her unharmed this instant. You bring her back . . . or so help me . . ." Finn tightened his grip. Her cold skin was like nothing he'd ever felt.

Maleficent's sickly green skin turned yellow.

"Release her!" Finn shouted. Looking behind himself, he saw the panther. It had yellow, unmoving eyes. Finn tightened his grip. Maleficent's eyes bulged. She waved her hand.

Amanda coughed and sat up, coming back to consciousness.

"Are you all right?" Finn asked, not taking his eyes off Maleficent.

Amanda coughed hard. "I'm okay!"

Finn squeezed even tighter. "Tell Chernabog it's over," he said. "You and him are over. The Overtakers are through."

He threw her to the floor. Grabbing Amanda by the hand, he ran past the panther. Luckily, at that moment, the fire sprinklers sprayed from the ceiling.

"You saved my life," Amanda said, holding fast to his arm as they ran. "Maleficent was actually *scared* of you!"

"I was . . . upset," Finn said.

"Because she'd hurt me," Amanda said. "I know. I saw you."

Finn slammed into an emergency door's panic bar. The door opened and together the two sprinted outside into the fading evening light.

50

THE KINGDOM KEEPERS stood behind Amanda as she controlled the security camera screen at the Vacation Club booth. Only Charlene was missing, still keeping watch on the area behind the bat enclosure. Amanda directed their attention to a camera view that showed the tiger yards. Another looked back at the arched bridge that separated the two tiger enclosures. The bridge helped to form the letter *C* on the satellite photo.

"Looks like tigers are kept on both sides of the bridge," she explained.

"So, if she's under the C, she could be anywhere in that area, including under the bridge," Finn said.

"That doesn't look possible," Philby said.

Amanda worked the screen, switching cameras. She placed her finger on the screen. "Look! The window! That's in her diary."

"Yeah," Finn said. "I remember."

"So she dreamed about this exact place," Amanda said.

Willa nudged closer for a better look at the screen.

"Zoom in on this."

Amanda made the one camera view larger, and then zoomed in.

What had looked like a patch of dirt surrounded by green grass took on a definite shape. The larger it grew, the more obvious. It wasn't just oddly shaped area of bare dirt, it was square. Man-made. Wood, not dirt. "It's a trapdoor!" Amanda's voice sounded ghostly. Filled with both excitement and concern, she sniffled.

"What's a trapdoor doing in a tiger yard?" Maybeck said, disbelieving. "More like a cover for a sprinkler system."

"She's in there," Amanda said. "Under there." She stared at Finn hoping for support. "I know she's in there."

"Philby?" Maybeck said, "Tell them there's no reason to put a trapdoor in the ground. It's got to be a sprinkler cover or maybe something electronic, or even just a place to put tools."

"There's no gate in the wall," Philby said.

"So what?" Maybeck said even more aggressively.

"So, Wayne told us that all the animals in the Animal Kingdom are counted and taken care of each day. Every day. Some are put into barns and pens backstage. The point being . . ." Philby gently stepped in front of Amanda to control the screen. He zoomed back. He switched cameras. "You're not going to get up close and cuddly with tigers every day. But you are going to count them."

"So?" Maybeck said.

"And tigers are cats, and cats fight, just like dogs. So . . ." He fiddled with the image of the grassy area on the other side of the high wall. "If you're going to separate big cats—put one in the lower area, one in the top area—how are you going to do that without a gate?"

Philby quickly zoomed the image of the lower grassy area, staying close to the wall. As he zoomed in, what looked like a patch of dirt could be seen.

"No way," Maybeck gasped.

"Another trapdoor," Amanda said, "on the *other* side of the wall."

Philby zoomed back so they could see two camera views, both showing similar sized wooden hatches in the ground. He used his finger to draw between the two images. "It's a tunnel. It's used to move the tigers safely between the two fields."

"But if they open the hatches at night to move them, and Jess is down there, doesn't that mean . . . ?" Maybeck's voice caught. He couldn't finish the thought.

Philby whispered so softly, it was hard to hear him. "Then the tiger gets her."

Willa coughed.

"You're saying she hid down there so no one could find her and now . . ." Maybeck had a difficult time speaking.

"She could have crossed the savannah," Willa proposed, "after escaping the tree trunk. Jumped a wall, or entered an open gate. Maybe she ended up here with the tigers, and went down there to get away from them."

Philby said, "The speaker wires for the Park might go through the tunnel. It would explain how she played the song over and over."

Amanda spoke up. Of everyone there, she knew Jess the best. "She has to be *under the C.* Philby's right. The song matters."

"Then what's with the *M* in her diary?" Maybeck asked.

"In her art there's a blob of ink on the lower right stem of the *M*," Philby said. "That could be a mistake, or it could mean something to her."

"Agreed," Finn said.

"Look where it is," Philby said. He unfolded his copy of the diary page. "In DinoLand." Philby studied each of their faces. "DinoLand is mostly for little kids. All except one attraction."

"The dinosaur research place—Dr. Grant Seeker," Willa said.

"As good a place as any," Philby said.

Maybeck looked ready to explode. "Listen to all of you. FYI: We don't know any of this for sure!"

"Not yet we don't," Philby said. "But while some of us check out the tunnel, I can get back on VMK. I'll bet Wayne can hack me into the game's control center. I should be able to track network bandwidth usage."

"Speak English," Maybeck snapped.

"DHIs, projecting holograms, require major bandwidth. The monkey, lions. All that is Overtaker technology, and the second server. I guess what I'm saying is that we *want* Maleficent to use her DHIs. When she does, I can track the bandwidth, locate the second server, and shut it down."

"Then let's split up," Finn said. "Maybeck and Willa will support Philby. Charlene, Amanda, and I will figure out how to get into the tiger yard and open into the hatch."

Philby said, "Maybe I can help with that once I'm inside VMK."

Amanda reminded everyone that there were other sketches in Jess's pages. She encouraged the others to keep watch for a hairy gorilla, an owl on the branch, an elephant, and "a dark-skinned hunchback guy." "The Park is closing soon. If we're seen after that we'll be told to leave," Finn warned.

"Let's get going," Philby said.

Maybeck apparently felt he deserved the last word. "No mistakes, people. If we mess this up, Jess becomes kitty chow."

51

CHARLENE INSISTED THAT she could slip over the wall of the upper tiger yard with no one the wiser.

"I don't think so," said Finn. He, Amanda, and Charlene were assembled along the edge of the Jungle Trek, very near the tiger yards.

"I can stay close to the wall, like I did at the bat enclosure," Charlene said. "No one'll see me, and that includes the tigers."

"Tigers are fast," Amanda reminded her. "Very fast. And they can jump, let's not forget."

Charlene nodded. "But also lazy. I'll be on the opposite wall. If the tiger moves or shows any interest, you can warn me. I can vault the wall in a nanosecond. It's not as if it's going to get me."

"No, probably not," Finn said. "But it's also not worth the risk. At the very worst, we wait until they try to move the tigers. If we're right, they'll open the hatches at that point. Jess will get out of there. Our jobs will be to distract the tigers so Jess doesn't get attacked."

"Tiger bait?" Amanda asked, horrified. "Your plan is to use us as tiger bait?"

"My plan is to rescue Jess. At the very worst, we wait out the Park's closing."

"Let's look for a maintenance entrance," Amanda encouraged. "If it actually exists, it can't be far from the bridge."

"Agreed. And Charlene promises not to jump the wall," Finn said, looking up at her. "I would suggest you scout the perimeter looking for other hatches, gates, or anything else we should know about."

"I can do that. But I can also—"

"Don't even think about it," Finn said, interrupting her.

Amanda and Finn set off down the path toward the tiger bridge. At Finn's suggestion, they kept a few yards apart in case they came under attack from the Overtakers. They sharpened their senses, alert to what was overhead and all around them for anything out of the ordinary—especially monkeys and orangutans.

They scouted both tiger yards from an old Indian temple made of stone and plaster, which was at the top of the tiger bridge. Amanda stared out the window that matched what Jess had sketched in the diary. An enormous tiger was stretched out in the shade about twenty feet below and across the yard. She couldn't see the trapdoor from where she stood but could place it just to her left in her mind's eye. She switched sides and kept looking around.

Finn patrolled the center of the bridge, also switching sides and looking into both tiger yards. He'd hoped to see a manhole cover in the path—some indication of maintenance access—but there was none.

"I think I have something," Amanda said from behind him. She faced some plants and a beautiful section of the wall, where four large stone panels had been carved, each depicting a unique scene. Finn recalled these from having seen them earlier, and he said so.

"I don't think we should be seen staring, so I'm going to turn my back, but check out the second panel," Amanda said, spinning around.

"The owl!" Finn said. "And the elephant with the headdress."

"Both of which she sketched in her diary," Amanda reminded.

"It's a secret panel," Finn said. "The access to the tunnel."

"We don't know that," Amanda protested.

"Screen me," Finn said. "I'm going back there and looking for some kind of switch to open it. The way it's on the corner, it's perfect for maintenance, because you're hidden to start with. No one's going to see me, but just to make sure . . ."

"I've got you covered," Amanda said.

Finn slipped into the vegetation and stepped into

shadow. The ground here was disturbed, and he noticed several large shoeprints in the mud, convincing him all the more that they were right about this.

He ran his hand along the edge of one of the large stone panels, hoping to find some kind of trigger. *Nothing.* He tapped on it lightly. It sounded hollow. "This has got to be it," he hissed. "But I can't find anything to open it."

"Try the owl," Amanda called over her shoulder.

Of course! he thought. He stretched to reach the owl, opened his hand, and pushed. The tile with the owl moved. The panel clicked and popped open an inch. Finn threaded his fingers behind it and pulled. It was incredibly heavy.

"I've got it!" he announced.

But behind the panel he saw a metal gate. And the gate was padlocked. This helped explain why, if Jess had found this entrance, she'd been unable to get out.

He didn't hesitate for a moment. Understanding the risk he took, Finn flushed all thought from his mind. He was neither anxious nor excited. Neither angry nor tired nor hungry. He felt the now familiar tingling in his arms and legs and witnessed a slight glow on the back of the stone panel that hung open: he had crossed over. He stepped through the wrought-iron gate, his glow illuminating a dank, stone stairway that spiraled down to his left. He turned around, his DHI already fading as fear crept into him. Fear of the dark. Fear of the unknown. He was himself again. He reached through the gate and grabbed a heavy iron handle on the inside of the panel. He pulled with all his strength, and the massive stone door clicked shut.

He'd acted a little too hastily: it was pitch-dark.

He couldn't see a thing.

52

Finn FELT HIS WAY DOWN the damp stones as the stairs beneath him fell away in a spiral to his left. It smelled at once of dust and mold, like his grandparents' basement. He counted the stairs as he went: *ten, eleven, twelve* . . . before they leveled off. He walked on the flat now, straight ahead, his left hand skimming a rock wall, the occasional cobweb tangling in his fingers and making him jump. Finn didn't like spiders.

The sound of his running shoes scraping the concrete changed; he could feel he was in a more open area. His vision, which had shown him nothing but sparkles and curlicues, improved to where he could make out a haze both to his left and right. It hung in the air like a gray mist. And now, slowly forming, a lump, an interruption in the mist. An imperfection in the horseshoe-shaped glow that continued to define itself.

"Jess?" he called out softly.

The lump moved. He thought it might have turned in his direction.

He called her name again, this time a little more loudly.

"If you're a dream, go away!" Jess's voice!

"It's Finn," he said, taking steps toward her, his hand still guiding him along the wall.

"Why can't I wake up?" she muttered.

Finn felt good. His heart swelled in his chest. It was not simply the pride of success, of beating the odds and finally finding her. It went beyond that, to something more. He felt an importance in being here. A significance. He was saving Jess. He was doing something that really mattered, not just studying or wasting time on his computer. It gave meaning to all the effort they had gone to, all the risks they had taken.

And then the tunnel filled with a colorful glow, like a light warming up. And it *was* a light warming up. *His* light. *His* DHI. It filled his end of the tunnel, and what had been a lump of darkness transformed into Jess. She stood up from her slumped position looking almost angelic and came toward him slowly, as if she were floating. He couldn't sustain his DHI, and it vanished. He pulled out the phone, using its glowing screen as a flashlight.

He thought of her as having jet-black hair and bone-white, almost translucent, skin. Intriguing eyes. That had been how she'd looked when he'd first met her on the Sports Complex soccer field, what seemed like years earlier. In fact, it had only been a matter of months. But Jess had made a radical transformation when Maleficent's spell had been lifted. Her hair was now a shocking blond—almost white. Her thin lips shined luminously red.

She came into his arms, like a young child hugging a parent, and then let go.

In the phone's bluish weird light, they both looked half-dead.

"I didn't think . . ." she stammered. "I hoped and even prayed, though I'm not very good at praying . . . I wired up my earbuds but couldn't be sure . . ."

"Amanda found a page in your diary," he explained. "We followed your sketches."

"I don't even remember what I drew."

"Dreams," Finn said. "Amanda said it was what you dreamed."

"Nightmares is more like it. I've had them here as well—down here in the dark."

She explained the ordeal she'd been through. It was much as the Kingdom Keepers had come to suspect: her detention on the savannah; her escape, which turned on a mistake made by one of the monkeys; her flight across the savannah and over a wall that turned out to be the tiger yard. The early morning release of the big cats and her finding herself following one down a wooden hatch and into the tunnel while being stalked by another left behind in the upper yard.

"The hatches both closed at the same time, and I

was trapped. At first I realized how lucky I was, because the Overtakers would never think to look in such a place, but then as time went on, it occurred to me that *no one* would look down here. That I was not just hidden, I was trapped. And that's when I realized that a dream I'd had—of a landscape, but from above, like from a plane—made all the more sense. I was in the tunnel, under the C in the photo."

"It was a satellite photo," Finn said, explaining. "One of your sketches led us to it."

"And that's when I realized the song on my iPod might help you find me. I used my earbud wire to connect to a box." She turned the glowing iPod, revealing a series of three junction boxes mounted to the stone wall and a number of wires leading from them. "I couldn't be sure it would work, but I thought it probably should. And maybe you'd hear it. *If* you were even here in the Park. And so I decided to save the battery and only play the song every few hours." She pointed at the glowing face of the device. "It still has some power, though not much, I'm afraid."

"We need to get out of here. Amanda and Charlene are up there waiting for us. Philby is on VMK with Wayne trying to see if they can control the hatches in the tiger yards."

He checked his phone. No bars, no signal.

"To get down here," Finn said, "I had to cross over to get through a maintenance gate. You can't turn yourself into a DHI the way I can. We're kind of stuck down here."

"But you can still get out, right?"

"I'm not leaving without you."

She untwisted the wires where her earbuds attached to the Park sound system. The tunnel's floor was concrete, its walls stone. At the far end, the tunnel floor began to rise, forming a ramp. The space became lower and tighter, ending in a box of concrete three feet square, a space Finn could just tuck himself into.

"It's exactly the same on the other end," Jess said.

"Have you tried opening it?" Finn asked.

"Yes. Of course. It's locked." Jess noticed Finn's nervous habit. "Why do you keep checking your watch, Finn? It's only a few minutes later than when you last looked."

"The Park closes soon."

"So Amanda and the others will have to leave. That's not the worst thing that could happen."

"They move the animals—all the animals—out of the Park at closing."

"Including the tigers." Jess sounded so sad.

"Yeah. Afraid so." In the hazy light, Finn and Jess

exchanged a look. It had to do with survival. Desperation. There was comfort there as well. A partnership. Friends. Teammates.

Finn's phone suddenly buzzed. Being close to the hatch had allowed a signal. A flurry of texts arrived, some older, some recent. He read them all and spoke to Jess. "Philby may have found a way to open the trapdoor."

"That's incredible!"

"Yeah, okay. The thing is," he took a breath, "Amanda says there are a bunch of orangutans in the tiger yard. Mean orangutans. So, if Philby gets the hatch open and we managed to get outside . . ."

"We get attacked."

"Something like that," Finn said. "Yeah."

"Well, we're not staying down here. Not if we can help it."

"No."

"Better orangutans than a tiger."

"I guess."

"Tell Philby to try to open the hatch," Jess said.

"Okay, but if it works, I go out first."

"Why are you looking at me like that?" she asked. "You don't think I'm going to argue with you, do you?"

53

Maybeck and Willa stood near the Garden kiosk on Discovery Island. It was a screen so guests could find restaurants offering various dietary choices like gluten-free. Philby had chosen it because late in the evening, no one would be making food decisions. It left him all alone at the screen.

Philby's avatar inside VMK was already busy tracing Ethernet cables, power supplies, and switches. Wayne had helped isolate the control switches for both tiger yard hatches.

Data flowed along colorful lines on the screen. Philby followed the darker red color that meant a high rate of data usage. Philby traced the source of the data. As expected, it led toward VMK's DinoLand.

Wayne's avatar appeared in the game and handed Philby's avatar two silver swords. The white-haired avatar warned in a text box to expect trouble. The Overtakers would have avatars as well. They would fight hard to defend the second server.

[ ] I hope you're a gamer.

Philby: Maybeck's better than me.

[ ] Well, then, I hope you're a fast learner.

Philby's avatar held the small sword. The other was slipped into his belt. Wayne stepped in front of him and the two sparred. Wayne fought well. Philby was clumsy with the sword. Wayne's avatar danced around Philby. Philby typed a message.

Philby: You're good at this

[ ]: I'm old. Rusty. A long time ago the Overtakers challenged the Kingdom. Uncle walt left the stonecutter's quill in case things went bad. I was a member of the team sent to repel the overtakers.

It was a bad battle.

Together their avatars continued inside the VMK game. They walked on catwalks. Up and down staircases. They followed the flow of data. As they crossed a bridge into DinoLand, six cables ran straight ahead. The second server, Philby thought.

Philby understood that if he shut down the second server he would weaken Maleficent. He would shrink her army of hologram animals.

The real Philby, not the avatar, turned around, to face Maybeck and Willa. He told them, "I need you two at the Dino Institute right now. The game . . . Wayne and I are going to have to fight. You may need to kill the server if I can't."

"We're on it," Maybeck shouted, already on the run.

When Philby looked back at the screen, he spotted his and Wayne's avatars. Wayne's sword was raised to strike.

They were under attack.

He turned his avatar to the left and lifted its right arm.

The tiger hatch switch was just out of reach.

54

"WHAT'S TAKING HIM so long?" Finn said, glancing at his watch. Without knowing why, he heard himself say, "The first time I saw you I was scared of you."

"Me? Why?"

The two were huddled close together just below the hatch.

"Your hair, maybe. The way you looked at me."

"Maleficent had cast a spell on me. I don't remember much."

"Yeah," he said. "The thing is, as it turned out, I liked you. So, there's that."

"Are you trying to tell me something?" she asked. Their faces were about a foot apart. Only a tiny bit of light seeped in from around the edges of the hatch, emitting a dull glow. He saw the shape of her head, not much more.

He said, "Fear is a weird thing. It can take over, or you can push it away. That's how I'm able to force myself in All Clear. I block out all fear. Suddenly I just cross over."

"You're saying it's going to be scary out there," Jess said.

"Yeah, probably."

"Why can't boys ever say what they actually want to say? If you were Amanda, you'd have just said, 'Heads up, girl! It's going to be freaky out there.'"

"Heads up, girl," Finn said.

"Ha-ha," she mocked him.

"When we leave the hatch, I'll try to cross over into All Clear. If Charlene's here, she'll be against a wall. Have you ever been to a rodeo?"

"Are you serious?"

"In a rodeo, the clown's job is to distract the bull. To draw the bull's attention. Think of Charlene and me as the clowns."

"You're saying the orangutans will be coming after me."

"They'll come after all of us," Finn said. "But if I go All Clear they can't hurt me. Only you. So we need to get you out of there."

"But you can't hold All Clear very long."

"Let me worry about that. You find Charlene. She can get you over the wall to safety. Don't even look at me. No matter what happens stay with Charlene."

"Finn, if you're trying to impress me . . . I already have a boyfriend . . ."

"Rob," Finn said. He saw her head cock to the side in curiosity. "'Change Rob'—it was in your diary. Amanda told us Rob was your boyfriend. It took us forever to realize why you'd written that."

"And why had I written that?"

"It's an anagram for Chernabog," Finn said.

"No kidding? The guy in *Fantasia*?"

"The same. We think he's Maleficent's leader, or partner, maybe."

"Oh my gosh."

"What?" Finn asked.

"I think I had a daydream," she said. "While I was down here in the dark. *King of the Mountain*, I called him. Big and ugly, and really hairy. He was trying to kill me. Me and Amanda. He had this club in his hand. No! It wasn't a club. It was—"

For the first time in the dull light he could see her face clearly: her eyes were squinted closed. "It was what?" he asked.

"It was . . . you, Finn. He had you by the legs and was swinging you like a club."

Finn knew the strength of Jess's dreams. He found it hard to breathe, his chest tight, his throat dry.

Fear!

He had to push it away. He had to find a sense of calm. He needed to cross over to his DHI.

Because at that moment, the hatch above their heads began to squeak and groan. Light flooded in and blinded them.

The hatch was open.

55

PHILBY'S AVATAR RAISED THE SWORD and blocked
the swipe of silver steel that aimed for his head.

Fighting two Overtaker avatars at the same time,
Wayne's sword was a blur of blinding light.

The four opposing avatars, hunchbacked trolls with
exaggerated noses, long hair, and strong arms, moved
quickly. They swung clubs and bludgeons, blunt bats
meant to crush Philby and Wayne and to remove them
from the Virtual Magic Kingdom game space.

Philby's sword blocked the blows as he backed up
defensively. The troll attacking him pivoted. Philby swung
his sword at the troll's head. His opponent cross-blocked
well, knocking the sword out of Philby's hands. Diving,
Philby caught the sword and swung. One of the troll's legs
fell off. It fell over onto its face and couldn't get up. Wayne
continued to defend himself against his two attackers.
Philby caught the remaining troll's club. The contact spun
the troll around. Philby launched a series of swift slices. But
he swung too hard. His avatar lost its balance and fell down.

Philby's sword cut a network cable. The cable lost its
color, fading to gray. Philby realized his avatar had cut an

actual data line in the real world. He considered cutting *all* the cables. Wouldn't that stop the Overtakers' DHIs? No more lions for Finn to battle. About to cut them all, he realized he needed to follow the data flow in order to locate the second server. As much as he wanted to help Finn and the others, he had a job to do.

One of the trolls turned away from Wayne. It jumped, landing in front of Philby. It raised its club. Philby had to deal with a one-legged enemy avatar on its knees and the new arrival. He struck the new arrival on its arm and the arm fell off.

The one-armed troll switched the club to its other hand. Philby moved out of the way as the club aimed for his leg. But Philby moved awkwardly. The avatar smashed Philby's foot. It looked like a swim fin flapping at the end of the leg of Philby's avatar.

Wayne dispatched the remaining troll. He attacked the wounded avatars that had ganged up on Philby. Philby watched as the two remaining trolls crawled away into the darkness.

[ ]: We have to hurry. The Overtakers will send more trolls. can you find the server?

Philby: I'm sure I can. Yes. It's in that direction. Philby's avatar pointed.

[ ]: We will need the help of our friends. The trolls are going to fight us. Count on it.

56

FINN AND JESS CLIMBED out of the open hatch. They squinted as their eyes adjusted to the evening light. They had entered the upper tiger yard, an open field of grass surrounded by high walls. They saw bamboo trees and shrubs. Jess heard a rustle to their left.

"Finn!"

A big tigress with amber eyes released a thunderous growl.

"More!" Finn said.

Two tigers were charging down the slope at them. A half dozen monkeys and four large orangutans came out of the bamboo. Finn and Jess froze.

Finn tried to cross over but it was no use. He was too freaked out by the animal attack. With a wall behind them, he and Jess had nowhere to go to escape the charge.

Jess pointed. The ivy on the wall near the bamboo was moving.

"It's Charlene," Jess said.

Finn said, "Stay close to the wall."

"But the monkeys!" she said.

"I know."

A hollow growl reverberated from behind them. The head of a tiger poked up out of the hatch.

Finn picked up a stick. He put himself between the monkeys and Jess. The two tigers coming down the slope were nearly upon them.

"Go!" Finn said, pointing. "Hurry!"

Jess took off.

Finn swung the stick at the monkeys and orang-utans. They skidded to a stop, forming a semicircle around him.

An orangutan turned its head toward Jess. In order to distract the orangutan, Finn swung the stick and lunged. Under his breath he whispered, *"Nothing can hurt me."* He pushed to go All Clear.

The orangutan flinched, jumping back. Finn ran past the ape, turning him.

Finn's effort bought Jess the time to continue along the line toward Charlene posing as DeVine. Seeing the two tigers, the monkeys startled.

As the monkeys spun, they focused on Finn. Jess continued toward Charlene.

Finn waved the stick and let out a war cry, trying to scare back the monkeys.

It didn't work. The monkeys moved closer, tighten-ing the circle around Finn.

Preparing to strike.

57

INSIDE VMK, THE AVATARS of Philby and Wayne moved along a catwalk following the colorful cables. Minutes later, they arrived at a thick line forming a box labeled "Dino Institute." Philby studied the wires. As he and Wayne reached the entrance, Wayne stopped.

[ ]: What now?

Philby: Why ask me?

[ ]: You're the computer expert.

Philby didn't consider himself any such thing. He liked computers. He knew a lot about them. But an expert? Not hardly.

Philby: We use the data lines to lead us to the second server. We try to cut the lines. But we're avatars. It's going to take Maybeck and Willa to actually find the server and shut it down.

Their avatars couldn't get through the black line that represented the wall of the institute. The color-coded figures moved along the wall looking for an entrance.

Philby: Finn and Jess won't be safe until we shut down the server and stop those DHIs of the animals. As in, we have to hurry.

Both avatars stopped at a doorway marked in the wall. A security pad flashed by the doorway.

Wayne's avatar stopped.

[ ] Hold on. I can get us through. I have the security clearance. But it will signal security. It could be a trap.

Philby: Why? There's no time. Besides, the cables right there on the other side are the ones we need to follow.

[ ]: And what if the cables are also part of a trap?
Philby hesitated. Wayne had gotten him this far.

[ ]: Please. They will expect us to use the first door we discover. I would suggest we continue along the wall. It's safer for all of us.
Philby moved his avatar away from the entrance.
Philby: Okay, but we have to hurry.

58

THE APES AND MONKEYS encircled Finn, closing around him like a net. How simple to cross over briefly into his DHI and just walk right through that hairy line, but it was not to be: he was terrified. He wasn't going to cross over on his own.

He spun, looking for the weak link in the circle. He considered charging some of the smaller monkeys, breaking the line there and running for it. But they all were ferociously fast on their feet and, at the moment, baring their teeth in a display of aggression and anger.

He caught sight of Jess as she reached Charlene. Excitedly, the two girls worked it out to where Charlene was leaning her back against the wall, and the nimble Jess now climbed up the stilts—using them as a ladder—toward Charlene's waiting hand. Finn looked away as the fingers of the two met, confident that Charlene would get Jess up and over to the other side.

"Over here!" a high-pitched voice called out.

Finn heard guests shout: "Check it out!" "Look at this!" "There are kids in with the tigers!"

Where had she come from? Finn wondered. It was

Amanda. She was *inside* the tiger yard, the huge, prowling cat to her left, the circle of monkeys directly in front of her.

Disney Security would be on them in minutes. They had to get Jess—and themselves—out before they were either eaten by the tigers or caught by Security.

The other two cats arrived at the same time. They, too, began to circle, along with the tiger that escaped the hatch—a wider circle than the monkeys, one that included Amanda.

The escaped tiger still confused Finn: *How had it gotten into the tunnel in the first place? Was the lower yard hatch open? If so, who had opened it?*

Only the prowling tigress that had emerged from the shadows remained on her own, majestically moving with long, confident strides, restlessly back and forth. She seemed to be agitated, studying the commotion in her yard, calculating a strike.

Several of the monkeys spun around, distracted by Amanda, and broke their chain. Finn took advantage of the distraction and shot for the opening.

The two charging tigers turned at the last minute, now aiming for Amanda.

Finn took two steps toward her, intending to defend her, but then witnessed her leaving the ground. She levitated, floating higher and higher. The monkeys, carried by their own momentum, ran right through the space she had occupied. The two charging tigers leaped into the air, reaching their claws toward her. One caught the leg of her jeans, but there was no sound of tearing fabric. No scream.

The leaping tiger flew through the air and landed with a roll.

The slinking tigress sat back on her haunches and sprang for the charging tiger. It looked as if the tigress were trying to defend Amanda. The two tigers growled at the tigress and the three cats began to circle each other.

Ignored, Amanda lowered herself to the grass.

"The wall!" Finn called out to Amanda as he raised his stick toward the remaining two monkeys.

Amanda sprinted toward Charlene.

Finn turned his back in their direction, battling most of the monkeys, who darted about him trying to sink their teeth into his legs. He knocked them back with his stick, but apparently they barely felt it.

Looking over the heads of the monkeys, Finn saw the tigress swiping her huge claws at the other two grand cats. It looked as if the cats made contact, but none of them reeled with pain—they held their ground.

Charlene let out a squeal as Amanda climbed up

her stilts; her hand had become caught between a stilt and the wall.

With that squeal, all three cats turned. One minute fighting each other; the next, acting like curious cats. They clearly saw the monkeys, then Finn, and finally the girl in the distance clambering up a wall.

They charged.

Finn had his hands full with the monkeys. He had not an ounce of strength nor a second of time to deal with three enormous cats barreling down toward him.

This is it, he thought. It was too late to turn and run. Too late to escape.

The cats were lightning fast. They seemed to pull the earth, and Finn with it, dragging him toward them. Without looking, the monkeys knew. They darted to their left, removing themselves from the tigers' line of sight.

Finn readied his pathetic stick; it was all the defense he had. He was going to be eaten alive.

The two smaller tigers leaped into the air when just five yards away, perfectly calculating the distance. They would land on Finn, crushing him, then snap his neck with their powerful jaws and start the feast.

Finn braced for the end.

59

WAYNE'S AVATAR RUSHED to keep up with Philby.

The two traveled around a corner of the institute's wall, following the data cables. Another virtual entrance appeared just up ahead. Wayne touched the security panel and the door opened and the two avatars moved inside.

Five of the data cables ran straight and then turned. A sixth cable branched away from the others. This cable burned bright blue, indicating a large amount of data moving across it.

Moments earlier, Wayne had messaged Philby to stop using the game's text bubbles. He didn't want anyone else being able to read what they were planning.

As a result, Philby had to make decisions—big decisions—all by himself. He wanted badly to ask Wayne what the former Imagineer thought of his ideas. But it wasn't to be.

Once inside the structure, Philby struck the five purple cables with his sword. It took several blows to cut them and watch the data color drain out of them.

Quickly, the cables turned gray—the data stream was stopped.

Wayne's avatar wasn't keeping up. Philby couldn't message him to tell him to hurry.

Then he realized that Wayne's avatar wasn't moving at all.

The white-haired figure dissolved and disappeared.

Philby panicked. He moved his avatar along the bright blue cable until reaching its end. The VMK floor plan indicated a small bathroom, or maybe a janitor's closet. Philby's avatar raised its sword and chopped the cable in two.

The real Philby, the boy controlling the video screen normally dedicated to dietary preferences, used the group text to reach Maybeck. He told him the location of the second server inside the Dino Institute. He warned him the Overtakers would know the Keepers were coming for the server. He instructed him to be super careful.

In typical Maybeck fashion, the reply text was short and to the point.

Maybeck: Yeah, whatever. Consider it done.

60

MAYBECK AND WILLA rode in the backseat of a Dino Institute exploration vehicle. With the Park nearing the closing hour, a large line had formed. But despite all those waiting, the front seat of their vehicle was empty. It should have concerned them if they hadn't been so focused on Philby's instructions.

The ride was dark and chilly. Its dinosaurs looked perfectly real. Asteroids fell to Earth in a shower of fiber optic lighting. The vehicle rounded a long turn. The prehistoric creatures lifted their heads and looked at the truck.

"How are we going to pull this off?" Willa asked Maybeck. "Even if we see a door to backstage, like Philby said, we can't jump out of the truck. We'd set off alarms."

"We'll figure it out," Maybeck said. "Philby said a janitor closet or small bathroom. Anything like that is going to be backstage. So first things first."

The attraction's next scene displayed a tyrannosaurus eating a lizard.

"It's majorly crazy the way their eyes move," Willa

hissed. "It feels like they're looking right at—"

She stopped talking, screeching "Eek!" instead. The dinosaur's tail swung quickly toward the truck and skimmed over its hood.

Maybeck yanked Willa down. A mirror broke loose and clanged onto the track.

Maybeck pulled at the safety belt. He and Willa were locked into their seats.

He stole a glance behind them. There were no other vehicles in sight.

There was no use calling for help.

"You remember what happened at Small World?" he asked her.

"I was inside Winnie the Pooh with Charlene at the time. We nearly drowned. So no, not personally, I don't."

"If we jump, the sensors will stop the ride."

"Note the seat belts," Willa reminded. "We aren't going anywhere."

A pterodactyl shot down at them from the ceiling.

Maybeck shouted a bad word.

With its six-foot wingspan and talons the size of garden shears, it looked monstrous. Maybeck ducked, but too late. The prehistoric bird latched on to his forearm.

His seat belt released inexplicably.

"Terry!" Willa cried out.

"I know!"

The timing of the seat belt unlocking could not be a coincidence.

The giant bird lifted Maybeck out of the vehicle.

Willa grabbed him by the boots, trying to keep him in the truck. Stretched between the bird and Willa, Maybeck cried out in pain.

Fighting back, Maybeck twisted free of the bird's hold. The pterodactyl craned back its neck to strike.

Maybeck grabbed the bird's bony leg and snapped it at the knee. The creature made a horrible sound. It flapped its long wings and rose into the overhead darkness.

Back in the truck, Maybeck studied the pterodactyl's broken leg. Shredded wires stuck out of the knee.

"You're bleeding," Willa said.

Maybeck studied the three holes in his arm, then shrugged. "You held on to me. You saved me."

"Maybe if I'd thought about it, I wouldn't have," Willa said. They laughed together.

"The ride is *trying* to hurt us!"

"You think?" he snapped sarcastically.

"The Overtakers know we're after the server. They'll keep trying to hurt us until they stop us."

Maybeck stood up in the seat. "We've got to get to the server."

"Note to Terry: my seat belt is locked," Willa reminded him. If the Overtakers got hold of them, things were about to get a lot worse.

"There has to be an emergency release," Maybeck said. "What would Philby do?"

"He'd think it through. Look, if the ride stops for an emergency, the seat belts must release."

"So all I have to do is stop the ride," he said.

The attraction's next scene featured a massive dinosaur that looked like a rhinoceros.

"I have an idea," Maybeck said.

"I don't like the sound of that."

"Oh, shut up!" he snapped.

Maybeck jumped from the vehicle.

Willa called out after him.

He crossed off the track expecting the emergency system to stop the ride.

It did not.

The truck continued moving. Maybeck waved at the giant rhinoceros.

"Terry! Stop! Don't do that."

But Maybeck not only waved his arms, he jumped up and down. "Here, kitty kitty!"

"Terry! NO!"

The beast broke loose from the fake jungle and stepped into the track. The truck was aimed at the rhino.

"Come and get 'em!" Maybeck shouted.

The beast put its head and massive horn down, announcing it would charge. It snorted.

"That's bad breath, dude!" Maybeck hollered.

The rhinoceros charged.

Maybeck counted: *one, two* . . . He jumped away from the truck.

The rhino stabbed the truck with its single tusk. The truck bucked up and landed back onto its front wheels.

Willa's seat belt released.

"Free!" she shouted.

She leaped from the backseat to the platform while the rhino tried to get its tusk out of the truck's grille.

"Door to your right!" Maybeck shouted. "Right behind you!"

Willa held open the backstage door for Maybeck.

The rhino pulled free of the truck. It pawed the floor, snorted, and charged.

Maybeck ran as fast as he'd ever run.

"It's . . . right . . . behind . . ." Willa called.

Maybeck dove through the open door. Willa slammed it shut. The entire wall shook as the dinosaur crashed into it. Willa took Maybeck by the hand and pulled him to his feet. "You shouldn't have done that," she scolded. "This isn't a competition! Just because I saved your life doesn't mean—"

"Everything's a competition," Maybeck said.

They reached a long, curving hallway. There were no markings or signs on its gray walls. Overhead, hundreds of data wires and power lines were strung in both directions.

"I think we follow the wires," Maybeck said.

"But which way?"

"I don't know," he said. "This way, I think." He pointed ahead.

"What if you're wrong?"

"Sometimes you just gotta have faith."

"Faith? Remember, this is you saying that, Terry."

"Yeah, well maybe I've changed."

"I don't think so," Willa said, her breath short from running so hard.

Alarms continued sounding but the hallway was empty.

"There!" she said, pointing out a massive group of blue wires. There were only a few breaking away from the others.

Maybeck swung open the door.

Workbenches ran along the far wall, covered with

spare parts, soldering guns, tools, and hydraulics. In the middle of the space to their left was a metal rack, floor-to-ceiling shelving holding dozens of computer servers, network hubs, and surge suppressors.

"We've got it!" Willa proclaimed.

"No!" Maybeck countered. "It's too big. Philby said it was a small room. And, anyway, it can't be this easy."

"Then where?" she asked. "This has to be right." She answered her own question. "The wires won't lie! We follow all the wires."

"There are a zillion of them!" Maybeck said.

But Willa was already working to see where all the wires led. Holding a group in her right hand, she looked up.

Footsteps . . . running quickly in the hallway.

"The door!" Maybeck whispered.

Willa raced to turn the door's lock.

Click!

The noise in the hall continued past.

"There!" she said, pointing to a narrow door painted green like the rest of the wall. It was easily missed among all the mess. Maybeck tried the door-knob.

Locked.

"Small, like a janitor's closet," Willa said. "Four

wires running through the wall near the floor. It's perfect!" She sounded elated.

Willa found a metal plate on a workbench and pushed it into the gap by the doorknob. The door came unlocked.

Maybeck pushed it open with the toe of his running shoe.

The room was small and dark. Carboard boxes, wires, and plastic milk crates were piled in a disorganized mess. Willa pushed through the stuff. She located a black box with a row of blinking orange, blue, and green lights.

"Found it," she said.

61

Two tigers midair and aimed at Finn opened their jaws and showed their fangs. Finn squinted and turned away from the attack, terrified. He was going to be eaten. . . . Nothing happened. Nothing bit him. No tigers.

He opened his eyes, shaking from fear. The big cats had vanished in midair.

So had four of the six monkeys and two of the orangutans.

The big tigress over in the shadows was still there. So was the enormous tiger that had come through the hatch.

Finn counted two monkeys and two orangutans. The ones that had vanished had been holograms. Their disappearance meant Philby and Wayne, or maybe Maybeck and Willa, had located and disconnected the second server.

What now? he wondered. Jess and Amanda were safe. Finn was not. He took off running. A caged-in jungle Jeep appeared from over the rise, a flashing light atop its roof.

The orangutans attacked Finn.

Incredibly fast, and as big as he was, the apes came at him with wild eyes and drooling snouts. The Jeep startled the orangutans, stealing their attention for a fraction of a second. Finn sprang for a clump of bamboo.

He pushed through the bamboo to reach Charlene. "How about a lift?" Finn shouted as the Jeep skidded to a stop.

Charlene gave Finn a hand. He reached the top of the wall, lay flat, and helped to pull Charlene up and over. Her stilts fell off.

Rangers from the Jeep hurried through the bamboo, shouting. By the time they reached the wall, the rangers found only a pair of abandoned stilts.

A few guests applauded, having watched all the excitement.

Not wanting to get caught, Charlene led the others directly across the formal gardens and into the jungle on a route she now knew well.

Jess took two steps and stopped. Finn nearly bumped into her.

"Come on! Let's go!" he said.

Jess appeared frozen in place.

Finn looked in the direction that Jess looked. Jess spoke softly. "That mountain was in my dream," she told Finn. "The bad dream I told you about."

"*King of the Mountain,*" Finn said. "Where you and

Amanda were under attack and the monster had me in his hand."

"Chernabog," Jess said. She reached out and took Amanda by the hand. She didn't speak, but something passed between the two girls.

"That's Expedition Everest," Charlene said.

"You and Finn go on," Jess said. "Amanda and I have to go into that mountain."

"That's absurd! Your dream was more like a nightmare." Finn could hardly believe what she was suggesting.

"She's right," Amanda said. "You go on. But if Jess dreamed it, then she and I were there."

"So was I," Finn said.

"Never once, not once, has one of my dreams lied to me. It ends there. If we leave now it doesn't end." Jess squeezed Amanda's hand all the tighter.

"Then we all go," Charlene said defiantly.

"You're crazy!" Finn said. "We could have been killed in there. In the tiger yard. We're so tired we're walking zombies. It was a *dream*."

Charlene spoke to Finn with kindness in her voice and eyes. "And what did Walt Disney say about dreams? 'If you can dream it—'"

"Yeah, yeah. 'You can do it,'" Finn said, interrupting. "So we all go. But just for the record, I never said this was a good idea."

62

HAVING RECONNECTED THROUGH the group text, all the Kingdom Keepers, along with Jess and Amanda, reunited in a small patch of jungle. Behind them towered Expedition Everest, and screams were heard periodically as the roller coaster thrilled its riders. After a quick celebration of Jess's return, Finn brought up the daydream she had had while trapped in the tunnel.

"But so what?" Maybeck asked. "We had two things we had to do: get Jess back and kill the second server. We've done both. I'm so tired I can barely stand. Let's get out of here while we still can."

"You all can go. It's all right," Amanda said matter-of-factly. "We will never be able to repay you for all you've done."

"But your dream," Charlene said. "The giant attacking you. Finn in his hands."

"All the more reason," Maybeck said, "we should just boogie and forget about all that."

He looked to the others for agreement but saw only vacant faces.

"Come on, people!" Maybeck chastised. "Quit while you're ahead. Ever heard of that?"

"Leave no stone unturned," Finn said, "might be more appropriate. Wayne has gone missing."

"Philby cut the data lines. Who knows how that affected the data flow in the Park? Besides, it wasn't Wayne. It was his VMK avatar! Are you kidding me? We're going to stay and try to find a missing avatar? Are you *serious*? Half the Park is out looking for us."

"Maleficent serves Chernabog. We know that Chernabog defeated Mickey at the Fantasmic show. Wayne told us that a long time ago. That means he has major powers. He's the one Disney demon that we know virtually nothing about—"

"And let's leave it that way!"

"But Jess dreamed something awful. And Maleficent could have hidden in any of the Parks. Why here? Why now? What's being planned? With Wayne missing, it's up to us to find out."

"You're hallucinating," Maybeck said.

Philby stepped forward. "Without Wayne we'd have failed. I promise you that. Maleficent's got him. Don't ask me to explain that, but I just know it. And if that's true, it's my fault—it's all of our faults. Can you honestly just go home and go to bed knowing that?"

Maybeck hung his head and shook it back and forth. "No." He sounded so despondent.

"No," Philby agreed. "I didn't think so."

Charlene unfolded the photocopied page of Jess's diary. She pointed to the sketch of what looked like a gorilla. "What if this isn't a gorilla at all? What if it's the yeti?"

Jess spoke up. "You just told us that Chernabog was missing from his float, remember? Maybe Maleficent thought that that was the real Chernabog, only to discover it a fake. The bat . . . the monkeys . . . something could have told her the real Chernabog was locked up here in AK."

"Or maybe this whole thing," Finn said, "was cooked up by Maleficent to use us to lead her to Wayne. Has anyone considered that possibility?"

He drew stunned expressions.

"What if we did *exactly* what she wanted us to do?" Finn asked in a softer voice. "We couldn't have gotten Jess without Wayne's help. He knew they were looking for him. So Maleficent cooks up this plan to basically use Jess as bait. We think she's after Jess to keep Jess's dreams from forecasting what Maleficent is up to—and that could be right. But it doesn't mean there wasn't a bigger plan."

A light breeze broke the silence between them

as, once again, it carried the cries from Expedition Everest.

"One thing we know," Willa said, "is that Everest is cold. At least, it represents the cold." She indicated the gorilla on Jess's diary page. "What if this is the yeti, like Charlene said?" The other kids stared at her with puzzled expressions. "What if, like Maleficent, the yeti can't handle the heat? So Maleficent's job is not only to get him out of the Park, but keep him cold. Keep them both cold."

"The ice truck!" Charlene said.

"Exactly!" agreed Willa.

"But to what purpose?" complained Maybeck.

"How do we know? A refrigerated truck can take him anywhere he wants to go."

"But where?" asked Finn.

"So Expedition Everest was a way for Wayne and the others to control Chernabog?" Charlene asked. "The Imagineers basically locked him up in a deep freeze?"

"It could be," agreed Willa. "They locked up Maleficent in the dungeons, let's not forget."

Philby spoke confidently. "I say we get inside Expedition Everest and check out the yeti. That could be where the answers lie. Jess drew it in her diary. It has to mean something!"

"It means that's where the danger lies," muttered Jess.

Finn said quietly, "Chernabog is using Maleficent—maybe to get him off of Everest or even out of the Park. Maleficent used us to reveal and capture Wayne. If they eliminate Wayne, then they take away years of knowledge about all the Parks, all the history of this place. If they're trying to gain control of the Parks, Wayne has to go. He's proved that."

"He has the knowledge and leadership," said Willa, "to stop them."

Leadership, Finn thought. Wayne had given him a lecture on how to be a good leader. *Had Wayne known what was coming?*

"Wayne is not the only one they need to get rid of," Maybeck reminded them. "I'd say we've become a pretty big pain in the—"

"But!" Finn said, interrupting, "there's obviously stuff we haven't figured out. Maybe a lot of stuff. It's pretty obvious we don't have it all. We can't make any conclusions without going in there, without knowing more. I'm going in there. And I have a hunch Amanda and Jess are, too, because Jess dreamed about it."

The two sisters nodded.

"This is stupid," Maybeck whined. "It could be a trap."

"Which is why you and Willa and Charlene will remain outside of Everest," Finn directed. "If we get nailed, you'll have to come save us." He knew if there was one thing Maybeck loved, it was being the hero.

Maybeck snorted. "Okay," he said, relenting.

"Philby will come with me because he's so good with tech stuff, and if there's one thing we know about Expedition Everest, it's that it's high-tech."

"I haven't studied it much," Philby cautioned.

"We'll take our chances," Finn said.

"The Park closes in, like, five minutes," said Charlene.

"That may work even better for us," Finn declared.

"What about the fact that Jess's daydream has Ape Man swinging you around like a drumstick?" Maybeck crossed his arms, believing he'd finally found a hole in Finn's plan.

"But what he doesn't know," Philby said, "is that we already know that, and that's gotta be to our advantage."

"Not if you're the one being swung around," said Maybeck, clearly challenging Finn.

"I'll take my chances," said Finn, staring back at Maybeck's twitching smile and wondering why he'd volunteered.

63

THE LINE FOR EXPEDITION EVEREST had been shut down fifteen minutes prior to the Park closing to make sure the roller coaster was free of passengers by the appointed time. The waiting area twisted through a startling reproduction of a Nepalese village, complete with prayer flags and Asian memorabilia.

Finn, Philby, Amanda, and Jess stuck together. They passed into the backstage area through a "Park Rangers Only" gate and simply walked into the enormous structure that housed the exotic roller coaster.

Finn had expected to need his ID and perhaps some quick talking to get them all inside, but with the closing of the ride to the public, someone had left the backstage door open, and the kids simply walked in.

"It's three structures in one," Philby explained in a hush. "The massive superstructure that supports the exterior building, the roller coaster, and the yeti."

"I thought you hadn't studied it," whispered Jess.

"I haven't studied it thoroughly," Philby replied, "but that doesn't mean I haven't read up on it a little."

"We may need the roller coaster for our escape,"

Finn said to Philby. "Why don't you stay and try to handle that?"

"Done," said Philby. He could be a handful when he showed off.

"See you up there," Finn said.

The metal stairs reminded him of a fire escape. The three of them climbed and climbed. Then they climbed some more. Far below they suddenly heard men's voices. The lights went out. Then a reverberating *thunk* as a door was slammed shut with such a finality that Finn felt it up his spine.

With the lights out, the building's vast interior was held in an unnatural haze caused by the few emergency lights strategically placed throughout.

No one said anything at first, but a tremor of fear passed between them.

Finn couldn't lose the image of his being swung around by his feet. Step by step he felt himself drawn to that fate.

Amanda started talking, possibly to break the mood established by the lights going out. "What is it that something—someone—like Chernabog wants?"

"Power," Jess answered.

"Exactly," Amanda agreed. "He's been locked up in here ever since they built the ride, and now he wants freedom and power, probably in that order."

"And you're saying he'd have gotten both if I hadn't dreamed what I dreamed," Jess said.

"He still may get both," Amanda cautioned. "And what's the one thing anyone seeking power is afraid of?"

"What is this?" Finn complained, "a social sciences class?"

"Answer the question," Amanda pushed.

"His enemies," Finn answered.

"Yes! His enemies," Amanda agreed. "In particular, any enemy who is potentially more powerful than he is. So who are his biggest enemies? You—the Kingdom Keepers—or Wayne, or Jess, or who?"

"All of the above," a winded Finn replied. The stairs seemed to go on forever. The trio passed along the roller coaster's high-tech tracks and the arctic scenery that only made the chill of the air all the more convincing. "Or none of the above," Finn said, his mind racing.

"You're messing with us?" Amanda said accusingly.

Finn answered, "Chernabog is rarely seen in any of the Disney stuff. *Fantasia* and Fanstasmic are it, I think."

"And all the postcards and stuff that show the Disney villains," Amanda corrected.

"That, too. But in Fantasmic—he's beaten by the sorcerer, Mickey," said Finn. "And in *Fantasia*, by the sun."

"Interesting," said Amanda.

Jess asked, "Are you saying he has to defeat Mickey before he can be assured of maintaining any power he gains?"

"Defeating Mickey," Finn said, "defeats us all. Without Mickey, there *is* no Magic Kingdom, no Animal Kingdom, no Disney at all."

"But then why kidnap Jess? Why involve the five of you? What do you guys have to do with Mickey?" Amanda asked.

"Nothing," Finn answered. "That's what's puzzling. But think about it: the sooner he eliminates Mickey, the sooner there's no one to stop him from overtaking the Park."

Maybeck: Ice truck just arrived!!!

Finn told the two sisters the news. "The ice truck pulled up around back."

"Then this is it," Jess said, her voice trembling. "Whatever Maleficent has been planning, it's happening right now."

They rounded a corner and then quickly jumped to one side to hide.

What they'd witnessed was emblazoned in their minds. Far above them towered the frightening figure of the yeti. It stood thirty feet tall or more, leaning out over the track—the embodiment of evil: monstrous and otherworldly.

At the yeti's feet stood a tall figure in a black robe. They were too far away to see the purple fringe on the cape or the green skin, but no one in the group doubted it was she. Hidden by an outcropping of rock, they continued higher until the steady chanting of her voice could be heard. She was conjuring a spell. The walkway curved. Finn raised a hand and the others stopped.

He didn't know exactly why they'd come here— only that they couldn't turn away from Jess's daydream. Perhaps they were here to witness whatever Maleficent planned, perhaps to stop it. He believed their attendance here critical to Wayne's rescue, yet he knew they were no match for the yeti. Not if Maleficent awakened the thing.

And then it became perfectly clear to him: they had to stop her from awakening the yeti in the first place. Chernabog must not come to power. This was the secret to preserving the peace in the Animal Kingdom. This was why Jess had dreamed it in the first place.

More than anything, Finn's concern for Wayne remained at the forefront of his thoughts. He had to find out what had happened to him, where he'd gone. And to that end, he must not be afraid.

This became his focus: *he must not be afraid*. He felt a tingling sensation wash over him.

It was true: he did not see the green skin or the fringe

on Maleficent's robe, and he was betting she couldn't make out the sudden slight shimmer to his skin, either.

He rose to his feet and called out boldly, "Do you really think you'll get away with it?" His electronically edged voice echoed in the cavernous building.

Amanda and Jess slunk back and down, once again hiding in the lee of the rock outcropping.

They all heard a loud *pop* followed by mechanical humming. The round rail to the left of the stairs carried a slight tremor.

The roller coaster had been switched on.

64

I t all happened so quickly: his words echoing around the building; the steady increase in electronic and mechanical sounds as the roller coaster started up; Maleficent's arms shooting up from her sides and lifting her robe like magnificent wings.

The twitching of the yeti's fingers, like the paws of a sleeping dog.

Too late! She had already awakened the giant.

His massive head moved side-to-side, and a loud *crack* thundered through the snowcapped mountains.

The hum and whir of the roller coaster grew steadily closer.

"Silly, silly, boy!" Maleficent spun around and shot a ball of fire at Finn. The size of a soccer ball, it exploded at his feet, flaming out.

And whereas once Finn would have been terrified by such things, would have stood transfixed by the power she displayed, something had come over him. She was nothing but an illusionist, a magician using her substantial skills to scare him. He was no longer convinced she even possessed the ability to kill him—or, if she did, then why hadn't she done so?

"If you were going to kill me," he shouted, "then you would have done that the first time we met. But you can't, can you? Walt Disney would never allow a creation of his imagination to take a life."

The tingling grew stronger; he felt it in a way, a degree, he'd never experienced. This confrontation was making his DHI stronger.

"But I am not of his imagination," Maleficent said. "I am of the old stories—tales that existed for hundreds of years in places all around the world. Tales of things that actually happened." She shot another ball at him. Again, he did not move from his spot. Again, the flames fell short.

The giant yeti was awake now, towering over them all, eyes blinking. Finn did not recoil. He could not picture Wayne and the other Imagineers building creatures designed to harm them.

The roller coaster sped closer.

"I will kill you," Maleficent said, "when you are no longer of use to me." She bent backward and looked up at the hairy creature above her. "When Lord Chernabog has no further use for you." She let out a laugh—a bloodcurdling cackle—that for the first time challenged Finn's DHI status. His feet and hands grew cold, and it took all his will to overcome this poison and return to his full DHI.

The beast had the reaction time of a snake. One moment Finn was standing on the stairs. The next, the yeti had him by the legs and was swinging him overhead.

His legs . . . not the legs of his DHI.

Amanda and Jess jumped out from their hiding places and Jess shouted, "Let him go!"

"Ah!" Maleficent cried out. "If it isn't the Fairlies."

Amanda craned forward, her neck thrust out. Maleficent knew way too much.

Finn knew the secret to his own survival was to push away his fear, but being swung at thirty miles an hour over the head of a forty-foot-tall giant proved a difficult challenge.

Maleficent suddenly floated—levitated—off the platform, clearly, nothing she'd planned for herself, for she flailed her legs and arms, dog paddling like a kid struggling to swim for the first time.

"You put me down, child!" she roared.

She hurled a ball of flame at Amanda, who leaned slightly left, allowing the asteroid to pass. It exploded into the Himalayas.

"PUT HIM DOWN!" cried out Amanda, "OR I WILL DROP YOU AS YOU WISH!"

Maleficent moved like a puppet twenty feet to the

left. Now there was nothing but a sixty-foot fall to concrete beneath her.

Finn felt the tingling return, and, as it did, the yeti's hand closed shut through his body—nothing but light. Finn clamored up the beast's arm toward its massive head. The yeti swiped at him, but again his hand passed through Finn's DHI, unable to touch him.

He caught a glimpse of Maleficent as she began to transform into a crow. But as she did, Amanda released her and the green-skinned creature fell fifteen feet straight down before stopping in midair.

"You try that again," Amanda warned, "and I'll drop you before you have the chance."

Maleficent looked down and seemed to consider her odds. Then she looked back at Amanda.

"You harm me, you little tart, and your friend will never see his precious Wayne again!"

With the mention of Wayne, Finn slipped. He fell off the yeti's shoulder, and the sensation immediately removed his DHI. He slid down the side of the creature, grasping at the matted gray hair and somehow controlling his fall. As he reached the yeti's leg, it moved. Then the other. The giant's feet broke free of the platform where it had stood for several years. The entire building shook.

A series of screams was followed by the roller

coaster shooting up at them through the darkness. Philby, Maybeck, and Willa zoomed past—backward—and out of sight.

Maybeck waved at Maleficent.

The witch proclaimed: "You will bring me the Stonecutter's Quill, or you will never see the white-haired man again."

At that moment, the yeti began to change. The hair was sucked inside its arms, turning the gray skin smooth; the legs and arms shrank, and the neck grew thinner, while the head also lost its hair and sprouted horns. The giant creature had been reduced to a figure much greater than Maleficent, but no longer a thirty-foot-high beast. Now black webbing formed under the thing's arms like . . . bat wings.

Chernabog.

Finn heard the roller coaster slowing in the distance. It would be returning—and when it did, he, Amanda, and Jess needed to be on it.

The pen, Finn realized. The Stonecutter's Quill was the pen Walt had used to imagine the first plans of the Parks. It had demonstrated great powers the one and only time Finn had seen it used. Powers, he assumed, that could be put to evil use as easily as they had been to good.

A wall of tension formed between Amanda and

Maleficent. The witch produced another ball of fire, but this time Amanda levitated it as well. It hovered next to the witch, burning hotly and illuminating her green face.

"You will regret this, little one," Maleficent muttered, clearly afraid of her own fire. "You are playing with things you know nothing about."

She grew the head of a vulture. Wings began to sprout.

Amanda released her. Again, Maleficent fell abruptly, before slowly being carried aloft. Evidence of the vulture was gone; the green-skinned fairy hovering over the precipitous fall.

The strain on Amanda was evident. She had quickly grown pale, her body now shaking.

Finn saw that Maleficent was merely playing for time. She knew Amanda couldn't keep this up forever.

"Release Wayne!" Finn called out, "or she'll drop you."

"The Quill," Maleficent said, "or you'll never see him alive again." She looked over at Finn, who held to Chernabog rather than drop to the platform where the creature might squash him like a bug.

Amanda's strength gave out, and she collapsed into Jess's arms.

"You harm any one of us and you will never see that

pen!" Finn shouted. He let go, jumped, slid down the mountain slope, and aimed straight for the two girls, hoping his timing was right, for he could see the roller coaster from the corner of his eye. Chernabog stepped forward, raising his arms in defiance. But he was too late.

Finn's wild slide down the mountainside connected with both girls at the exact moment the roller coaster arrived. He stretched out his arms and caught both Amanda and Jess, his momentum carrying all three of them headfirst into the passing roller coaster. They tumbled into a middle car.

But the safety bars on the ride were already set, having been locked at the start; and, as the cars gained substantial speed, Finn held on to the weakened Amanda as Jess reached out to cling to the car, and with Maybeck, Philby, Charlene, and Willa calling out from the back, the Kingdom Keepers plummeted down into the dark.

65

CHERNABOG MOVED WITH surprising agility for something that was a beastly demon with a pair of batlike wings the size of boat sails.

To the surprise of all, Chernabog made no attempt to stop the Kingdom Keepers. He flew toward the bottom of the ride. For once in his life Finn willed a roller coaster to go even faster.

Finn had ridden on Expedition Everest before. Within a matter of seconds they would be thrown into a spiral that would crush them against each other if they couldn't hold on tightly.

Holding on with one hand each, he and Jess wrapped their free arms around the other's shoulders and, with Amanda pinned between them, leaned forward, braced for the spinout.

Expedition Everest roared into its climactic spiral, the G-force driving Finn and Jess to their right, their hands slipping along the restraining bars. The force nearly threw them from the car, but together Finn and Jess managed to keep Amanda pinned in, and soon the roller coaster began to slow to a stop.

As it came to rest, the restraining bars released, and Maybeck and the others hurried to join Finn, Amanda, and Jess.

Finn left Amanda in the care of her sister and led the others through the building and out an enormous garage door that was standing wide open.

They ran out into the street where they caught a final glimpse of the back of the ice truck as it sped away.

"What now?" a gasping Philby said, clutching his sides.

"They got away," Finn said.

"But we can't just let them go!" Maybeck said.

"We got Jess back," Finn said, "and we crippled the second server." He looked at each one of his friends. "I think it's safe to say that Jess and Amanda are now officially Kingdom Keepers."

The others nodded.

"We have work to do," Willa mumbled.

"Let's get some sleep," Finn said. His suggestion met with no resistance.

66

THE STORY MADE THE morning news: a refrigerator truck, being driven poorly, had been pulled over by the local police. The officer swore that he'd been knocked over when he'd gone to open the back of the truck, and that two creatures had been seen hurrying away. He refused to describe them. He said only that they had traveled in the general direction of Disney's Hollywood Studios theme park, and that from everything he'd seen, that was where they belonged.

* * *

For nearly two weeks, Finn—who'd been grounded for a month—sneaked onto VMK the way Wayne had told him. He hoped to find Wayne by typing the name into a text screen. When the white-haired avatar failed to appear, Finn organized the other kids, most of whom were also currently grounded.

So it was that exactly a month after the event at Expedition Everest, Finn went to sleep fully dressed, a small black remote button in his pocket.

As he fell asleep that night, he intentionally dreamed

of the Magic Kingdom, and he awakened there on a Park bench, his body glowing under the moonlight.

He was at the hub near the entrance, at the end of Main Street, USA.

Soon, the other Kingdom Keepers joined him. Only Charlene was still in her nightgown, having forgotten to change into street clothes before going to sleep. Or maybe this was how she wanted to dress.

The five headed up and into Wayne's small apartment above the firehouse in the Magic Kingdom. It was exactly twelve midnight.

This was Wayne's apartment. Most had visited it before. There was incredibly sour milk in the refrigerator and food that now wore a coat of green fuzz—Wayne had not been here in a very long time.

They searched for over an hour for the Stonecutter's Quill, but to no avail. If Wayne had hidden it, he'd hidden it well.

"What now?" Charlene asked.

"Is there any choice?" Finn asked.

"But without the pen," Philby said, "what leverage do we have? We can't win his release without that pen."

"We'll think of something," Finn said.

"Or maybe Jess will dream it," said Charlene, "and give us more clues to follow."

"The point is, we did save Jess, and we pretty

much saved the Animal Kingdom from being over-run by DHIs. We can't be giving DHIs a bad name, after all."

They laughed. Five shimmering kids, glowing as they enjoyed a rare moment of levity.

"Maleficent used us to bring Wayne out of hiding," Finn said. "We failed him. And although we don't know enough about Chernabog, we've seen his power. And I have a hunch that the bat with green wings was him all along, although I'm not sure how to explain that."

"We know that even Maleficent cannot transform herself for very long," Philby said. "Especially in this heat. She and her animal army may have been planning to take over AK. They had the ice truck as their backup, in case they failed. It was only when we crashed the server that she resorted to moving Chernabog. What's strange is that if they hadn't captured Jess, if she hadn't been in that tunnel to have that daydream, we might never have known what Maleficent was planning, might never have been there when she was freeing Chernabog."

"I think it was intended—us being there. I think if we'd failed to defeat the server, then the animals would have caught us all and taken us to her. I don't know what would have happened, but I think she had plans for us. Amanda saved us all by levitating her. Without that . . ."

"I always thought staying up that late would be fun," said Charlene. "But it—"

"Stank." Although Maybeck used another word.

"We've got work to do," Finn said. "And we need to act quickly. Who knows what secrets Wayne might have in that old head of his? Secrets no one should know."

"Tell us what to do," Willa said.

All eyes fell on Finn. They waited for him to say something.

He smiled, a warmth filling him and making his DHI glow even brighter.

Wayne would have been proud.

"We'll meet after school. We've got to find Wayne."

He raised his right hand. In it was the black remote with the small button at its center.

"Ready?" he said.

The others nodded.

He pushed the button.

ACKNOWLEDGMENTS

The Kingdom Keepers novels depend on a team, in part because the research conducted inside the Parks, and also *about* the Parks, is both complex and time-consuming, and ultimately essential to the story.

First, I want to thank my co-writer (from other novels), Dave Barry, who, during a car ride to Orlando's airport made suggestions to the outline that formed and framed the book, forever changing it. He jokes how I'm the "plot guy" in our partnership, but for once he *is* "making this up." He set the clock in the book ticking and gave me one of the most important twists. Thanks.

The real dedication of the book should probably be to Alex Wright, a Disney Imagineer, a man with tireless patience, who has endured (and I am *not* making this up!) *hundreds* of e-mails where I picked his brain for details. Alex also hosted several behind-the-scene tours for me in Animal Kingdom and introduced me to:

Dr. Joseph Soltis—Wildlife Tracking Center
Dr. Don Neiffer—Veterinary Hospital
Debbie Weber—Animal Nutrition Center
Matt Hohne—Animal Barns
Jason Surrell—Disney Imagineer (and AK tour host/insider)

I'd also like to thank my niece, Blair M. Daverman.

My wife, Marcelle, along with Laurel and David Walters, as always, copyedited the various drafts. And Tanner Walters, who in sixth grade reads more than I do, gave me an early read and caught a bunch of problems. So did my daughter Paige. And thanks to daughter Storey for reading KK1 and telling me what she liked!

Special gratitude to Nandy Litzinger, my office manager; Wendy Lefkon, Disney editor; Amy Berkower, agent; Matthew Snyder, film agent; and Jennifer Levine, Disney publicist.

It obviously takes a village.

—Ridley Pearson
January 2008
St. Louis, Missouri

UPDATE 2020: Special thanks to Brooke Muschott, without whom this 2nd Edition would not have been possible. And to New Leaf Literary for the continued support and management.

GET A SNEAK PEAK OF RIDLEY PEARSON'S NEW KINGDOM KEEPERS BOOK
FIRST LIGHT

Coming March 2021

1

ELI WHITMAN LIFTED HIS HANDS and screamed. He was sitting in the front row of the Animal Kingdom's roller coaster, Expedition Everest. The thing was older than his parents! He could imagine the views from outside. Giraffe and hippos in the Kilimanjaro Safari. White seagulls perched atop the Tree of Life.

His friends cried out as the roller coaster dove. Parents weren't on the ride. Fine with him. At twelve and thirteen, he and his friends didn't need hand-holding.

As the roller coaster stopped, Eli had a brief view of Pandora, an attraction more than twenty years old. The Siberian Forest Climb and the Great Barrier Reach had opened two years earlier. That had been Animal Kingdom's fortieth birthday. Other kids might have gone there for a birthday party. Not Eli. Expedition Everest was his favorite. And this was, after all, his birthday party.

Animal Kingdom was super crowded. Tomorrow there would be a total solar eclipse. The Disney Parks had special shows planned, including a Star Wars Sky Search.

When the roller coaster entered the double loop, Marie-Claire grabbed Eli's hand. She squeezed and held on tight. That made it the best day-before-his-birthday ever.

When he got off the ride, he stopped at the show wall to see a video of himself on the ride. The other kids looked strong or pretty. He saw himself as boring-looking. Freckles. Brown hair. Darkish skin. (His mother was part Asian; his father, Caucasian.) Eli didn't think of himself as good-looking. In the video, the wind pushed back his hair. It gave away a secret: He kept his hair long to hide his gigantic ears.

The July air felt hot and damp. He was sweaty. Jungle trees and vines lined the path back toward the Monkey Temple. It was a place Eli liked to stop and watch for a while. He and Marie-Claire and a few other friends did just that. The sound of laughter filled the air. *Happy birthday*, he thought.

The group explored the rock canyons leading to Harambe. His parents had once tried to explain what the park had looked like back in 2020. But it was impossible for Eli not to see the solar holograms of the Disney Cast Members—Solograms—moving around throughout the park. He knew the hover carts were new. And so were attractions like Lock Nest Nessie that he counted as favorites.

He knew he was lucky. Not everyone got to live in a place like Epcot's CommuniTree. He had things others didn't. But he also wanted to travel more, like his parents did. They were currently riding the Boring Hyperloop from Atlanta to Los Angeles. Instead of being with them, he was in the park. His parents listened; they just didn't seem to ever hear him.

Maybe things would change tomorrow. Thirteen had to be better than twelve.

"Did you know that people in India don't eat during

a solar eclipse because they think any food would be poisoned?" At ten, Lily Perkins was too young to hang out with sixth and seventh graders. There were unwritten rules about such things. But she was funny and smart, and she always made him feel better. To Eli, that was the definition of a good friend, and so he'd invited her.

"I did not," he admitted.

"In some cultures, pregnant women stay indoors during an eclipse." Her eye color matched her straight hair perfectly—brown with flecks of highlight in both. Her hair was very fine, and hung past her shoulders. She smiled for Eli and giggled, sounding like a complaining squirrel.

"Because?" he asked.

"Superstition." Lily wore a light-blue T-neck pullover, dandelion-yellow baggy cropped pants, and aquamarine retro-Moana flip-flops.

Eli's parents listened to extremely old music, including a singer named Stevie Wonder who'd written a pretty good song, "Superstitious." The music started swirling in Eli's head and he felt his foot tapping. *Ver-y super-sti-tious.* He loved music. Any kind. But he didn't tell his friends that. So-called friends judged you on all kinds of stuff that shouldn't matter. He'd learned that the hard way.

"It's not all scary," Lily said. Thing about Lily: if you let her get going, it was hard to stop her.

"Is that so?" An only child, Eli was really nice to other kids, especially younger girls, whom he saw as little sisters. Like little Lily. Lily was the best, funniest, most unexpected creature on the planet.

"In Italy, some people think that flowers planted

during a solar eclipse turn out more colorful than others. So, what do you think it means when a boy's thirteenth birthday is on the solar eclipse?"

"I dunno," Eli said, nervously.

"Maybe you'll grow a beard or something."

"Doubtful." Eli longed for the day he would start shaving.

"Maybe you'll start to age faster than everyone else your age."

"Now you're just being creepy," Eli said.

"Or find a princess." She giggled. "Other than Marie-Claire."

Eli swung to hit her playfully, but Lily saw and dodged the hit. Marie-Claire, who was French like her single mom, had transitioned from being Eli's lab partner, to friend, to someone he now regularly texted with. The more they texted, the more Eli had trouble not texting her back. It was becoming a habit. If someone like little Lily had noticed, he had big problems.

"You know what I think?" Lily said.

"I'm not sure I want to." Eli hoped she would stop.

"I think you only wanted to ride Expedition Everest so Marie-Claire would freak out and hold your hand in the dark."

"Are you a mind-reader?"

"Not exactly," Lily said sheepishly. "Kinda close, though." She giggled nervously.

Something about the way she said that interested Eli. He made a mental note to ask her more later.

"Keep that to yourself, will you, Lily?"

She ran off, skipping like a six-year-old. Eli smiled.